The Captain of the Kansas

Louis Tracy

Contents

THE CAPTAIN OF
THE KANSAS

BY

Louis Tracy

CHAPTER I
ITEMS NOT IN THE MANIFEST

I think I shall enjoy this trip," purred Isobel Baring, nestling comfortably among the cushions of her deck chair. A steward was arranging tea for two at a small table. The *Kansas*, with placid hum of engines, was speeding evenly through an azure sea.

"I agree with that opinion most heartily, though, to be sure, so much depends on the weather," replied her friend, Elsie Maxwell, rising to pour out the tea. Already the brisk sea-breeze had kissed the Chilean pallor from Elsie's face, which had regained its English peach-bloom. Isobel Baring's complexion was tinged with the warmth of a pomegranate. At sea, even in the blue Pacific, she carried with her the suggestion of a tropical garden.

"I never gave a thought to the weather," purred Isobel again, as she subsided more deeply into the cushions.

"Let us hope such a blissful state of mind may be justified. But you know, dear, we may run into a dreadful gale before we reach the Straits."

Isobel laughed.

"All the better!" she cried. "People tell me I am a most fascinating invalid. I look like a creamy orchid. And what luck to have a chum so disinterested as you where a lot of nice men are concerned! What have I done to deserve it? Because you are really charming, you know."

"Does that mean that you have already discovered a lot of nice men on board?"

Elsie handed her friend a cup of tea and a plate of toast.

"Naturally. While you were mooning over the lights and tints of the Andes, I kept an eye, both eyes in fact, on our compulsory acquaintances of the next three weeks. To begin with, there's the captain."

"He is good-looking, certainly. Somewhat reserved, I fancied."

"Reserved!" Isobel showed all her fine teeth in a smile. Incidentally, she took a satisfactory bite out of a square of toast. "I 'll soon shake the reserve out of him. He is mine. You will see him play pet dog long before we meet that terrible gale of yours."

"Isobel, you promised your father--"

"To look after my health during the voyage. Do you think that I intend only to sleep, eat, and read novels all the way to London? Then, indeed, I should be ill. But there is a French Comte on the ship. He is mine, too."

"You mean to find safety in numbers?"

"Oh, there are others. Of course, I am sure of my little Count. He twisted his mustache with such an air when I skidded past him in the companionway."

Elsie bent forward to give the chatterer another cup of tea.

"And you promised to read Moliere at least two hours daily!" she sighed good-humoredly. Even the most sensible people, and Elsie was very sensible, begin a long voyage with idiotic programs of work to be done.

"I mean to substitute a live Frenchman for a dead one--that is all. And I am sure Monsieur le Comte Edouard de Poincilit will do our French far more good than 'Les Fourberies de Scapin.'"

"Am I to be included in the lessons? And you actually know the man's name already?"

"Read it on his luggage, dear girl. He has such a lot. See if he doesn't wear three different colored shirts for breakfast, lunch, and tea. And, if *you* refuse to help, who is to take care of le p'tit Edouard while I give the captain a trot round. Don't look cross, there's a darling, though you *do* remind me, when you open your eyes that way, of a delightful little American schoolma'am I met in Lima. She had drifted that far on her holidays, and I believe she was horrified with me."

"Perhaps she thought you were really the dreadful person you made yourself out to be. Now, Isobel, that does not matter a bit in Valparaiso, where you are known, but in Paris and London--"

"Where I mean to be equally well known, it is a passport to smart society to be *un peu risque*. Steward! Give my compliments to Captain Courtenay, and say that Miss Maxwell and Miss Baring hope he will favor them with his company to tea."

Elsie's bright, eager face flushed slightly. She leaned forward, with a certain squaring of the shoulders, being a determined young person in some respects.

"For once, I shall let you off," she said in a low voice. "So I give you fair warning, Isobel, I must not be included in impromptu invitations of that kind. Next time I shall correct your statement most emphatically."

"Good gracious! I only meant to be polite. Tut, tut! as dad says when he can't swear before ladies, I shan't make the running for you any more."

Elsie drummed an impatient foot on the deck. There was a little pause. Isobel closed her eyes lazily, but she opened them again when she heard her friend say:

"I am sorry if I seem crotchety, dear. Indeed, it is no pretense on my part. You cannot imagine how that man Ventana persecuted me. The mere suggestion of any one's paying me compliments and trying to be fascinating is so repellent that I cringe at the thought. And even our sailor-like captain will think it necessary to play the society clown, I suppose, seeing that we are young and passably good-looking."

Isobel Baring raised her head from the cushions.

"Ventana was a determined wooer, then? What did he do?" she asked.

"He--he pestered me with his attentions. Oh, I should have liked to flog him with a whip!"

"He was always that sort of person--too serious," and the head dropped again.

The steward returned. He was a half-caste; his English was to the point.

"De captin say he busy, he no come," was his message.

Elsie's display of irritation vanished in a merry laugh. Isobel bounced up from the depths of the chair; her dark eyes blazed wrathfully.

"Tell him--" she began.

Then she mastered her annoyance sufficiently to ascertain what it was that Captain Courtenay had actually said, and she received a courteous explanation in Spanish that the commander could not leave the chart-house until the *Kansas* had rounded the low-lying, red-hued Cape Caraumilla, which still barred the ship's path to the south--the first stage of the long voyage from Valparaiso to London.

But pertinacity was a marked trait of the Baring family; otherwise, Isobel's father, a bluff, church-warden type of man, would not have won his way to the chief place in the firm of Baring, Thompson, Miguel & Co., Mining and Export Agents, the leading house in Chile's principal port. Notwithstanding Elsie's previous outburst, the steward was sent back to ask if the ladies might visit the bridge later. Meanwhile, would Captain Courtenay like a cup of tea? All things considered, there was only one possible answer; Captain Courtenay would be charmed if they favored him with both the tea and their company.

"I thought so," cried Isobel, triumphantly. "Come on, Elsie! Let us climb the ladder of conquest. The steward will bring the tea-things. The chart-house is just splendid. It will provide a refuge when the Count becomes too pressing."

There was a tightening of Elsie's lips to which Isobel paid no heed. The imminent protest was left unspoken, for Courtenay's voice came to them:

"Please hold on by the rail. If a foot were to slip on one of those brass treads the remainder of the day would be a compound of tears and sticking-plaster."

"I think you said 'reserved,'" whispered Isobel to her companion with a wicked little laugh. To Courtenay, peering through a hatch in the hurricane deck, she cried:

"Is the brass rail more dependable than you, captain?"

"It will serve your present purpose, Miss Baring," said he, not taking the hint.

Gathering her skirts daintily in her left hand, Isobel tripped up the steep stairs. Elsie followed. Courtenay, who had the manner and semblance of the first lieutenant of a warship, stood outside a haven of plate glass, shining mahogany, and white paint. The woodwork of the deck was scrubbed until it had the color of new bread. An officer paced the bridge; a sailor, within the chart-house, held the small wheel of the steam steering-gear. Somewhat to Isobel's surprise, neither man seemed to be aware of her presence.

"So this is your den?" she said, throwing her bird-like glance over the bright interior, before she gave the commander a look which was designed to bewitch him instantly. "Surely you don't sleep here, too?"

"Oh, no. This room is the brain of the ship, Miss Baring. We are always wide-awake here. My quarters are farther aft. I think I can find a chair for you if you care to sit down while I have my tea."

The captain led the way to a spacious cabin behind the chart-house.

"I hope you don't mind the chairs being secured to the deck," he said, taking off his hat. "So far above sea line, you know, everything that is loose comes to grief when the ship rolls."

"Then what becomes of your photographs?" demanded Isobel, promptly, her quick eyes having discovered the pictures of two ladies in silver frames on a writing-table.

"I take care to put them away. There is always plenty of warning. No ordinary sea can trouble a big hulk like the *Kansas*."

"Is that your mother, the dear old lady in the lace cap?"

"Yes, and the other is my sister."

"Oh, really! Is she married?"

"No. Like me, she is wedded to her profession."

"Will you think it rude if I ask what that is?"

"She is a hospital nurse; the matron, indeed, of a public institution in the suburbs of London."

"How wonderful! I do admire hospital nurses so much. They are so clever and self-sacrificing, and they always have a smile on their sweet faces. Only dad wouldn't hear of such a thing, I should love to be a nurse myself."

And Isobel sighed, dropped her long eyelashes, and examined the toe of a smart brown shoe with a wistful resignation. Courtenay was politely incredulous, but the arrival of the steward with the replenished tea-tray created a diversion.

"Do let me pour your tea," cried Isobel. "I make lovely tea, don't I, Elsie?"

Elsie laughed so cheerfully that Isobel flashed an interrogatory glance at her. Certainly, the notion of Isobel Baring claiming the domestic virtues was amusing. But Elsie answered at once:

"I know few things that you cannot do admirably, dear."

So Isobel filled a cup, asked if Captain Courtenay took milk and sugar, and said demurely, with a sip of a spoonful:

"Let me see if I can guess your tastes."

Elsie's blue eyes assumed a deeper shade. Men might like that kind of thing, but she felt that her face and neck would be poppy red in another moment. Thus far she had not addressed a word to Courtenay, though by his manner he had included her in the conversation. She now resolved to break in on the attack which Isobel was beginning with the adroitness of a skilled campaigner. And she, too, could use her eyes to advantage when she chose.

"What a curious library you have, Captain Courtenay," she said, looking, not at him, but at a row of books fitting closely into a small case over the writing-table. Instantly the sailor was interested.

"Why 'curious,' Miss Maxwell?" he asked.

"First, in their assortment; secondly, in the similarity of their binding. I have never before seen the Bible, Walt Whitman, and Dumas in covers exactly alike."

"That is easily explained. They are bound to order. My real trouble was to secure editions of equal size--an essential, you see--otherwise they would not pack into their shelf."

"But what a gathering! Shakespeare, the *Pilgrim's Progress*, Montaigne's Essays, Herbert Spencer, *Goethe's Life*, by Lewes, Marcus Aurelius, Martial, Wordsworth, *The Egoist*, Thoreau, Hazlitt, and Mitford's *Tales of Old Japan*! Where have I heard or read of that particular galaxy of stars before?"

"Go on. You are on the right track," cried Courtenay, setting down the tea-cup and hastening to Elsie's side. She was leaning on the table, reading the titles of the books. The motive of her exclamation was merged now in the fine ardor of the book-lover. She had an unconscious trick of placing the forefinger of her right hand on her lips when deeply engaged in thought. Elegant as Isobel Baring might be in her studied poses, Elsie need fear no comparison as she examined the contents of the bookcase with eager attention.

"Why the *Vicomte de Bragelonne* only, and not the *Three Musketeers*?" she mused aloud. "And if the *Life of Goethe*, why not his poems, his essays, *Werther*?-- Ah, I know--'the crowning offence of *Werther*.' A Stevenson library! Each volume he recommends in 'Books which have influenced men,' I suppose? What a charming idea! I shall never forgive myself for not having thought of it long ago."

Courtenay laughed and blushed like any schoolgirl. Elsie's appreciation had a downright, honest ring in it that went far beyond the platitudes. She accorded him the ready comradeship of a kin soul.

"Many people have been surprised by my collection; you are the first to discover its inspiration," he said.

"That is not strange. There are so few who read. Reading means discerning, interpreting. I am a worshiper of R. L. S., but I have been shocked to find that for a hundred who can talk glibly of his novels there is hardly one who has communed with him in his essays."

"We have actually hit upon a topic that should prove inexhaustible. Believe me, Miss Maxwell, that is my pet subject. More than once, needing a listener, I have even lectured my long-suffering terrier, Joey, on the point."

Isobel laughed softly. The two standing in front of the bookcase started apart, with a sudden consciousness that they were speaking unguardedly, for Isobel's mirth had mockery in it--"there was a laughing devil in her sneer."

"By the way, where is Joey?" she asked.

The dog answered her question by appearing, with a stretch and a yawn, from beneath a bunk. He had heard his name in Courtenay's voice. That sufficed for Joey at any time.

"What a strange animal!" went on Isobel. "I should have thought that he would bark, or peep out at us, at the least, when we came in."

"Joey had a disturbed night," said Courtenay. "We passed the evening in the Hotel Colon, and he regards South American hotels as the natural dwelling-place of cats, and other bad characters. Here, he is at home, and he knew that I was present."

"Otherwise, he would have classified us as suspicious?"

"He is far too discriminating. What do you say, pup?"

Joey looked up at his master. Apparently, he found the conversation trivial; he yawned again, capaciously.

"You darling! You must have slept with one eye open," said Elsie, stooping to pat him.

"Oh, take care!" cried Isobel. "He may bite you."

"Not he! When you see that wistful look in a dog's eyes, have no fear. He wants to speak then. You won't bite me, will you, dear?" And Elsie sank on one knee, to stroke Joey's white coat; whereupon Joey tried to lick her face.

"Between the Stevenson Library and the captain's dog you are installed as a prime favorite on board the *Kansas*," commented Isobel. The other girl rose hurriedly. She had caught the touch of malice in the smooth voice.

"Captain Courtenay is too polite to remind us that we are intruders," she said lightly. "We forget that he is busy. Joey, candidly canine, did not try to hide his feelings."

Isobel swung her chair round to face the door.

"This is quite the best place in the ship," she said. "I am very comfortable, thank you. Please don't send us away, captain."

Before Courtenay could answer, the officer of the watch looked in.

"Cape Caraumilla bearing sou'west of the Buei Rock, sir," he announced, and vanished again.

"Don't hurry," said Courtenay, taking up his cap. "I must leave you for a few minutes."

He was gone, with Joey at his heels, and there was a brief silence.

"Really, Isobel, we should go back on deck," urged Elsie, uneasily. Already she half regretted the impulse which led her to intervene in her friend's special hobby.

"I like that. I didn't credit you with such guile, Elsie Maxwell. You snap up my nice captain beneath my very nose, and coolly propose that I should vacate the battlefield. Oh dear, no! I can't talk literature, but I *can* flirt, and I have not finished with Arthur yet by a long chalk."

"Isobel, if you knew how you hurt me--"

Miss Baring crossed her pretty feet, folded her arms, and gave her companion a smiling glance.

"So artful, too. 'Love me, love my dog,' eh? You actually took my breath away."

"It may amaze you to learn that I meant to achieve that much, at any rate," was Elsie's quiet retort as she turned to select a volume from the queer miscellany in the bookcase.

"Oh, don't be cruel. Leave me my Frenchman! Say you won't wheedle Edouard by quoting the classics of his native tongue! Poor me! Here have I been warming a serpent in my bosom."

With a *moue* of make-believe anguish Isobel leaned back in her chair. She was insolently conscious of her superior attractions. Was she not the richest heiress in Valparaiso? Had not her father chartered this ship? And was not Elsie even now flying from an unwelcome suitor? She knew full well that her friend would resent the slightest semblance of love-making on the part of any man on board. Already her astonishment at Elsie's unlooked-for vivacity was yielding to the humor of meeting such a rival. The Count might serve as a foil, but the real quarry now was the captain. That very night there would be a moon. And the sea was calm as a sheltered lake. Isobel's lips parted in a delighted smile as she tried to imagine Courtenay deserting her to discuss those celebrities whom Elsie had made the most of. And how she would play off the Count against the captain! They ought to be at daggers drawn long before the Straits of Magellan were reached. Certainly she never expected such sport on board such a humdrum ship as the *Kansas*.

Suddenly they both heard an excited bark from the dog, and the quick rush of feet along the deck; Courtenay's voice reached them with a new and startling note in it.

"Stop that!" he shouted.

There was an instant's pause. Their alert ears caught the sounds of a distant scuffle. Then a pistol shot jarred the peaceful drone of the ship.

"Sheer off, there!" roared Courtenay again. "Next time I shoot to kill!"--

With terror in their eyes, with blanched cheeks, they rushed to the door and peeped out. Courtenay was not to be seen, but the officer of the watch was swinging himself over the canvas shield of the bridge. He disappeared. Joey, barking furiously, trotted into view and ran back again. Creeping forward, they saw the stolid sailor within the chart-house squint at the compass and give the wheel a slight turn. That was reassuring. Yet another timorous pace, and through the curving window they could discern Courtenay, holding a revolver in his right hand, but behind his back.

Even in their alarm they realized that nothing very terrible would happen now. But why had the shot been fired, and what had given that tense ring to Courtenay's threat?

Venturing a little further, they gained the bridge. On the main deck, a long way beneath, near an open hatch, a half-caste Chilean was lying on his back. He had evidently been wounded. Blood was flowing from his leg; it smeared the white deck. The officer who had climbed down so speedily from the bridge was directing two other men how to lift him. Close by, the chief officer, Mr. Boyle, was stanching a deep cut on his chin with a handkerchief. At the same time he curtly ordered off such deck hands and stewards as came running forward, attracted by the disturbance.

The girls were gazing wide-eyed at this somewhat unnerving scene, when

Courtenay approached.

"Better go below," he said quietly. "I am sorry this trouble should have happened, at the beginning of the voyage, too. I hope it will not upset you. That rascally Chilean tried to knife Mr. Boyle, and those other blackguards were ready to side with him. I had to shoot quick and straight to show them I meant what I said."

"Is he dead?" asked Isobel, with a contemptuous coolness as to the fate of the mutineer which Courtenay found admirable.

"Not a bit of it. Fired at his legs. Only a flesh wound, I fancy."

"Poor wretch!" murmured Elsie. "Was there no other way?"

"There is only one way of dealing with that sort of skunk," was the gruff answer. The pity in her voice implied a condemnation of his act. He resented it. He knew he had done rightly, and she knew that she had given offence by her involuntary sympathy with the suffering Chilean, who, with the passing of the paralyzing shock of the bullet, was howling dolefully now as the sailors carried him towards the forecastle.

The man's groans tortured her. Her eyes filled with tears. Joey, yelping with frenzy, leaped up to invite her to lift him above the canvas screen so that he might see what was going on. But Elsie could only reach blindly for the rail of the companion-way, and Isobel, after a smiling word of farewell to Courtenay, followed her.

So it came to pass that neither Stevenson nor the moon had power to draw the captain of the *Kansas* to the promenade deck that night.

CHAPTER II
WHEREIN THE CAPTAIN KEEPS TO HIS OWN QUARTERS

Doctor Christobal brought some additional details to the dinner-table. He was not the ship's doctor. The *Kansas*, built for freight rather than passengers, did not carry a surgeon on her roll; Dr. Christobal's presence was due to Mr. Baring's solicitude in his daughter's behalf. It chanced that the courtly and gray-haired Spanish physician had relinquished his practise in Chile, and was about to pay a long-promised visit to a married daughter in Barcelona. Friendship, not unaided by a good fee, induced him to travel by the *Kansas*.

He had been called on to attend Mr. Boyle and the wounded Chilean, and he reported now that the chief officer's injury was trifling, but the Chilean's wound might incapacitate him during the remainder of the voyage.

"So far as I can gather," he said, "Mr. Boyle had a narrow escape. These half-breeds have a nice anatomical knowledge of the situation of the lung; they also know the easiest way to reach it with a sharp instrument. Captain Courtenay fired as the knife fell, otherwise our first mate would have attended his own funeral this evening."

"What was the cause of the affair?" Isobel asked.

"The man is not one of the ship's crew, I understand. His name is Frascuelo, and it appears that he was engaged to place some bunker coal aboard early this morning. He says that he was drugged, and his clothes stolen; that he came off to the ship at a late hour, and that some one flung him headlong into a hold which, luckily for him, was nearly full of cotton bales. He was stunned by the fall, and were it not for Captain Courtenay's custom of having all hatches taken off and a thorough examination of the cargo made before the holds are finally battened down for the voyage, Frascuelo might now be in a tight place in more than one sense."

Dr. Christobal was proud of his idiomatic English. He spoke the language with the careless freedom of a Londoner.

"Frascuelo seems to have passed an eventful day," said the little French Comte, who had been waiting anxiously for a chance to join in the conversation.

"But why should he want to kill poor Mr. Boyle?" inquired Isobel, after giving the Frenchman an encouraging glance. Incidentally, she smiled at Elsie. "Why puzzle one's brains over foreign tongues when all the world speaks English?" she telegraphed.

"Mr. Boyle is a peculiar person," said the doctor dryly. "I happen to have known him during some years. You and I might regard him as a man of few words, but he has acquired a wonderful vocabulary for the benefit of sailor-men. I believe he can swear in every known lingo. His accomplishment in that direction no doubt annoyed Frascuelo, who became frantic when he heard that the ship would not call at any South American port. I imagine, too, that the unfortunate fellow is still suffering from the drug which, he says, was administered to him. Anyhow, you know how the affair terminated."

"I, for one, think some consideration might have been shown him," said Elsie.

"There is no time for argument when a Chilean draws a knife, Miss Maxwell."

"But, if his story is true--"

"There never yet was a stowaway who did not invent a plausible yarn. Nevertheless, I believe, and Mr. Boyle agrees with me, that the man is not lying."

They felt the ship swing round on a new course, and the rays of the setting sun lit up the saloon table through the open starboard ports.

"Due south now, ladies!" cried Dr. Christobal cheerily. "We have rounded Cape Cardones. We practically follow the seventy-sixth degree until we approach Evangelistas Island. Thus far we are in the open sea. Then we pick our way through the Straits discovered by that daring Portuguese, Fernando de Magallanes, to whose memory I always drink heartily once we are clear of the Cape of the Eleven Thousand Virgins. I never pass through that gloomy defile without marveling at his courage, and thinking that he deserved a better fate than murder at the hands of some painted savage in the Philippines. Peace be to his ashes!"

And the doctor lifted his glass of red wine with a quasi-masonic ritual which lent solemnity to his discourse.

"You are a long way ahead of your toast," said Isobel.

"Just as Magellan was ahead of his times," was the rejoinder.

"Yet he was a man of leisurely habit," put in Elsie, who found Dr. Christobal's old-world manners full of charm and repose.

"How so?" said he, puzzled, for the worthy Portuguese navigator was notoriously a swashbuckler.

"Otherwise he never could have christened any unhappy promontory by such a long-winded name," she explained.

"Perhaps he met a contrary wind in that region," said Christobal, laughing. "Monsieur de Poincilit here, were he in a very bad temper, might exclaim, 'Mille diables!' Why should not our excellent Fernando rail against the almost inconceivable fickleness which could be displayed by eleven times as many young ladies?"

"I came out last time on the **Orellana**, and I don't even remember passing such a place," said Isobel. She was a Chilean born and bred, but she always affected European vagueness as to the topography of South America. Dr. Christobal knew this weakness of hers; he also remembered her beautiful half-caste mother, from whom Isobel inherited her flashing eyes, her purple-red lips, and a skin in which the exquisite flush of terra-cotta on her checks merged into the delicate pallor of forehead and neck.

But, being a tactful man, he only answered: "Your English sailors, my dear, who gruffly dubbed the adjacent point 'Cape Dungeness,' have shortened Magellan's mouthful into 'Cape Virgins.'--Yet, Ursula was a British saint, and her memory ought to be revered, if only because it keeps alive a classic pun."

A born raconteur, he paused.

"Go right ahead, doctor," came a voice from the lower end of the table.

"Well, the story runs that Princess Ursula fled from Britain to Rome to escape marriage with a pagan--"

"How odd!" interrupted Isobel, and Elsie alone understood the drift of her comment.

"Not at all odd if she didn't happen to like him," said Christobal. "She reached Cologne, and was martyred there by the Huns. Long afterwards a stone was found

with the inscription ***Ursula et Undecimilla Virgines***, which was incorrectly translated into 'Ursula and her Eleven Thousand Virgins.' Some later critic pointed out
that a missing comma after Undecimilla, the name of a handmaid, made all the
difference, assuming that two young ladies were a more reasonable and probable
number than eleven thousand. But what legend ever cared for a comma, or reached
a full stop? If you go to Cologne, the verger of the Church of St. Ursula will show
you the bones of the whole party in glass cases, and, equally amazing, the town of
Baoza in Spain claims to be the birthplace of the lot. Clearly, Magellan had a man
from Baoza on board his ship."

"All mail steamers ought to provide a lecturer on things in general and interesting places passed in particular," said Isobel.

Dr. Christobal bowed.

"I am sure that some of the officers of the ***Orellana*** could have told you the
history of Cape Virgins, but they, not to mention the other young gentlemen in the
passenger list, would certainly find you better sport than puzzling your pretty head
about the ship's landmarks."

"I also came out on the ***Orellana***, but there was no Miss Baring to be seen,"
murmured the Frenchman.

"You had a dull trip, I take it?" said the doctor, quietly.

"I was very ill," was the response; but, after a stare of surprise, he joined in the
resultant laugh quite good-naturedly.

"It is a standing joke that my countrymen are poor sailors," he protested, "and
that is strange, don't you think, seeing that France has the second largest navy in
the world?"

"Console yourself, monsieur," said Christobal. "Three great sea-captains, Nel-
son, Cook, and, it is said, Columbus himself, always paid tribute to Neptune. And,
if I am not mistaken," he added, glancing through the port windows, "we shall all
have our stamina tested before twenty-four hours have passed."

Heads were turned and necks craned to see what had induced this unexpected
prophecy. Behind the distant coast-line the inner giants of the Andes threw heavenward their rugged outlines, with many a peak and glacier glinting in vivid colors
against a sky so clear and blue that they seemed strangely near.

"Yes, this wonderful atmosphere of ours is enchanting," said the doctor, when assailed by a chorus of doubts. "But it carries its deceptive smiles too far. The very beauty of the Cordillera is a sign of storm. I am sorry to be a croaker; yet we are running into a gale."

"I shall ask the captain," pouted Isobel, rising.

The Count twisted his mustache. He knew that both ladies were in the forbidden territory of the bridge when the fracas occurred.

"You, perhaps, are a good sailor?" said he, addressing Elsie.

"I am afraid to boast," she answered. "I have been in what was called a Number Eight gale, whatever that may mean, and weathered it splendidly, but I am older now."

"It cannot have been long ago, seeing that you recall it so exactly."

"It was six years ago, and I was seventeen then," said Elsie, her eyes wandering to the purple and gold of the far-off mountains.

"But you are English. You are therefore at home on the rolling deep," murmured Monsieur de Poincilit, confidentially. She did not endeavor to interpret his expressive glance, though he seemed to convey more that he said.

"Not so much at home at sea as you are in my language," she replied, and she turned to Dr. Christobal, whom she had already known slightly in Valparaiso.

"Are you coming on deck?" she inquired. "I am sure you are a mine of information on Chile, and I want to extract some of the ore while the land is still visible. It is already assuming the semblance of a dream."

"You are not saying a last farewell to Valparaiso, I hope?" said her elderly companion, as they quitted the salon.

"I think so. I have no ties there, save those of sentiment. I shall not return, unless, if a doubtful fortune permits, I am able some day to revisit two graves which are dear to me."

There was a little catch in her voice, and the doctor was far too sympathetic to endeavor forthwith to divert her sad thoughts.

"I knew your father," he said gently. "He was a most admirable man, but quite unsuited to the environment of a new country, where the dollar is god, and an unstable deity at that. He was swindled outrageously by men who stand high in the community to-day. But you, Miss Maxwell, with your knowledge of Spanish and your other acquirements, should do better here than in Europe, provided, that is, you mean to earn your own living."

"I am proud to hear you speak well of my father," she said. "And I am well aware that he was badly treated in business. I fear, too, that his advocacy of the rights of the Indians brought him into disfavor. Of all his possessions the only remnant left to me is a barren mountain, with a slice of fertile valley, in the Quillota district. It yields me the magnificent revenue of two hundred dollars per annum."

"How in the world did he come to own land there?"

"It was a gift from the Naquilla tribe. He defeated an attempt made to oust them by a big land company. The company has since asked me to sell the property, and offered me a fair price, too, as the cultivable land is a very small strip, but it would be almost like betraying the cause for which he fought, would it not?"

"Yes, indeed," agreed the doctor, though his heart and not his head dictated the reply. "May I ask you to tell me your plans for the future?" he went on.

"Well, when Mr. Baring heard I was going to England, he was good enough to promise me employment in his London agency as Spanish correspondent. That will fill in two days a week. The rest I can devote to art. I paint a little, and draw with sufficient promise to warrant study, I am told. Anyhow, I am weary of teaching; I prefer to be a pupil."

"I cannot imagine what the young men of Valparaiso were thinking of to allow a girl like you to slip off in this fashion," said Christobal with a smile.

"Most of them hold firmly to the belief that a wife's wedding-dress should be made of gilt-edged scrip."

"Poor material--very poor material out of which to construct wedded happiness. And as to my young friend, Isobel? She joins her aunt in London, I hear?"

"That is the present arrangement. She means to have a good time, especially in Paris. I should like to live in Paris myself. Dear old smoke-laden London does not appeal so thoroughly to the artist. Yet, I am content--yes, quite content."

"Then you have gained the best thing in the world," cried the doctor, throwing out his arms expansively.

The two became good friends as the voyage progressed. Christobal was exceedingly well informed, and delighted in a thoughtful listener like Elsie. Isobel, tiring at times of the Count, would join in their conversation, and display a spasmodic interest in the topics they discussed. There were only six other passengers, a Baptist missionary and his wife, three mining engineers, and an English globe-trotter, a singular being who appeared to have roamed the entire earth, but whose experiences were summed up in two words--every place he had seen was either "Fair" or "Rotten."

Even Isobel failed to draw him further, and she said one day, in a temper, after a spirited attempt to extract some of his stored impressions: "The man reminds me of one of those dummy books you see occasionally, bound in calf and labeled 'Gazetteer of the World.' When you try to open a volume you find that it is made of wood."

So they nicknamed him "Mr. Wood," and Elsie once inadvertently addressed him by the name.

"What do you think of the weather, Mr. Wood?" she asked him at breakfast.

He chanced to notice that she was speaking to him.

"Rotten," he said.

Perhaps he wondered why Miss Maxwell flushed and the others laughed. But, in actual fact, he was not far wrong in his curious choice of an adjective that morning. Dr. Christobal's dismal foreboding had been justified on the second day out. Leaden clouds, a sullen sea, and occasional puffs of a stinging breeze from the southwest, offered a sorry exchange for the sunny skies of Chile.

Though the *Kansas* was not a fast ship, she could have made the entrance to the Straits on the evening of the fourth day were not Captain Courtenay wishful to navigate the most dangerous part of the narrows by daylight. His intent, therefore, was to pick up the Evangelistas light about midnight, and then crack ahead at fourteen knots, so as to be off Felix Point on Desolation Island by dawn.

This was not only a prudent and seamanlike course but it would conduce to the comfort of the passengers. The ship was now running into a stiff gale. Each hour the sea became heavier, and even the eight thousand tons of the *Kansas* felt the impact of the giant rollers on her starboard bow. Dinner, therefore, promised to be a meal of much discomfort, cheered only by the knowledge that as soon as the vessel reached the lee of Desolation Island the giant waves of the Pacific would lose their power, and all on board would enjoy a quiet night's rest.

There were no absentees at the table. Dr. Christobal strove to enliven the others with the promise of peace ere many hours had passed.

"Pay no heed to those fellows!" he cried, as the ship quivered under the blow of a heavy sea, and they heard the thud of many tons of water breaking over the bows and fore hatch, while the defeated monster washed the tightly screwed ports with a venomous swish. "They cannot harm us now. Let us rather thank kindly Providence which provided Magellan's water-way; think what it would mean were we compelled to weather the Cape."

"I am beginning to catch on to the reasonableness of that toast of yours, doctor," said one of the mining engineers, a young American. "I happen to be a tee-totaler, but I don't mind opening a bottle of the best for the general welfare when we shove our nose past the Cape of the large number of young and unprotected females."

Christobal raised his hand.

"All in good time," he said. "Never halloo for the prairie until you are clear of the forest. If the wind remains in its present quarter, we are fortunate. Should it happen to veer round to the eastward, and you see the rocks of Tierra del Fuego lashed by the choppy sea that can run even through a land-locked channel, you will be ready to open two bottles as a thanks-offering. Is this your first trip round by the south?"

"Yes, I crossed by way of Panama. Guess a mule-track over the Sierras is a heap better than the Pacific in a gale. Jee-whizz!"

A spiteful sea sprang at the *Kansas* and shook her from stem to stern. The ship groaned and creaked as though she were in pain; she staggered an instant, and then swung irresistibly forward with a fierce plunge that made the plates dance and cutlery rattle in the fiddles.

"I suppose we must endure five hours of this," said Elsie, bravely.

"I don't like it. Why does not Captain Courtenay, or even Mr. Boyle, put in an appearance? I have hardly seen either of them since the day I came aboard."

Isobel was petulant, and perhaps a little frightened. She had not yet reached that stage of confidence familiar to all who cross the open seas. The first period of a gale is terrifying. Later there comes an indifference born of supreme trust in the ship. The steady onward thrust of the engines--the unwavering path across the raging vortex of tumbling gray waters--the orderly way in which the members of the crew follow their duties--these are quietly persistent factors in the gradual soothing of the nerves. Many a timid passenger, after lying awake through a night of terror, has gone to sleep when the watch began to swab the deck overhead. Not even a Spartan sailor would begin to wash woodwork if the ship were sinking.

"All ladies like to see an officer in the saloon during a storm," commented Christobal. "I plead guilty to a weakness in that direction myself, though I know he is much better employed on the bridge."

"The captain cannot be on the bridge always," said Isobel.

"He is seldom far from it in bad weather, if he is faithful to his trust. And I fancy we would all admit that Captain Courtenay--"

A curious shock, sharper and altogether more penetrating than the Thor's hammer blow of a huge wave, sounded loud and menacing in their ears. The ship trembled violently, and then became strangely still. The least experienced traveler on board knew that the engines had stopped. They felt a long lurch to port when the next sea climbed over the bows; at once the *Kansas* righted herself and rode on even keel, while the stress and turmoil of her fight against wind and wave passed away into a sustained silence.

The half-caste stewards glanced at each other and drew together in whispering groups, but the chief steward, an Englishman, who had turned to leave the saloon, changed his mind and uttered a low growl of command which sent his subordinates' attention, if not their thoughts, back to their work. In the strained hush, the running along the deck of men in heavy sea-boots was painfully audible. Water could be heard pouring through the scuppers. Steam was rushing forth somewhere with vehement bluster. These sounds only accentuated the extraordinary truce in the fight of ship against sea. The *Kansas* was stricken dumb, if not dead.

"Something has gone wrong," said Elsie in a low voice.

Doctor Christobal nodded carelessly.

"A burst steam-pipe, probably. Such things will happen at times. We are hove to for the moment."

He traded on the ignorance of his hearers. The chief steward heard his explanation and looked at him fixedly. Christobal caught the glance.

"I suppose we shall lose an hour or so now?" he asked.

"Yes, sir. It will be all right by the time you have finished dinner."

The meal drew to its close without much further talk. The American engineer was the first to rise, but the chief steward whispered in his ear; he returned to the table.

"Say," he said calmly, "we can't quit yet. The companion-hatch is closed. We must remain here a bit."

"Do you mean that we are battened down?" demanded Isobel, shrilly, and her face lost some of its beauty in an ashen pallor.

"Something of the sort, Miss Baring. Anyway, we can't go on deck."

"But--I insist on being told what is the matter."

The American knew little of ships, but he knew a great deal about mines, and, in a mine, if an accident happens, the man in charge cannot desert his post to give information to those who are anxious for it. So he replied laconically:

"Guess the captain will tell us all about it after a while, Miss Baring."

"Que diable! I feel like the rat in the trap," said Count Edouard, suppressed excitement rendering his English less fluent.

At another time the phrase would have sent a ripple of amusement through that cheery company. Now, no one smiled. They knew too well what he meant to pay heed to the mere form of his words. No matter how large or sumptuously equipped the trap, the point of view of the rat was new to them.

CHAPTER III
WHEREIN THE CAPTAIN REAPPEARS

The fierce hissing of the continuous escape of steam excited alarm in those not accustomed to machinery. Men and women share the unreasoning panic of animals when an unknown force reveals its pent-up fury. They forget that safety-valves are provided, that diminished pressure means less risk; the knowledge that restraint, not freedom, is dangerous comes ever in the guise of a new discovery.

The mining engineers, of course, did not share this delusion.

"There must be something serious the matter, or they would not be wasting power like that," murmured the American to one of his fellow-professionals.

"A smash-up in the engine-room. Nada es mas seguro,"[1] was the answer.

"Wonder if any one is hurt?"

The Spaniard bent a little nearer. "What can you expect?" he whispered sympathetically.

In the unnatural peacefulness of the ship's progress, disturbed only by the roar of the superheated vapor, they all heard the opening of a door at the head of the saloon stairway. The third officer appeared--his wet oilskins gleaming and dripping.

"Dr. Christobal, the captain wishes to speak to you," he said.

Christobal rose and crossed the saloon.

"As you are here, won't you tell the ladies there is nothing to be afraid of in the mere stopping of the engines?" he suggested.

"Oh, the ship is right enough," was the hasty response. "There has been an accident in the stokehold. That is all."

"Want any help?" demanded the American.

---

1 Nothing is more certain.

"Well--I'll ask the captain."

Evidently anxious to avoid further questioning, he ran up the companion. Christobal followed, the door was closed and bolted again.

"I hate the word 'accident.' It covers so many horrid possibilities," said Isobel.

"I am afraid some poor fellows have been injured, and that is why Captain Courtenay sent for Dr. Christobal," said Elsie.

"Oh, of course, I meant that. I was not thinking of the mere delay, though it is annoying that a breakdown should occur here."

"It would be equally bad anywhere else," put in the missionary's wife, timidly.

"By no means," was the sharp response. "If we were in the Straits, for instance, we could signal to San Isidro or Sandy Point; and there would be other vessels passing. Here, we are in the worst possible place."

Miss Baring's acquaintance with the chief features of the South American coast-line had seemingly improved. To all appearance, she alone among the passengers, now that Christobal was gone, realized vaguely the perilous plight of the *Kansas*. The fact was that even a girl of her apparently frivolous disposition could not avoid the influences of environment.

In a maritime community like that of Valparaiso there was every reason to know and dread the rock-bound coast which fringed the southern path towards civilization. Strange, half-forgotten stories of the terrors which await a disabled ship caught in a southwesterly gale on the Pacific side of Tierra del Fuego rose dimly in her mind. And the advancing darkness did not tend towards cheerfulness. In her new track, the *Kansas* had turned her back on the murky light which penetrated the storm-clouds towards the west. Unhinged by the external gloom and the prevalent uncertainty, and finding that no one cared to dispute with her, Isobel felt that a scream or two would be a relief. For once, pride was helpful--it saved her from hysteria.

The curious sense of waiting, they knew not for what, which dulled the thoughts and stilled the tongues of the small company at the table, soon communicated itself to the stewards. The men stood in little knots, exchanging few words, and those mostly meaningless; but the chief steward, whose trained ear caught the regular beat of the donkey-engine, woke them up with a series of sharp orders.

"Switch on the lights," he said loudly. "Clear the table and hurry up with the coffee. Get a move on those fellows, Gomez. Have you never before been in a ship when the screw stopped?"

The Gomez thus appealed to was the Englishman's second-in-command; he acted as interpreter when anything out of the common was required. He muttered a few words in the Hispano-Indian patois which his hearers best understood, and the scene in the saloon changed with wondrous suddenness. The glow of the electric lamps banished the gathering shadows. The luxurious comfort of the apartment soon dispelled the notion of danger. Coffee was brought. The smoking saloon was inaccessible, owing to the closing of the gangway, but the chief steward suggested that the gentlemen might smoke if the ladies were agreeable. Under such circumstances the ladies always are agreeable, and the instant result was a distinct rise in the social barometer.

The noise of the steam exhaust ceased as abruptly as it began. The ship was riding easily in spite of the heavy sea. Drifting with wind and wave is a simple thing for a big vessel. There is no struggle, no tearing asunder of resisting forces. Thus might a boat caught in the pitiless current of Niagara glide towards the brink of the cataract with cunning smoothness.

And then, while the occupants of the saloon were endeavoring to persuade each other that all was well, the loud wail of the siren thrilled them with increased foreboding. It was not the warning note of a fog, nor the sharp course-signal for the guidance of a passing ship, but a sustained trumpeting, which announced to any steamer hidden in the darkening waste of waters that the *Kansas* was not under control. It was a wild, sinister appeal for help, the voice of the disabled vessel proclaiming her need; and the answer seemed to come in a fiercer shriek of the gale, while the added fury of the blast brought a curling sea over the poop. The *Kansas* staggered and shook herself clear. The wave smashed its way onward; several iron stanchions snapped with reports like pistol-shots, and there was an intolerable rending of woodwork. But, whatever the damage, the powerful hull rose triumphantly from the clutch of its assailant. Shattered streams of water poured off the decks like so many cascades. Loud above the splash of these miniature cataracts vibrated the tense boom of the fog-horn.

It was a nerve-racking moment. It demanded the leadership of a strong man, and there are few gatherings in Anglo-Saxondom which cannot produce a Caesar when required.

"Say," shouted the American, his clear voice dominating the turmoil, "that gave us a shower-bath. If we could just stand outside and see ourselves, we should look like an illuminated fountain."

That was the right note--belief in the ship, contempt of the darkness and the gale. The crisis passed.

"There really cannot be a heavy sea," said Elsie, cheerfully inaccurate. "Otherwise we should be pitching or rolling, perhaps both, whereas we are actually far more steady than when dinner commenced."

"I find these lulls in the storm most trying," complained Isobel. "They remind me of some wild animal hunting its prey, creeping up with silent stealth, and then springing."

"I have never before heard a fog-horn sounded so continuously," said the missionary's wife, a Mrs. Somerville. "Don't you think they are whistling for assistance?"

"Assistance! What sort of assistance can anybody give us here? Unless the ship rights herself very soon we don't know what may happen."

Isobel seemed to have a premonition of evil, and she paid no heed to the effect her words might have on the others. Although the saloon was warm--almost uncomfortably hot owing to the closing of the main air-passages--she shivered.

Mr. Somerville drew a book from his pocket. "If that be so," he said gently, "may I suggest that we seek aid from One who is all-powerful? We are few, and of different religions, but in this hour we can surely worship at a common altar."

"Right!" said the taciturn Englishman, varying his adjective for once. The missionary offered up a short but heartfelt prayer, and, finding that he carried his congregation with him, read the opening verse of Hymn No. 370, "For those at Sea."

The stewards, most of whom understood a few words of English, readily grasped the fact that the *padri* was asking for help in a situation which they well knew to be desperate. They drew near reverently, and even joined in the simple lines:

O hear us when we cry to Thee
For those in peril on the sea.

During the brief silence which followed the singing of the hymn it did, indeed, seem to their strained senses that the fierce violence of the gale had somewhat abated. It was not so, in reality. A steady fall in the barometer foretold even worse weather to come. Courtenay, assured now that the main engines were absolutely useless, thought it advisable to get steering way on the ship by rigging the foresail, double-reefed and trapped. The result was quickly perceptible. The **Kansas** might not be pooped again, but she would travel more rapidly into the unknown.

Yet this only afforded another instance of the way men reason when they seek to explain cause from effect. The hoisting of that strip of stout canvas was one of the time-factors in the story of an eventful night, for it was with gray-faced despair that the captain gave the requisite order when the second engineer reported that his senior was dead, the crown of two furnaces destroyed, and the engines clogged, if not irretrievably damaged, by fallen debris. None realized better than the young commander what a disastrous fate awaited his ship in the gloom of the flying scud ahead. There was a faint chance of encountering another steamship which would respond to his signals. Then he would risk all by laying the **Kansas** broadside on in the effort to take a tow-rope aboard. Meanwhile, it was best to bring her under some sort of control, the steam steering-gear, driven by the uninjured donkey-engine, being yet available.

In the saloon, Elsie had shielded her face in her hands, to hide the tears which the entreaty of the hymn had brought to her eyes. Some one whispered to her:

"Won't you sing something, Miss Maxwell?"

It was the American. He judged that the sweet voice which unconsciously led the singing of the hymn must be skilled in other music.

She looked up at him, her eyes shining.

"Sing! Do you think it possible?" she asked.

"Yes. You can do a brave thing, I guess, and that would be brave."

"I will try," she said, and she walked to the piano which was screwed athwart the deck in front of the polished mahogany sheath of the steel mainmast. It was in her mind to play some lively excerpts from the light operas then in vogue, but the secret influences of the hour were stronger than her studied intent, and, when her fingers touched the keys, they wandered, almost without volition, into the subtle harmonies of Gounod's "Ave Maria." She played the air first; then, gaining confidence, she sang the words, using a Spanish version which had caught her fancy. It was good to see the flashing eyes and impassioned gestures of the Chilean stewards when they found that she was singing in their own language. These men, owing to their acquaintance with the sea and knowledge of the coast, were now in a state of panic; they would have burst the bonds of discipline on the least pretext. So, as it chanced, the voice of the English senorita reached them as the message of an angel, and the spell she cast over them did not lose its potency during some hours of dangerous toil. Here, again, was found one of the comparatively trivial incidents which contributed materially to the working out of a strange drama, because anything in the nature of a mutinous orgy breaking out in the first part of that soul-destroying night must have instantly converted the ship into a blood-bespattered Inferno.

Excited applause rewarded the song. Fired by example, the dapper French Count approached the piano and asked Elsie if she could play Beranger's "Roi d'Yvetot." She repressed a smile at his choice, but the chance that presented itself of initiating a concert on the spur of the moment was too good to be lost, so M. de Poincilit, in a nice light tenor, told how

> Il etait un roi d'Yvetot
>
> Pen connu dans l'histoire,
>
> Se levant tard, se couchant tot,
>
> Dormant fort bien sans gloire.

The Frenchman took the merry monarch seriously, but the lilting melody pleased everybody except "Mr. Wood." The "Oh, Oh's" and "Ah, Ah's" of the chorus apparently stirred him to speech. He strolled from a corner of the saloon to the side of Gray, the American engineer, and said, with a contemptuous nod towards the singer:

"What rot!"

"Not a bit of it. He's all right. Won't *you* give us a song next?"

If Gray showed the face of a sphinx, so did "Mr. Wood," whose real name was Tollemache. He bent a little nearer.

"Seen the rockets?" he asked.

"No. Are we signaling?"

"Every minute. Have counted fifteen."

"You don't say. Things are in a pretty bad shape, then?"

"Rotten."

"Well, like Brer Rabbit, we must lie low and say nothing."

This opinion was incontrovertible. Moreover, Tollemache was not one who needed urging to keep his mouth shut. Indeed, this was by far the longest conversation he had indulged in since he came aboard; nor was he finished with it.

"Ship will strike soon," he said.

Gray turned on him sharply. "Oh, nonsense!" he exclaimed. "What has put that absurd notion into your head?"

"Know this coast."

"But we are far out at sea."

"Fifty miles from danger line, two hours ago. Thirty now."

"Are you sure?"

"Certain."

"Do you mean to tell me that in three hours, or less, the ship may be a wreck?"

"Will be," said Tollemache. "Have a cigar," and he passed a well-filled case to his companion.

The American was beginning to take the silent one's measure. He bit off the end of a cigar and lit it.

"What's at the back of your head?" he asked coolly. The other looked towards the Chileans.

"Those chaps are rotters," he said.

"You think they will cut up rough? What can they do? We must all sink or swim together."

"Yes; but there are the women, you know. They must be looked after. You can count on me. Tell the chief steward--and the padri."

Gray felt that here was a man after his own heart, the native-born American having a rough-and-ready way of classifying nationalities when the last test of manhood is applied by a shipwreck, or a fire.

"Got a gun?" he inquired.

"Cabin. Goin' for it first opportunity."

"Same here. But the captain will give us some sort of warning?"

"Perhaps not. Die quick, die happy."

Then Gray smiled, and he could not help saying: "Tell you what, cousin, if you shoot as straight as you talk, these stewards will come to heel, no matter what happens."

"Fair shot," admitted Tollemache, and he stalked off to his stateroom, while the Count was vociferating, for the last time:

Quel bon p'tit roi c'etait la!
La, la!

Between Elsie and de Poincilit the chorus made quite a respectable din. Few noticed that the saloon main companion had been opened again, until the sharp bark of a dog joining in the hand-clapping turned every eye towards the stairway. Captain Courtenay was descending. In front ran Joey, who, of course, imagined that the plaudits of the audience demanded recognition. Courtenay had removed his oilskins before leaving the bridge. His dark blue uniform was flecked with white foam, and a sou'wester was tied under his chin, otherwise his appearance gave little sign of the wild tumult without. Joey, on the other hand, was a very wet dog, and inclined to be snappy. When, in obedience to a stern command, he ceased barking, he shook himself violently, and sent a shower of spray over the carpet. Then he cocked an eye at the chief steward, who represented bones and such-like dainties.

Courtenay, removing his glistening head-gear, advanced a couple of paces into the saloon. He seemed to avoid looking at any individual, but took in all present in a comprehensive glance. Elsie, who had exchanged very few words with him since the first afternoon she came on board, thought he looked worn and haggard, but his speech soon revealed good cause for any lack of sprightliness.

"I regret to have to inform you," he said, with the measured deliberation of a man who has made up his mind exactly what to say, "that the ship has been disabled by some accident, the cause of which is unknown at present. The unfortunate result is that she is in a position of some peril."

There was a sudden stir among the Chilean stewards, whose wits were sharpened sufficiently to render the captain's statement quite clear to them. Isobel uttered a little sob of terror, and Mrs. Somerville gasped audibly, "Oh, my poor children!" Elsie, her lips parted, sat forward on the piano-stool. Her senses seemed to have become intensified all at once. She could see everything, hear everything. Some of the Chileans and Spaniards crossed themselves; others swore. Count Edouard breathed hard and muttered "Grand Dieu!" She wondered why the captain and Mr. Tollemache, who had returned from his stateroom, and was standing in the half light of a doorway, should simultaneously drop their right hands into a coat pocket. Mr. Tollemache, too, gave a queer little nod to the American, who had moved near to Isobel and placed a hand on her shoulder. Elsie was quite sure that Gray whispered: "For goodness' sake, don't cause a scene!" And, indeed, he did ask Isobel and Mrs. Somerville, with some curtness, to restrain themselves.

Courtenay, with one cold glance, chilled into silence the muttered prayers and curses of the Chileans.

"It may be necessary, about daybreak, to endeavor to beach the ship," he continued. "I wish you all, therefore, to guard against possible exposure by wearing warm clothes, especially furs and overcoats. Money and jewelry should be secured, but no baggage of any sort, not even the smallest handbag, can be carried, as all other personal belongings must be left on board. Passengers will gather here, and remain here until I send one of the officers for them. The companion doors will not be closed again, but the decks are quite impassable. You hear for yourselves that they are momentarily swept by heavy seas."

He turned to the chief steward.

"Your men, Mr. Malcolm," he said, "will begin at once, under your directions, to draw stores for each boat. There need be no hurry or excitement. We are, as yet, many miles distant from the nearest known land. If the wind changes, or one of several possible things happens, the *Kansas* will suffer no damage whatever. I wish all hands to be prepared, however, for the chance, the remote chance, I trust, of the ship's being driven ashore, and I beg each one of you to remember that discipline and strict obedience to orders are not only more necessary now than ever, but also that they will be strictly enforced."

The concluding sentence was uttered very slowly and clearly. It was evident he meant the ship's company to understand him. Before any of his hearers attempted to question him, he jammed the sou'wester on his head and ran up the stairs. The dog followed, somewhat ruefully, the cozy saloon being far more to his liking than the wind-swept, spray-lashed chart-house. Mr. Malcolm promptly stirred his myrmidons with a command to fall in by boats' crews, and Gomez won his chief's approval by quietly translating the captain's orders. Beyond Mrs. Somerville's subdued sobbing there was little outward manifestation that another crisis in the history of the **Kansas** and her human freight had come and gone.

"The skipper did turn up, you see," said the American, when Tollemache came to him. The silent man screwed his lips together as if he would put a padlock on them.

"From your knowledge of the coast, do you think he will be able to beach the ship?" went on Gray, some humorous imp prompting him, even in that tense moment, to draw the expected answer from his new friend and ally.

"Yes, in pieces," said Tollemache, and the reply was neither humorous nor expected.

CHAPTER IV
ELSIE GOES ON DECK

As a little yeast leavens much flour so does the presence of a few stout-hearted men give strength and courage to a multitude. Although the rumor soon went the rounds that the giant wave which pooped the ship had carried away two of her six boats, there were no visible signs of flurry in the measures taken to equip the remaining boats for use. The men had confidence in their officers; every one worked smoothly and well.

All told, there were eighty persons on board when the *Kansas* left Valparaiso. Of these, seventeen, including the officers, were of European birth or lineage. The remaining sixty-three were men of mixed nationalities, ranging from Spanish-speaking Chileans to negroes. There were eight under-stewards, a cook and his assistants, and nearly fifty sailors and firemen. Unfortunately, the explosion in the stokehold had killed the chief engineer and one of his juniors, while six stokers were dead and several injured.

It was discovered that, before he died, the chief had shut off steam, and thus prevented the accident from assuming far more serious proportions. The second engineer, a Newcastle man named Walker, who rushed to the engine-room at the first indication of a mishap, found his chief lying in collapse on the lever platform. Walker promptly opened certain levers which allowed the steam to escape freely; then he carried his comrade out of the spume to the deck. It was too late. Partial suffocation had placed too great a strain on a diseased heart; by the time Dr. Christobal was summoned, a brave man was dead.

Courtenay, who had left instructions that he was to be called when the Evangelistas light was sighted, was sound asleep. In the elevated quarters assigned to the captain, the noise of the explosion differed little from the thunderous blows of the sea. But the stopping of the engines awoke him instantly. He felt the ship lurch away from her course, and saw the quick swerve of the compass indicator over his head. As he ran down the gangway leading from the bridge he heard the officer of the watch say:

"Something given way in the engine-room, sir."

Several minutes elapsed before he, or Walker, aided by willing volunteers, could penetrate the depths of the stoke-hold. The place was a charnel-house, a stifling pit, filled with the charred contents of the furnaces, which gave off the most noisome fumes owing to the rapid condensation of steam and water escaping from the damaged pipes. But the gale raging without served one good purpose in driving plenty of air down the ventilating cowls. Gradually, the choking atmosphere cleared. Courtenay was the first to reach the lowermost rung of the iron ladder, whence he looked with the eyes of despair on a scene of death and ruin.

The electric light was uninjured. It revealed the bodies of several men, either dead or insensible, lying amidst the scattered coal. Shovels, stoking-rods, and pieces of iron plate had been hurled about in wild confusion. The door of one furnace was blown clean out of its bolts; furnace bars and fire-bricks strewed the iron deck, while, each time the ship rolled, the heavy clank of loose metal somewhere in the engine-room proved that the damage was not confined solely to the stoke-hold.

If Courtenay could have dropped quietly into the sea through the stout hull of the **Kansas** he would have welcomed the certain result in that bitter moment. But he was the captain, and men would look to him for salvation. Well, he would do all that was possible, and, at any rate, die at his post. So, choking back his misery, he organized the work of rescue. Slings were formed of ropes, and those men in whom any signs of life were visible were the first to be lifted to the upper deck. The stoke-hold was quickly emptied of its inanimate occupants; living and dead alike were carried to the untenanted second-class saloon forward. Then Courtenay left Walker to solve the puzzle of the accident and report on its extent, while he climbed back to the bridge, there to tackle the far more pressing problem of the measures to be adopted if he would save his ship.

It was typical of the man that his first act was to wipe the grime of the stoke-hold off his face and hands. Then he drew a chart from the locker in which he had placed it two hours earlier. Mr. Boyle, who had been attending to the signals both by siren and rocket, joined him. Courtenay pointed to a pin-mark in the sheet.

"We were there at six o'clock," he said, and his voice was so steady that he seemed now to be free from the least touch of anxiety. "The course was South-40-East, and, against this wind and sea, together with a strong current to the nor'east, we would make eight knots under easy steam. Therefore, by eight o'clock, when the furnaces blew out, we were here."

He jabbed in a pin a little further down the chart. Mr. Boyle, whose peculiar gifts in the way of speech were accurately described by Dr. Christobal, grunted agreement.

"Huh," he said.

Courtenay glanced at a chronometer.

"It is now a quarter to nine," he went on, "and I reckon that since the ship swung round we have been carried at least six knots to the nor'east."

"Huh," growled Mr. Boyle again, but he bent a trifle nearer the chart. To his sailor's eyes the situation was quite simple. Unless, by God's providence, some miracle happened, the **Kansas** was a doomed ship. The pin stuck where the Admiralty chart recorded soundings of one hundred fathoms with a fine sand bed. The longitude was 75-50 west of Greenwich and latitude 51-35 south. Staring at them from the otherwise blank space which showed the wide expanse of the Pacific was an ominous note by the compilers of the chart:

"Seamen are cautioned not to make free with these shores, as they are very imperfectly known, and, from their wild, desolate character, they cannot be approached with safety."

Right in the track of the drifting ship lay a vaguely outlined trio of dread import: "Breakers; Islet (conical); Duncan Rock." Behind this sinister barrier stood the more definite White Horse Island, while, running due north and south a few miles away to the eastward, was a wavering dotted line which professed to mark the coast of Hanover Island. Lending a fearful significance to the unknown character of the region, a printed comment followed the dotted line: "This coast is laid down from distant observations on board the Beagle." So the sea face of Hanover Island had not been visited by civilized man for nearly sixty years! There, not three hours' steaming distance from the regular track of Chilean commerce, was a place so guarded by reefs on one hand, and impenetrable, ice-capped mountains on the other, that a proper survey was deemed impracticable even by officers of the British Navy, a service which has charted nearly every rock and shoal and tiny islet on the face of the waters.

Neither man spoke while their practised scrutiny took in these details. The roaring chaos of the gale told what fate awaited them. The elemental forces had donned the black cap of the judge and sentenced them to speedy destruction.

Mr. Boyle pursed his lips; he looked sideways at Courtenay.

"Huh," he said. "What's to be done?"

"I propose," answered the captain, coolly, "to endeavor--"

It was then that the giant wave leaped madly over the poop, as though the sea were resolved to swallow its prey without further warning. The second officer, outside on the bridge, had to cling to a stanchion for his life. Courtenay and Boyle saw two boats wrenched from their davits and carried overboard, while a bulkhead forward was smashed into matchwood. The half-caste quarter-master at the wheel muttered "Madonna!" and tried to remember a prayer.

"I propose," continued Courtenay, raising his voice so that the other might hear, "to give the ship steering-way by hoisting the foresail. Will you see to it? Then I intend to warn the passengers, and make such preparations as are possible before we strike."

"Huh," agreed Mr. Boyle. He took the short cut over the rails. In a few seconds the captain heard a flow of ornate Spanish, and he knew that Mr. Boyle was getting the scared Chileans to work.

Then Courtenay went to his own cabin, in which, in the haste of his exit, he had imprisoned Joey. The dog received him with delight, for Joey knew a real gale from a sham one, as well as any man before the mast. Courtenay patted his head, opened a drawer in the writing-table, and drew forth two photographs, which he kissed. He replaced them, locked the drawer, and went out, letting the dog come with him. That was his farewell to his mother and sister; it was the first and last sign of sentiment he exhibited during that night of great endurance.

When he returned from the saloon, he found the chief officer examining the chart.

"Do you think we have any chance of making Concepcion Strait?" he asked, pointing to the doubtfully marked channel which separates Hanover and Duke of

York Islands.

"If we set the mains'le we might bear up a bit."

"Try it."

"Huh," said Mr. Boyle, and he was off again into the spindrift.

Be it understood that the sails carried by a big vessel like the *Kansas* are of little practical value save under certain conditions of wind and sea, when they are rigged to steady her, and thus give help to helm and propeller. Still, they might serve now to carry the ship a point or two towards the north, and this was the sole avenue of escape which remained. Here, again, was one of those trivial circumstances which are so potent in the shaping of events. Had either of the sails blown out, or had the mainsail been set at the same time as the foresail, the course followed during the next few hours must have been deviated from to some extent, and the alteration of a cable's length in direction could not fail to exercise the most momentous result on the fortunes of the *Kansas*. But ships are singularly akin to men in respect to the apparent vagaries of fate. A moment's hesitation, a mere pace to right or left, may mean all the difference between success and failure, safety and danger.

Leaving the chart on the table, where it was secured by drawing-pins, Courtenay went back to his cabin to obtain a pair of sea-boots. Seeing Joey sitting on his tail and shivering, unable to indulge in a comfortable lick because the taste of salt water was hateful, he hunted for a padded mackintosh coat which he had procured for the dog's protection in cold latitudes. He ransacked two lockers before he found it. Several articles were tumbled in a heap on the floor in his haste, and he did not trouble to pack them away again. He buckled Joey into the garment, fastened his own oilskins, and rejoined the second officer on the bridge. A glance showed him the dark wall of the mainsail rising abaft the after funnel. The quarter-master at the wheel, having recovered his wits, was keeping the ship's nose up to the wind by a steady pressure to port. The gale was as fierce as ever. The second officer shouted in Courtenay's ear:

"I am afraid, sir, the wind has shifted a point."

Courtenay looked at the compass. The ship was bearing exactly northeast. He had hoped that the sails would enable her to shape due north, at least; unquestionably some spiteful fiend was urging her headlong to ruin. Had the wind but veered as much to the south, he might have chanced the run through Concepcion Strait, or even weathered Duke of York Island. He nodded to his junior, whose presence on the bridge was a mere matter of form, owing to the powerless condition of the ship and the impenetrable wrack of foam and mist that barred vision ahead, and strode off on a tour of inspection. As wind and sea were now beating more directly on the port side, there was some degree of shelter along the covered-in deck to starboard. He found that two boats had been cleared of their hamper and lowered on the davits until they could be swung in on the promenade deck. The men were thus able to provision them more easily than in their exposed berths on the spar deck. He watched the workers for a few minutes, showed them how to stow and lash some biscuit tins more securely, and continued his survey, meaning to look in on Walker and the doctor.

He had to pass the cabins set apart for the two girls. The ports were lighted, and through one window he could see some one peering out at him. Owing to the thickness of the glass and its blurred condition, he could not tell whether the occupant was Elsie or Isobel, or Isobel's maid, but, whoever it was, a hand seemed to signal to him to open the door.

He unfastened the bolts, and held a half door slightly ajar. Joey, ever eager to be out of the pelting storm, hopped inside, and Courtenay heard Elsie exclaim:

"Good gracious, Joey! Where is your life-belt?"

"Do you want anything?" asked Courtenay, through the chink.

Elsie smiled at him. She was wrapped in a heavy ulster, and had a Tam o' Shanter tied firmly on her head by a stout veil.

"Mr. Malcolm thought we had better bring life-belts from our cabins. I came for mine, and I looked out and saw you. I wanted to ask you what had become of Dr. Christobal. I hope you don't mind?"

"Not in the least. I am just going to him. Would you care to come?"

"Oh, I shall be most pleased."

"He is attending the injured men, you know. And there are--others there, who are beyond his help."

"Perhaps I may be of some assistance."

"Come, then. When I open the door, step out quickly and hold tight to that rail. And don't move until I tell you."

His manner was curt enough to please the superioress of a nunnery. Elsie was awed instantly by the glimpse she obtained of the flying scud within the narrow area of the saloon lights, but she obeyed directions, and presently found herself clinging desperately to the brass hand-rail which ran, breast high, along the outer wall of her cabin. She saw Courtenay kneel to fasten a bolt, and she wondered how a man encumbered with heavy boots could be so active. Then she felt an arm grip her tightly round the waist, and she heard a voice, which sounded as if it had traveled down a long corridor, shouting in her ear:

"Lean well back and trust to me. Let go!"

She had no idea that wind could blow like that, especially when the ship was going in the same direction. It shrieked and whistled and tore at the canvas side-awnings with a vehemence that threatened to rip them from their stays. Courtenay held her glued to his left side, and there was something reassuring in his vice-like grasp. She had a dim notion that he need not squeeze her quite so earnestly, until she passed a gangway which led to the port side, between the deck cabins and the music-room. Then she changed her opinion; were it not for the strong arm which held her she would have been blown into the sea.

To reach the forward saloon they had to pass the boats near which Courtenay had halted. The sailors saw them. During the first lull one of the men said:

"The senor captain is escorting one of the English senoritas from the saloon."

"Where is he taking her to?" asked another.

"Who knows?"

"It will be all the same wherever she is. If the ship goes, we go."

"Who can tell? These English are stupid. They always try to save women first. Once, when I was on the--"

A few words in Spanish reached them from Mr. Boyle, and they went on with their work. But such muttered confidences are eloquent of mischief when the pinch comes.

At the forward end of the promenade deck, just beneath the bridge, Elsie received another reminder of the force of the wind, which was rendered almost intolerable by the lashing of the spray.

"I--can't--go on," she gasped. Courtenay felt, rather than heard, that she was speaking to him. Without further ado, he picked her up in his arms, and deposited her, all flushed and breathless, in the shelter of the fore saloon hatch. If she were so anxious to see her friend the doctor, he was determined she should not be disappointed.

"No time for explanations," he said, while she tremblingly clutched at a rail which gave support down the companion-way. "Dr. Christobal is below. But--I fear you will find a shocking scene. Perhaps you had better let me take you back."

"No, no, not on my account. I think I am past feeling any sentiment. I would far rather do something, be of some use, however slight."

A pungent smell of iodoform came to them up the hatchway. Joey, who had followed bravely in their wake, and was now a few steps down the stairs, crept back, awed.

"At least, let me ask Dr. Christobal if you may come. You will be quite safe here if you grip the rail. Even if a sea breaks over the hatch it cannot touch you. May I leave you? And do you mind holding Joey?"

Elsie detected a return to his earlier manner, and she was grateful to him for it. She did not like him so well when he was stern and curt.

"Yes," she said. "That is only reasonable; but please tell him I shall not be in the way, I know that there are wounded men to be attended, and dead men down there, too. I shall not scream or faint, believe me."

"I am sure of that. Not one woman in a thousand could have played and sung to cheer others, as you did after the accident happened."

It might have been the reaction from her exciting passage along the deck, but Elsie experienced a sudden warm glow in her face. Somehow, it was delightful to hear those words from such a man in the hour of his supremest trial. For she realized what it meant to him, even though his life were saved, if the **Kansas** became a wreck.

She stooped, ostensibly to grasp the dog's collar.

"Before you leave me," she said, "let me tell you how sorry I am for you."

He ran down the stairs, and entered the small saloon, which had been hastily converted into a hospital. Perhaps it would be better described as a mortuary, for it held more dead than living. Christobal, aided by two sailors, was wrapping lint round a fireman's seared arm. Happily, there was an abundance of cotton sheets available, and the men tore them into strips. But the comparatively small supply of cotton wool carried in the ship's stores, and in the doctor's private medicine chest had long since given out.

"Miss Maxwell is here. She asked me to bring her to you in case she might be able to render you some assistance," explained Courtenay.

Christobal drew himself upright, with the slowness of an elderly man whose joints are stiffening.

"Miss Maxwell here?" he repeated, obviously surprised, if not displeased. He waved a hand towards the men laid on mattresses on the deck. Most were quite motionless; others writhed in agony. "She cannot come--it is impossible."

"It is her wish."

"Quite impossible. Where is she?"

"Standing in the companion."

Courtenay saw that the girl could do no good now in that chamber of death; the mere memory of it would be an abiding horror. He wanted Christobal himself to send her away, but the doctor had taken off his coat and bared his arms. His appearance was grimly business-like.

"Will you tell her how much I am obliged to her for her kind thought. But you see--it cannot be permitted. Please say that I hope to join her in the saloon in a quarter of an hour. My work is nearly ended. I am sure you will make her understand that this is not a place for a woman."

Again he swept the row of silent bodies with a comprehensive hand. Yet the trivial thought intruded itself on the sailor that this elegant old Spaniard delegated the task of explanation to him solely because he did not wish to appear before Miss Maxwell in a somewhat disheveled state. He dismissed the notion at once.

"How many?" he asked, glancing at the quiet forms which bore no bandages.

"Eleven, now. By the way, just one word. What chance have we?" Christobal put the concluding sentence in French.

Courtenay answered in the same language: "A very poor one. But I shall come to the saloon and warn you. That will be only fair, don't you think?"

"Most certainly. Well--I may as well finish here." And the doctor signed to his helpers to lift the next sufferer on to the table.

Courtenay returned to the stairway. At the top stood Elsie, looking eagerly for his reappearance. A sense of unutterable anguish shook him for a second as he saw the sweet face, instinct with life and beauty, gazing down at him. How monstrous it was to think of such a fair woman being battered out of recognition against the rocks. He bit his lip savagely, and it is to be feared the words he swallowed were not those of supplication. But his eyes were calm and his voice well under control when he said:

"Dr. Christobal is captain below there, Miss Maxwell, and he absolutely vetoes your presence. He was exceedingly distressed at being compelled to send you such a message. However, he will soon explain matters to you in person, as he is coming aft almost at once."

Elsie was disappointed. She dreaded the return to the saloon, with its queerly assorted company. When she quitted them, they were in a state of indescribable distress. Gray and the Englishman were helping the chief steward to adjust life-belts; but Isobel was in a frenzy of despair, her maid had fainted, de Poincilit and the Spaniards were muttering alternate appeals to the saints and oaths of utter abandonment, and Mrs. Somerville was almost unconscious, while her husband knelt by her side and wrung his hands in abject misery. Anything was better than to go back to that woful assembly, yet she choked down a protest and said quietly:

"I am ready. I am afraid I have been a bother to you, Captain Courtenay."

"Say, rather, you have given me hope. I think Heaven has work for you to do in the world. Let me go out first. Never mind Joey. He can struggle along behind. Steady now. Head down and lean well against the wind."

Elsie found, to her amazement, that there was less sense of danger in facing the wind than in being driven along before it. Moreover, she had greater confidence during this second transit over the exposed portion of the deck. She felt Courtenay dragging her on irresistibly until they gained the lee of the smoking-room. He let her rest there, beneath the ladder leading to the bridge. Then a strange revulsion of feeling came to him. He experienced an overwhelming desire not to be parted from her; he had a sickening fear that he might never see her again; so he shouted, very close to her cheek:

"Would you like to sit in my cabin a little while, if I bring Miss Baring?"

She thought that would be splendid. Courtenay, if any one, would succeed in calming Isobel. In order to make herself heard she, in turn, had to put her lips quite near to Courtenay's face.

"Yes," she cried, "I shall be only too pleased. But be patient with her; she is very frightened."

There is no accounting for the workings of a man's mind. Courtenay, at no time a lady's man, most certainly had other matters to attend to just then. Yet here he was thinking only of a woman's comfort. His dismal forebodings were banished by a rush of absurd delight at the thought that he would have an opportunity of speaking to her occasionally. What a brave girl she was! What a wife for a sailor! In truth, these were mad notions that jostled in his brain when his life and her's were not worth an hour's purchase. He drew her to the foot of the ladder.

"Run ahead, Joey!" he cried. The dog, a weird little figure leaning forward at a ridiculous angle against the tearing wind, obeyed instantly. "Now, you," he said to Elsie, "but wait until I pass you at the top."

Though her skirts were troublesome, she managed the ascent. Then she was taken off her feet again, and hardly knew where she was until she found herself in the haven of Courtenay's cabin. Joey was glad to be there, too. He shook himself noisily in his heavy coat.

"You won't mind if I fasten the door on you?" and the captain so far forgot his anxiety as to smile.

"No, indeed," and she smiled in response.

"Very well. I shall bring Miss Baring in about five minutes. You won't stir till we come?"

"What? Face that gale without you?" She almost laughed at the idea. He bolted the door, and he ran into the chart-house to tap the barometer. It moved appreciably. It was rising! Ah, if only the wind moderated, he could save the *Kansas* yet! He glanced at the compass. Still the same course. Not a fraction of a point gained to the north. That was bad. The ship was already within the danger zone. Pray Heaven for a falling wind, or even a change to the southward! Still, it was in an altogether more cheerful mood that he regained the promenade deck and made his way towards the saloon.

He was in the very act of entering the doorway when a shudder ran through the ship, and she lifted slightly. Clinging to a rail, he waited, rigid as a statue. A second time the great steel hull shook, but much more violently. Then the *Kansas* ran her nose into a shoal, swung round broadside to the sea, lifted again, struck heavily, and listed to port.

Courtenay was on the starboard side. He heard a yell of dismay from the men attending to the boats. Screams came from the saloon. The sea leaped triumphantly over the rails and nearly smothered him with its dense spray. So this was the end? It had come all too soon. And what a place for the ship to be cast away! Twenty miles from the nearest land, in the midst of a sea where no boat could live. God help them all!

CHAPTER V
THE KANSAS SUSTAINS A CHECK--

Once, in early days, when Courtenay was a middy an a destroyer, his ship ran ashore on the Manacles. After a bump or two, and a noise like the snapping of trees during a hurricane, the little vessel broke her back, and the after part, with the engines, fell away into deep water. Courtenay happened to be on the bridge; the forward half held intact, so he and the other survivors clambered ashore at low water.

He waited now for the rending of plates, the tearing asunder of stanch steel ribs and cross-beams, which should sound the knell of the ship's last moments. But the *Kansas* seemed to be in no hurry to fall in pieces. She strained and groaned, and shook violently when a wave pounded her; otherwise, she lay there like a beaten thing, oddly resembling the living but almost unconscious men stretched on the mattresses in the forward saloon.

Courtenay did not experience the least fear of death. Emotion of any sort was already dead in him. He found himself wondering if an unexpectedly strong current, setting to the southeast, had not upset his reckoning--if there were any broken limbs among the occupants of the saloon--if Elsie had been injured by being thrown down into his cabin. He looked at his watch; it was past eleven. In four hours there would be dawn. Dawn! In as many minutes he might see the day that is everlasting. . . . Ah! Perhaps not even four minutes! The *Kansas*, with a shiver, lifted to the embrace of a heavy sea, lurched to port, and settled herself more comfortably. The deck assumed an easier angle. Now it was possible to walk. There were no rocks here, at any rate. Courtenay at once jumped to the conclusion that the powerful current whose existence he suspected had cut out for itself a deep-water channel towards the land, and the ship had struck on the silt of its back-wash. Anyhow, the **Kansas** was still living. The lights were all burning steadily. He could detect the rhythmic throb of the donkey-engine. He felt it like the faint beat of a pulse. In her new position the ship presented less of a solid wall to the onslaught of the sea. The tumultuous waves began to race past without breaking so fiercely. Had she started her plates? Were the holds and engine-room full of water? If so, Walker and his helpers were already drowning beneath his feet. And, when next she moved, the vessel might slip away into the depths!

These and kindred thoughts, thoughts without sequence and almost without number, flew through his mind with incredible speed. They were lucid and reasoned, their pros and cons equally dealt with--he could have answered any question on each point were it propounded by a board of examiners--and all this took place within a few seconds, between the impact of one big wave and another.

A man rushed by, or tried to do so. Courtenay recognized him as a leading stoker who had temporary charge of the donkey-boiler and seized him wrathfully, his eyes ablaze.

"Go back!" he roared.

"Senor! The ship is lost!"

"Go back, and await my orders."

He could have strangled the fugitive in his sudden rage. The fireman endeavored to gasp his readiness to obey. Courtenay relaxed his grip, and, for a time, at least one member of the crew stuck to his post, fearing the mad captain more than death.

A mob of stewards and kitchen hands came in a torrent up the saloon stairs. Courtenay met them, a terrifying figure, and thrust a revolver in their faces.

"Back!" he shouted, "or some of you will die here."

Even in their frenzy they believed him. The foremost slunk away, and fought in a new terror with those who would urge them on. Gray, bleeding from a cut across the forehead, knocked down a man who brutally tore Isobel out of his path. Tollemache, a revolver in each hand, set his back against the corner of the saloon at the foot of the stairs.

"I'm with you, captain," he yelled.

Courtenay saw that he had conquered them--for the instant. He raised his hand.

"Behave like men," he cried. "You can do no good by crowding the deck. I am going to the bridge to see if it is possible to lower the boats. Each boat's crew will be mustered in turn, passengers and men alike. If you are cowards now you will throw away what chance there is of saving your lives."

His voice rang out like a trumpet. His attitude cowed while it reassured them. Men turned from one to another to ask what the senor captain was saying. They understood much, but they wanted to make sure of each word. Was there any hope? Now that the gates of death were opening, he was a god in their eyes--a god who promised life in return for obedience.

A revolver barked twice somewhere on deck. A bullet smashed one of the windows of the music-room and lodged in a panel behind Courtenay. They all heard the reports, but the captain promptly turned the incident to advantage.

"You see we mean to maintain order," he said. "Mr. Malcolm, take care that every one has a lifebelt."

A sort of cheer came from the men. Who could fail to believe in a leader so cool and resourceful? He ran out into the darkness to discover the cause of the shooting. A number of sailors and firemen were striving to launch a boat. There was a struggle going on. He could not distinguish friend from foe in the melee, but he threw himself into it fearlessly.

"You fools!" he shouted. "You may die soon enough without killing each other. Make way there! Ah! would you?" He caught the gleam of an uplifted knife, and struck savagely at the face of the man who would have used it. The butt of the revolver caught the sailor on the temple. He went down like a stone. Courtenay stumbled over another prostrate body. It was Mr. Boyle, striving to rise. Their eyes met in the gloom. Courtenay stooped and swung the other clear of the fight, for the second and third officers were using their fists, and Walker, even in the hurry of his ascent from the stoke-hold, had not let go of a spanner. The yells and curses, the trampling of dim forms swaying in the fight, the roaring of the gale, and the incessant crash of heavy spray made up a ghastly pandemonium. It was an orgy of terror, of wild abandon, of hopeless striving on the edge of the pit--a stupid madness at the best, as the ship's life-boats on the port side were on the spar deck; in their panic the men were endeavoring to lower a dingy. Yet Courtenay saw that discipline was regaining its influence. He thought to inspire confidence and stop useless savagery by a sharp command.

"All hands follow me to starboard!"

The struggle ceased instantly. The captain's order seemed to imply some new scheme. Men who, a moment ago, would have killed any one who sought to restrain them from clearing the boat's falls, now raced pell-mell after their officers. No heed was paid to those who lay on the deck, wounded or insensible. Herein alone did these Chilean sailors differ from wolves, and wolves have the excuse of fierce hunger when they devour their disabled fellows.

Still carrying Boyle, Courtenay led the confused horde through a gangway to the higher side of the deck.

"Swing those boats back to the spar deck!" he said. "Get falls and tackle ready to lift them to port. Don't lose your heads, men. You will all be clear of the ship in ten minutes if you do as you are told."

Two officers and a quarter-master sprang forward. In an incredibly short space of time the crew were working with redoubled frenzy, but under control, and with a common object. For an instant, Courtenay was free to attend to his chief officer. He bore him to the lighted saloon companion. Boyle was deathly pale under the tan of his skin. The captain saw that his own left hand, where it clasped the other round the waist, was covered with blood.

"Below there!" he cried. "Bring two men here, Mr. Malcolm."

When the chief steward came he gave directions that Mr. Boyle should be taken to the saloon and Dr. Christobal summoned.

"Send some one you can trust to return," he continued. "Go then to the lee of the promenade deck. You will find others there."

He did not stop to ask himself if solicitude for the unfortunates wounded in the fight were of any avail. His mind was clear, the habit of command strong in him. Not until the sea claimed him would he cease to rule. The clank of pulleys, the cries of the sailors heaving at the ropes, told him that the crew were at work. At last he was free to go to the bridge.

He found the quarter-master in the chart-house, on his knees. When the ship struck, the officer of the watch had been thrown headlong to port. Recovering his feet before a tumbling sea could fling him overboard, he hauled himself out of danger just in time to take part in the fray on deck. He came back now, hurrying to join the captain. Courtenay, standing in the shelter of the chart-house, was peering through the flying scud to leeward. The sea was darker there than it had been for hours. Around the ship the surface was milk-like with foam, but beyond the area of the shoal there seemed to be a remote chance for a boat to live.

"We 're on a sort of breakwater, sir," said the second officer.

"Seems like it. Is the ship hard and fast?"

"I am afraid so."

"I think the weather is moderating. Go and see how the barometer stands."

"Steady improvement, sir," came the report.

"Any water coming in?"

"Mr. Walker said he thought not."

"Perhaps it doesn't matter. Try to get the first life-boat lowered. Let her carry as many extra hands as possible. We have lost two boats. But do not send any women in her. If all is well, let them go in the next one. Take charge of that yourself."

"Would you mind tying this handkerchief tightly just here, sir?"

The second officer held out his left forearm.

"Were you knifed, too?" asked Courtenay.

"It is not much, but I am losing a good deal of blood."

"The brutes--the unreasoning brutes!" muttered the captain. As he knotted the linen into a rough tourniquet the other asked:

"Shall I report to you when the first boat gets away, sir?"

"No need. I shall see what happens. When she is clear I shall bring the ladies to you."

Pride of race helped these men to talk as collectedly as if the ship were laid alongside a Thames wharf. They knew not the instant the *Kansas* might lift again and turn turtle, yet they did not dream of deviating a hair's breadth from their duties. The second officer went aft to carry out the captain's instructions. Courtenay followed a little way, passing to leeward of the chart-house, until he reached his own quarters. There was no door on that side, but light streamed through a couple of large port-holes across which the curtains had not been drawn. He looked in. Elsie was leaning against the table to balance herself on the sloping deck. She held Joey in her arms. She seemed to be talking to the dog, who answered in his own way, by trying to lick her face. The glass was so blurred that Courtenay could not see that she was crying.

"Better wait," he muttered, and turned his gaze seaward again. Yes, there could be no doubt that the almost unbroken swell within half a cable's length of the ship promised a possibility of escape. There was no telling what dangers lay beyond. To his reckoning, the nearest land was twenty miles distant, but the shoal water might extend all the way, and, with a falling wind, waves once disintegrated would not regain any considerable size. It was a throw of the dice for life, but it must be taken. He indulged in a momentary thought as to his own course. Would he leave the ship in the last boat? Yes, if every wounded man on board were taken off first; and how could he entertain even a shred of hope that his cowardly crew would preserve such discipline to the end as to permit of that being done?

The answer to his mute question came sooner than he expected. He had been standing there alone about five minutes, intently watching the set of the sea, so as to determine the best time for lowering a boat, when, amid the sustained shriek of the wind and the lashing of the spray, he heard sounds which told him that the forward port life-boat was being swung outward on the davits. The hurricane deck was a mass of confused figures. The two boats to starboard, a life-boat and the jolly-boat, had been carried across the deck in readiness to take the places of the port life-boats. A landsman might think that medley reigned supreme; but it was not so. Sailor-like work was proceeding with the utmost speed and system, when an accident happened. For some reason never ascertained, though it was believed that the men in the leading boat were too anxious to clear the falls and failed to take the proper precautions, the heavy craft pitched stern foremost into the sea. She sank like a stone, and with her went a number of Chileans; their despairing yells, coming up from the churning froth, seemed to be a signal for the demoniac passions latent in the crew to burst forth again, this time in a consuming blaze that would not be stayed. Each man fought blindly for himself, heedless now of all restrictions. The knowledge of this latest disaster spread with amazing rapidity. Up from the saloon came a rush of stewards and others. Overborne in the panic-stricken flight, Gray, Tollemache, Christobal, the French Count and the head steward, not knowing what new catastrophe threatened, brought Mr. Somerville and the almost inanimate women with them, leaving to their fate those who, like Boyle, were unable to move. Some of the mob rushed up the bridge companion; others made for the after ladders used only by sailors; others, again, swung themselves to the spar deck by the rails and awning standards. Even before Courtenay could reach the scene, both the second and third officers were stabbed, this time mortally. He saw one of the infuriated mutineers heave the third officer's body overboard--a final quittance for some injury previously received.

He emptied his revolver into the tumbling mass of men, but he was swept aside by the fresh gang from the saloon, and perhaps owed his escape from instant death by falling on the slippery deck. He was up again, shouting, entreating, striking right and left, but he felt bitterly that his efforts now were of no avail, and he bethought him that there was only one resource left. These frenzied wretches would destroy themselves and all others--so, if he would save even a few of the lives entrusted to his care, at least one of the boats must be protected. The struggle was fiercest for the possession of the two life-boats. By a determined effort the jolly-boat might be secured.

So he ran to obtain help from the few he could trust, from the tiny company of white men he had left in the saloon; he met them, a forlorn procession, coming up to the bridge. The all-powerful instinct of self-preservation, aided, no doubt, by the stinging, drenching showers of spray, had gone far towards reanimating Isobel and her maid, while Mrs. Somerville, a woman advanced in years, was able to walk, though benumbed with the sudden cold. Courtenay unlocked the door of his cabin. Elsie, her face pale and tear-stained, but outwardly composed, was yet standing near the table, and the dog sprang from her arms the moment his master appeared.

"Thank God!" she said, all of a flutter now that the solitary waiting for a death which came not was ended. "I feared I should never see you again. Is the ship lost?"

The wild soughing of the wind rendered her words indistinct. And the captain had no time for explanations.

"In here!" he shouted to Gray, who had helped Isobel to enter the chart-room, the first refuge available on this exposed deck.

"Sharp with it!" he thundered, when Isobel was unwilling to face the storm again. The men took their cue from his imperative tone. Gray clasped Isobel in his arms and lifted her bodily through the doorway. The others followed his example. Soon the three women were with Elsie in the cabin. Isobel, by sheer reaction from her previous hysteria, was sullen now, and heedless of all considerations save her own misery. When she set eyes on Elsie she snapped out:

"You here!"

"Yes. Captain Courtenay brought me to his cabin after our return from the fore saloon."

"Oh, did he? And he left me with those devils beneath!"

They both heard Courtenay's hurried order:

"Leave the ladies here until we can come for them. Follow me at once."

The door slammed behind the men. Even the missionary was fired to action by Courtenay's manner. Elsie helped Mrs. Somerville to a chair. Then she turned to Isobel, and said gently:

"It is a slight thing to discuss when any moment may be our last, but the captain placed me here while he went to bring you. He had gone only a few seconds when the ship struck."

The crest of a wave combed over the upper works and pounded the solid beams and planks of the cabin until they creaked. The ship lifted somewhat as the sea enveloped her.

"Oh, this is awful!" shrieked Isobel. "If I must die, let me die quickly. I shall go mad."

"Calm yourself, dear. There must be an end of our sufferings soon. Perhaps we may escape even yet."

"Yes, I know. If any one is saved it will be you. You left me down there to take my chance among those fiends. You have been here hours, with your precious captain, no doubt. Were he looking after his ship this might not have happened. . . . Why did I ever come on this wretched vessel? And with you, who ran away from Ventana! I should have been warned by it. When he could work me no other evil he sent you. . . . Oh, you have taken a fine vengeance, Pedro Ventana! May you be denied mercy as I am denied it now! . . . Go away! If you touch me I shall strike you. I hate you! I tell you I am losing my senses. Do you wish me to tear your face with my nails?"

Elsie, who would have soothed her distraught friend with a loving hand, drew back in real fear that she was confronted by a maniac. The utter outrageousness of this new infliction brought tears to her eyes. Yet she choked back her grief for the sake of the others.

"Isobel, darling, please try to control yourself," she pleaded. "Don't say such cruel things to me. You cannot mean them. I would do anything to serve you. I am more sorry for you than for myself. I have little to bind me to this life, whereas you have everything. Indeed, indeed, I have not been away from you many minutes."

Another heavy sea pitched on board. The *Kansas* trembled and listed suddenly. Isobel screamed shrilly, and burst into a storm of dry-eyed sobs. Her mood changed instantly into one of abject submission. She sprang towards Elsie with hands outstretched.

"Oh, save me, save me!" she wailed. "God knows I am not fit to die!"

There are some noble natures which find strength in the need to comfort the weakness of others. Elsie drew the distracted girl close to her, and placed an arm round her neck.

"It is not for us to say when we shall die," she murmured. "Let us try to be resigned. We must bear our misfortunes with Christian faith and hope. Somehow, I feel that I have endured so much to-night that death looks less terrible now. Perhaps that is because it is so near. To me, the specter seems to be receding."

"Did the captain tell you we had any chance of escape, senorita?" asked the Spanish maid.

"What hope did Captain Courtenay hold out?" demanded Mrs. Somerville, who had listened to Isobel's raving with small comprehension.

Elsie left unuttered the protest on her lips. They all thought she possessed Courtenay's confidence in the same extraordinary degree. Well, she would try to impart consolation in that way. It was ridiculous, but it would serve.

"Of course we are in a desperate situation," she said, "but while the ship holds together there is always a chance of rescue, and you can see quite clearly that she is far from breaking up yet."

"Rescue! Did he speak of rescue?" cried Isobel. "That is impossible, unless we take to the boats. And the cry in the saloon was that two boats were lost long ago and a third just now. That is why we were brought on deck. Were they launching a boat?"

"I don't know," said Elsie. "I was here quite alone, except for Joey."

"Ah, it was true then. He was acting secretly, and the men broke loose as soon as they heard of it."

Elsie found this recurring suspicion of Courtenay's motives harder to bear than the preceding paroxysm of unreasoning rage. She had heard the shooting, bellowing, and tramping on deck, and she knew that some terrible scene was being enacted there, while the mere fact that the captain himself placed the female passengers in his cabin proved that he was doing his best for all.

"I do not believe for one instant that Captain Courtenay was acting otherwise than as a brave and honorable gentleman," she said; and then the fantastic folly of such a dispute at such a moment overcame her. She drew apart from Isobel, leaned against the wall of the cabin, and wept unrestrainedly.

Her companions in misfortune did not realize how greatly her calm self-reliance had comforted them until they witnessed this unlooked-for collapse. The Spanish maid slipped to her knees, Mrs. Somerville began to rock in her chair in a new agony, and Isobel, to whom a turbulent spirit denied the relief of tears when they were most needed, buried her face in a curtain which draped one of the windows.

It was thus that Courtenay found them, when he appeared at the door after a lapse of time which none of them could measure.

"Now, Miss Maxwell, you first," he said with an air of authority which betokened some new move of utmost importance.

"First--for what?" she managed to ask.

"You are going off in a boat. It is your best chance. Please be quick."

"No, Miss Baring goes before me. Then the others, I shall come last."

"Have it as you will. I addressed you because you were nearest the door. Come along, Miss Baring."

He waited for no further words. He grasped Isobel's arm and led her out into the darkness. It seemed to be a very long time before he returned.

"Now, Mrs. Somerville," he said, but that unhappy lady was so unnerved that he had to carry her.

"Can you manage to bring the maid?" he asked over his shoulder to Elsie. This trust in her drove away the weakness which had conquered her under Isobel's taunts. She stooped over the maid, but the girl wrestled and fought with her in frantic dread of the passage along the deck and of facing that howling sea in a small boat.

Elsie herself was almost worn out when Courtenay came back. He took in the situation at a glance. He picked up the shrieking maid in his strong arms.

"You won't mind waiting for me," he said to Elsie.

"Don't attempt to come alone. You are too exhausted."

It was a fine thing to do, but she smiled at him to show that she could still repay his confidence.

"I shall wait," she said simply.

So she was left there, all alone again, without even the dog to bear her company.

CHAPTER VI
--BUT GOES ON AGAIN INTO THE UNKNOWN

This final waiting for the chance of succor seemed to be the hardest trial of all. The door had been hooked back to keep it wide open, so wind and sea invaded the trim privacy of the cabin. Spray leaped over the ship in such dense sheets that a considerable quantity of water quickly lodged on the port side where Courtenay's bunk was fixed. There was no means of escape for it in that quarter, and the angle at which the *Kansas* lay would permit a depth of at least two feet to accumulate ere the water began to flow out through the door to the starboard.

At the great crises of existence the stream of thought is apt to form strange eddies. Courtenay, when the ship struck, and it was possible that each second might register his last conscious impression, found himself coolly reviewing various explanations of the existence of an uncharted shoal in a locality situate many miles from the known danger zone. Elsie, strung half-consciously to the highest tension by the affrighting probability of being set adrift in a small boat at the mercy of the sea roaring without--a sea which pounded the steel hull of the *Kansas* with such force that the great ship seemed to flinch from each blow like a creature in pain--Elsie, then, faced by such an intolerable prospect, was a prey to real anxiety because the wearing apparel scattered by Courtenay on the floor was becoming soaked in brine.

She actually stooped to rescue a coat which was not yet saturated beyond redemption. As she lifted the garment, a packet of letters, tied with a tape, fell from its folds. She placed the coat on the writing-table, and endeavored to stuff the letters into a pigeon-hole. They were too bulky, so she laid them on the coat. In doing this she could not avoid seeing the words, "Your loving sister, Madge," written on the outer fold of the last letter in the bundle.

And that brought a memory of her previous visit to the captain's stateroom; the contrast between the careless chatter of that glorious summer afternoon and the appalling midnight of this fourth day of the voyage was something quite immeasurable; it was marked by a void as that which separates life and death. She was incapable of reasoned reflection. A series of mental pictures, a startling jumble of ideas--trivial as the wish to save the clothes from a wetting, tremendous as the near prospect of eternity--danced through her brain with bewildering clearness. She felt that if she were fated to live to a ripe old age she would never forget a single detail of the furniture and decorations of the room. She would hear forever the dolorous howling of the gale, the thumping of the waves against the quivering plates, the rapid, methodic thud of the donkey-engine, which, long since deserted by its cowardly attendant, was faithfully doing its work and flooding the ship with electric light.

She could scarcely believe that it was she, Elsie Maxwell, who stood there on the tremulous island of the ship amidst a stormy ocean the like of which she had never seen before. She seemed to possess an entity apart from herself, to be a passive witness of events as in a dream; presently, she would awake and find that she was back in her pleasant room at the Morrisons' hacienda, or tucked up in her own comfortable cabin. Yet here was proof positive that the terror which environed her was real. Bound up with the thunder of the gale were the words, "Your loving sister, Madge"--evidently the sister Captain Courtenay had spoken of--"matron of a hospital in the suburbs of London," he said. Would he ever see her again? Or his mother? Had he thought of them at all during this night of woe? Beneath his iron mask did tears lurk, and dull agony, and palsied fear--surely a man could suffer like a woman, even though he endured most nobly?

And then, not thinking in the least what she was doing, she scrutinized the closely tied packet. She wondered idly why he treasured so many missives. Each and every one, oddly enough, was written on differently sized and variously colored note-paper. And it could be seen at a glance that they were from as many different people. The outside letter was the most clearly visible. Miss Courtenay wrote a well-formed, flowing hand. If handwriting were a clue to character, she was a candid, generous, open-minded woman.

But what was this? Elsie suddenly threw down the letters. She had read a sentence at the top of the page twice before she actually grasped its purport. When its significance dawned on her, she flushed violently. For this was what she read:

"I am glad of it, too, because under no other circumstances would I wish to greet and embrace the woman destined to be your wife."

The knowledge that she had involuntarily intruded on Captain Courtenay's private affairs brought her back with a certain slight shock to a sense of actualities. The storm, the horrible danger she was in, emerged from shadow-land. Why had he not come for her? Surely there must have been some further mishap! Heavens! Was she alone on the ship, alone with the dead men and the dying vessel? Her head swam with a strange faintness, and she placed a hand to her eyes. She felt that she must leave the cabin at once, and strive to make her way unaided along the deck. Yes, whatever happened, she would go now. It was too dreadful to wait there any longer in ignorance as to her fate.

Then Joey sprang in through the doorway, and, with that splendid disregard for sentiment displayed by a fox-terrier who has just come out of a first-rate fight, shook his harness until it rattled.

But he eyed the inrush of the sea with much disfavor, so he leaped up on the table beside Elsie, and looked at her as though he would ask why she had permitted this sacrilege.

Though the dog was apparently unscathed and in the best of condition, his head and forepaws were blood-stained. His advent dispelled the mist which was gathering in the girl's brain. She feared a tragedy, yet Joey assuredly would not be so cheerful, so daintily desirous to avoid the splashing water in the cabin, if his master were injured. She was doubtful now whether to go on deck or not. The mere presence of the dog was a guarantee that Courtenay had not quitted the ship. Indeed, Elsie colored again, and more deeply, at the disloyalty of her ungoverned fear. Joey's master would be the last man to desert a woman, no matter what the excuse. She strove to listen for any significant noises without, but wind and sea rendered the effort useless to untrained ears, and there was no shooting or frenzied yells to rise above the storm.

"Oh, Joey," she said, "I wish you could speak!"

The sound of her own voice startled her. In a fashion, it gave her a measure of time. It seemed so long since she had heard a spoken word. The captain could certainly have gone round the whole ship since he left her. What could have detained him? She was yielding to nervousness again, and was on the point of venturing out, at least as far as the deck-house ran, to see if she could distinguish what was taking place on the after part of the vessel, when Dr. Christobal entered.

"I suppose you thought you were forgotten," he cried with a pleasant smile, for Christobal would have a smile for a woman even on his death-bed. "There, now! Don't try to explain your feelings. You have had a very trying time, and I want you to oblige me by drinking this."

"This" was a glass of champagne, which he hurriedly poured out of a small bottle he was carrying into a glass which he produced from a pocket. The trivial action, no less than Dr. Christobal's manner, suggested that they were engaged in some fantastic picnic. The outer horrors were not for them, apparently. They were as secure as sight-seers in the Cave of the Winds, awe-smitten tourists who cling to a rail while mighty Niagara thunders harmlessly overhead.

The mere sight of the wine caused Elsie to realize that her lips and palate were on fire with salt. At one moment she had not the slightest cognizance of her suffering; at the next, she felt that speech was impossible until she drank. Never before had she known what thirst was. A somewhat inferior vintage suddenly assumed a bouquet which surpassed the finest cru ever dreamt of by Marne valley vigneron.

"Ah, that is better," said the doctor. "Now, if you don't mind, we shall have the door closed."

With peace suddenly restored to the room, and her faculties helped more than she suspected, Elsie began to wonder what had happened.

"Where are the others?" she asked; "and why are you taking things so coolly? Captain Courtenay said--"

"Captain Courtenay said exactly what he meant. But circumstances proved too strong for him. We shall not be able to leave the ship just yet."

"Can't they lower any of the boats?"

"Most decidedly. Two boats have been gone some time. I imagined you knew that. Did not the captain tell you?"

At another time Elsie would have laughed at the prevalent delusion that she enjoyed Courtenay's confidence so thoroughly. But she felt that her companion's glib tone was artificial. Something had occurred which he was keeping from her.

She believed that he had gone to the saloon to procure the wine so that she might have what men called Dutch courage when bad news came.

"I have not exchanged a dozen words with the captain since you refused my help in the fore cabin," she said. "He had other matters to attend to than explaining the progress of events to me. Why cannot you trust me? I shall not scream, nor faint, nor hinder you in your work; I ask you again-- Where are the others?"

"You mean Miss Baring and Mrs. Somerville?"

"Yes."

"If they are living, they are far enough away by this time. When their boat was lowered it was cast off prematurely--"

"Purposely?"

"Well--yes. Courtenay had just placed Miss Baring's maid on board when some of the crew let go the ropes. What could we do? We were forced to depend on them."

"Is there no other boat?"

Christobal threw out his hands in his characteristic gesture. He was so emphatic that he spilled some of the wine.

"You take it bravely," he said. "I may as well give you the whole story. The first boat lowered was lost, through the men's own bungling, the captain says. Then there was a desperate fight for the three remaining craft. Most of the officers were killed. Courtenay got a few of us together when Isobel and Mrs. Somerville joined you here, and we held off such of the madmen as tried to seize the jolly-boat. They managed to lower two life-boats, but, between murder and panic, not half of the crew escaped in that way. Four men, who were left behind, promised obedience, and Malcolm, the steward, was placed in charge, with Mr. Gray as second in command. One of the engineers, acting on the captain's orders, brought a can of oil from the engine-room and threw it over the side in handfuls. The result was magical. We lowered the boat easily, placed Monsieur de Poincilit on board, because he was worse than the women, and then Courtenay, as you know, brought Isobel, the minister's wife--who refused to go without her husband--and the maid. There was room for you and another, so, at the captain's request, Tollemache and I tossed for the vacancy. Meanwhile, Courtenay had turned to go for you, when we heard a shout from Gray; two of the Chileans had cast off the ropes which kept the boat alongside. Gray, who was fending her from the ship with the boat-hook, jabbed one fellow in the face with it; but he was too late. The boat raced off into the darkness. And here we are!"

That Christobal left several things unsaid Elsie knew quite well. He plumed himself on the reserve he had acquired from his English mother, though in all matters pertaining to nationality he was a true hidalgo. Indeed, there was a touch of vanity in the way he examined the sparkle of the champagne he now poured into Elsie's empty glass. He scrutinized the wine with the air of a connoisseur. He was looking for the gas to rise in three or four well-defined spirals. And he nodded doubtfully, before drinking it, as one might say:

"The right brand, but of what year?"

Then it dawned on the girl that both her elderly friend and she herself were accepting an extraordinary situation with remarkable nonchalance.

"How many of us remain on the ship?" she asked.

"Very few--on the effective list. The captain, an engineer whose name I do not know, Mr. Tollemache, and ourselves make up the total."

"Where is Mr. Boyle?"

"Ah, poor Boyle! I fear he is done for. He is very badly wounded. I bandaged him as well as I could, but the call on deck was imperative."

"Is he in the saloon? Should we not go to him?"

"I have only just left him. The hemorrhage has stopped, and I gave him some brandy. Believe me, we can do nothing more for him. I told Courtenay it was quite useless to place him on board the boat. You may be sure he was not forgotten."

"I did not imagine that any one would be forgotten," said Elsie, and, for some reason, the light in her eyes caused Christobal to go on rapidly:

"We have a whole crowd of injured men on board, Miss Maxwell. At present we can render them no aid. I thought it wisest to obey orders. The captain told me to bring you some wine and remain with you here. It will not be for long."

"Why do you say that?"

"The ship appears to be lodged hard and fast on a reef or sandspit. I am told the tide is rising. If that is so, our only hope is in the raft which our three allies are now constructing. With a falling tide we might have a breathing-space at low water. As it is, well--"

Christobal, with a bottle in one hand and a glass in the other, nevertheless waved them. Elsie, whose nervous system at this juncture was proof against any but the last pang of imminent death, could almost have laughed at the queer figure he cut, brandishing his arms and standing awkwardly on the inclined deck. She bent her head to hide the smile on her lips; she noticed that Joey was panting, the use of his teeth on various wet legs during the tussle for the jolly-boat having caused him to swallow more salt-water than he cared for. Elsie's sympathies were aroused. While assuaging her own thirst she had neglected the dog. She took a carafe of water from its wooden stand near the table, and poured some of the contents into a tumbler. Joey's thanks were ecstatic. He yelped with delight at the mere thought of a drink.

While the dog was lapping a second supply, the *Kansas* shifted again with a disconcerting suddenness. The water in the cabin swirled across the floor as the ship was restored to an even keel. The movement dislodged the packet of letters. It fell, and Elsie rescued it a second time. Christobal watched her with undisguised admiration.

"Really," he said, "I find you wonderful."

"Why?" Certainly she might be pardoned for seeking an explanation of any compliment just then.

"Why? Por Dios! Excuse me, but that slipped out sideways. Just imagine any woman being able to attend to a dog and pick up a bundle of letters at the very instant the ship appeared to be slipping off into deep water!"

"Is not that the best thing that can happen?"

"My dear young lady, we should sink instantly."

"How do you know?"

"Well--er--I don't exactly know, but I assume that the hull was broken long since."

"I don't see why you should take that for granted. These very movements seem to me to argue buoyancy. Somehow, I feel far safer here than if I were--"

She was interrupted by the opening of the door, and the consequent roar of the gale. It was Walker, the engineer, a lank, swarthy man, with long black mustaches which drooped forlornly down the sides of his mouth. He shouted, with the inimitable accent of Tyneside:

"Yo' wanted, Docto' Chwistobal. The captain thinks Mr. Boyle is bettaw."

"May I come, too?" asked Elsie.

"No, missie. You bide he-aw."

"Please tell me before you go--is the ship full of water?"

"She's dwy as a bone," said Walker. A sea splashed over him and sent a shower into the cabin. "A vewy wet bone," he added, with a broad grin, for the Northumbrian had a ready wit though he had such a solemn jowl, and he could not pronounce an "r" to save his life.

"Between you and the captain, I am beginning to be infected by belief," said Christobal to Elsie. "Let me recommend you to close the door behind us."

And she was left with the dog for company once more. A chronometer showed that the hour was past midnight. She knew sufficient of the sea to understand that the clock was probably accurate, as the course had practically followed the same meridian since the *Kansas* quitted Valparaiso. So the ship and those left on board had entered on another day! How little she had thought that to be possible when the awful knowledge first came to her that the *Kansas* was ashore! How long ago was that? Then she remembered that when Courtenay placed her in his cabin with the promise to bring Isobel to her, she had noticed the time--eleven o'clock. Was it conceivable that only one hour had elapsed since she and her four-footed friend were flung all of a heap into a corner by the impact of the vessel against the sandbank? One hour! Surely there was some mistake; she puzzled over the problem, recounting each event since the conclusion of dinner, and finally convinced herself that her recollection was not at fault. An hour--one of eternity's hours! A verse of the 90th Psalm came to her mind:

"For a thousand years in Thy sight are but as yesterday when it is past, and as a watch in the night."

The words had a new and solemn meaning to her. Yesterday was her thousand years--this was her watch in the night--and it would pass as a tale that is told. Involuntarily she turned to the bookcase behind her, and took the Bible from the little library of books which she had laughingly described as "a curious assortment." It was her intent to find the psalm containing that awe-inspiring verse, and read the whole of it, but, in turning over the leaves, she came upon a scrap of paper with notes on it. The handwriting was scholarly and legible. She thought that Captain

Courtenay would probably write just such a hand. Though her cheeks tingled a little at the memory of the words in his sister's letter, there was no harm in reading a memorandum evidently intended to mark a passage in the book. The items were sufficiently striking:--"Meribah--a place of strife; Selah--a repetition, or sort of musical *da capo*."

This stirred her to seek an explanation. She searched the two pages which opened at the marker, and, in the seventh verse of the 81st Psalm, she found the key:

"Thou calledst in trouble, and I delivered thee; I answered thee in the secret place of thunder; I proved thee at the waters of Meribah. Selah."

The phrases were strangely appropriate to her present environment. They were almost prophetic, and there was even a sinister sound in the concluding instruction to the "chief musician upon Gittith" in this psalm of Asaph. That was the terrible feature of her vigil. There was no knowing when or how it would end. She closed the book in a state more closely approximating to hysterical fright than she had been at any previous time during that most trying night. The truth was, though she could not realize it, that her senses were far too alert, her brain too preoccupied, to permit of such an ordered task as reading. In her mind's eye, she saw the boats, with their cowering occupants, plunging and tossing in that frenzied sea. By contrast, she was far better off on the ship. Yet, were it not for the action of some cowardly Chilean, she must have gone with Isobel and the others. It was torturing to think that her fancied security was really more perilous than the more apparent plight of the storm-tossed boats. No wonder she could not read, though the words were inspired!

And Joey was becoming restless. He danced backwards and forwards on the table where he had taken refuge from the invading flood. Indeed, the dog knew, long before Elsie, that the **Kansas** was afloat again. At last she noticed that the water in the cabin was gurgling to and fro, and, in the same instant, she felt the regular swing of the moving ship. She was speculating on the outcome of this new condition of affairs when the door opened and Walker thrust his lantern-jawed face within. He grinned cheerfully.

"I've come to fetch you to yo' cabin, miss," he announced. "The ship's under weigh, an', as yo' pwobably winging wet, the captain says you ought to change yo' clo'es."

Joey followed her out, but deserted her instantly. She saw the reason, when Walker helped her to reach the bridge companion. Courtenay was in the chart-house, at the wheel. He gave her a friendly nod as she passed. Somehow, Elsie felt safe now that the ship was in the captain's hands again.

CHAPTER VII
UNTIL THE DAWN

Walker was about to take her to the saloon, whence an inner staircase communicated with the principal staterooms, but she knew that the door leading to the promenade deck had been left unlocked, so she signaled him to lead her the speediest way. Speak she could not. Although there was a perceptible improvement in the weather, Elsie found the wind even harder to combat than when she traversed the deck with Courtenay. This apparent contradiction arose from the fact that during their early dealing with the boats the sailors had cut away the greater part of the canvas shield rigged to protect passengers from adventurous seas.

Nevertheless, all flustered and breathless as she was, she held Walker back when he would have left her in the shelter of her cabin.

"Do spare me one moment," she pleaded. "When I have put on dry clothing, what am I to do? Where am I to go? I will do anything rather than remain alone."

Walker jammed himself in the doorway to break the violence of the unceasing deluge of spray.

"Well, missie," he said, "I'm examining the engines, Mistaw Tollemache is fi-wing up the donkey-boiler, an' Doctaw Chwistobal is with Mistaw Boyle. You know whe-aw the captain is, so I weckon yo' best place is the saloon."

"Dr. Christobal said you were making a raft?"

"That's wight. But when the ship got off, we tackled othaw jobs. She is ow-ah best waft."

"And--do you think--we have any chance."

"Nevah say 'die,' missie. Owt can happen at sea."

She made a guess at the meaning of "owt."

"May I not look after some of the injured men?"

"That you can't," was Walker's prompt assurance. "You'd bettaw stick to the saloon. I'll tell the captain yo' the-aw."

"Tell him? Are you returning to the bridge?"

"Telephone!" shouted Walker, as an unusually heavy sea caused him to slam the door unceremoniously. He bolted it, too. Not if he could help it would his charge come out on that storm-swept deck unattended.

The electric light glowed brightly in Elsie's cabin, exactly as she had left it an hour ago. This was one of the anomalous conditions of the disaster. It lent a queer sense of Midsummer madness to the night's doings. In a few days it would be Christmas, the Christmas of sunshine and flowers known only to that lesser portion of the habitable earth south of the line. In Valparaiso the weather was stifling, yet here, not so very far away, it was bitterly cold. And the ship was driving headlong to destruction, though electric bells and switches were at command in a luxuriously furnished apartment, while the engineer had just spoken of the telephone as a means of conversing with the captain. Away down in her feminine heart the girl wondered why Courtenay himself had not come to her. Why had he sent Christobal first and Walker subsequently? Oh, of course he had more urgent matters to attend to, though, in the helpless condition of the ship, it was difficult to appreciate their precise degrees of importance.

Anyhow, he had sent word that she was to change her clothes, and he must be obeyed, as Dr. Christobal said. Then she discovered, as a quite new and physically disagreeable fact, that her skirts were soaked up to her knees, while her blouse was almost in the same condition owing to the quantity of spray which had run down inside her thick ulster.

It was an absurd thing to be afraid of after all she had endured, but Elsie cried a little when she realized that she had been literally wet to the skin without knowing it. In truth, she had a momentary dread of a fainting fit, and it was not until she untied the veil which held her Tam o' Shanter in its place that she learnt how the knot had come near to suffocating her.

The prompt relief thus afforded brought an equally absurd desire to laugh. She yielded to that somewhat, but busied herself in procuring fresh clothing and boots. The outcome of the pleasant feeling of warmth and comfort was such as the girl

herself would not have guessed in a week. The mere grateful touch of the dry garments induced an extraordinary drowsiness. She felt that she must lie down--just
for a minute. She stretched herself on the bed, closed her eyes, and was straightway
sound asleep. At the captain's suggestion, Christobal had given her a strong dose of
bromide in the wine!

It was better so. If the ship were dashed to pieces against the rocks which unquestionably lay ahead, Elsie would be whirled to the life eternal before she quite
knew what was happening. If, on the other hand, some miracle of the sea enabled
the men to construct a seaworthy raft in time, or the rising tide permitted the *Kansas* to escape, in so far as to run ashore again in a comparatively sheltered position,
she would be none the worse for an hour's sleep. And now that the ship was afloat,
there were things to be done which only men could do. The saloon, the decks,
the forecabin, were places of the dead. Fearing lest Elsie might pass, Christobal,
before attending to Boyle, had thrown table-cloths over the bodies of men slain in
the saloon, for Gray and Tollemache had sternly but vainly striven to repress the
second revolt. Tollemache and Walker had dragged out of the smothering spray
near the port davits three men who seemed to be merely stunned. These, with the
chief officer, and perhaps four survivers of the explosion, made up the list of living
but non-effective members of the ship's company. There was one other, Gulielmo
Frascuelo, who was bawling for dear life in his bunk in the forecastle, but in that
dark hour no one chanced to remember him, and it needed more than a human
voice to pit itself against the hurricane which roared over the vessel. The unhappy
wretch knew that something out of the ordinary had taken place, and he was scared
half out of his wits by the continued absence of the crew. Luckily for himself, he
did not appreciate the real predicament of the ship, or he would have raved himself
into madness.

Walker, in his brief catalogue of occupations, had suppressed one. To make
sure, Christobal closed a water-tight bulkhead door which cut off the principal
staterooms from the saloon. Then he and his two helpers carried out a painful but
necessary task. It was his duty to certify whether or not life was extinct. There
were very few exceptions. The three men lifted the bodies and threw them overboard. When they reached the corpses of the second officer and a Spanish engineer
who had been knifed in the defense of the jolly-boat--his comrade had scrambled

into one of the life-boats--Tollemache took possession of such money, documents, and valuables as were in their pockets, intending to draw up an inventory when an opportunity presented itself.

Though they knew not the moment when a sickening crash would herald the final dissolution of the ship, they proceeded with their work methodically. In half an hour they had reached the end. All the injured men--seven nondescript sailors and firemen--were carried to the saloon and placed under Christobal's care. Walker dived below to the engine-room, where he had already disconnected the rods broken or bent by the fracture of a guard ring, which, in its turn, was injured by the blowing out of a junk-ring, a stout ring of forged steel secured to one of the pistons. He could do nothing more on deck. Whether he was destined to live fifty seconds or as many years he was ill content to hear his beloved engines knocking themselves to pieces with each roll of the ship.

Tollemache, who undertook the firing of the donkey-boiler, which was situated on the main deck aft of the saloon--for the *Kansas* was built chiefly to accommodate cargo--during his wanderings round the world had picked up sufficient knowledge of steam-power to shovel fuel into the furnace and regulate the water-level by the feed valve and pump. The small engine, more reliable and quite as powerful as a hundred men, was in perfect order. It abounded in valves and taps, but Walker's parting instructions were explicit:

"Keep yo' eye on the glass, an' pitch in a shovel of coal evewy ten minutes: she'll do the west."

So the new hand, satisfied that the gage was correct and the furnace lively, lit his pipe, sat down, and began to jot in a note-book the contents of his coat-pockets. The Spaniard's letters he could not read, though he gathered that one of them was from a wife in Vallodolid, who would travel overland early in January to meet her husband. But the Englishman's correspondence was terribly explicit. A "heart-broken mother" wrote from Liverpool that "Jack" had been shot during one of the many cold-weather campaigns on the Indian frontier. "I have no news, simply a telegram from the War Office. But of what avail to know how my darling died. My tears are blinding me. You and I alone are left, and you are thousands of miles away. May the Lord be merciful to me, a widow, and bring you home to comfort me." Yet the knife which killed him must have gone very near that letter.

Tollemache tried to grip his pipe in his teeth. He failed. It fell on the iron floor.

"Oh, this is rotten!" he growled. "Why couldn't he have been spared? No one would have missed me. I don't suppose Jennie would care tuppence."

The *Kansas* rolled heavily. He waited a few seconds for the expected shock, but she swung back to an even keel. Then he stooped to pick up his pipe, and his mouth hardened.

"'Spared!' by gad!" he said. "What rot!" That roll of the ship was caused by an experimental twist of the wheel. Courtenay, peering into the darkness through the open window of the chart-house, saw that the weather was clearing. He had evolved a theory, and, for want of a better, he was determined to pursue it to a finish. The *Kansas* was being swiftly carried along in a strong and deep tidal current. Happily, the wind followed the set of the sea, else there would be no chance of success for his daring plan. His expedient was the desperate one of keeping the vessel in the line of the current, and, if day broke before he reached the coast, he would steer for any opening which presented itself in the fringe of reefs which must assuredly guard the mainland.

With his hands grasping the taut and, in one sense, irresponsive mechanism of a steering-wheel governed by steam, a sailor can "feel" the movement of his ship, a seaworthy vessel being a living thing, obedient as a docile horse to the least touch of the rein. But, in the unlikely event of fortune favoring Courtenay to the extent of giving him an opportunity to see the coming danger, it was essential that the ship should have a certain radius of action apart from the direction and force of the ocean stream. The two sails were helpful, and it was to assure himself of their efficiency that he put the helm to starboard. The *Kansas* obeyed with an answering roll to port, showing clearly that she was traveling a little faster than the inrushing tide would take her unaided. He brought her head back to nor'east again, and glanced over his shoulder at the ship's chronometer. It was a quarter to one. Two hours must pass before he would discern the first faint streaks of light. At any rate, if he were spared to greet the dawn, it would be right ahead, and, as a few seconds might then be of utmost value, that was a small point in his favor. Yet, two hours! Could he dare to hope for so long a respite? How could the ship escape the unnumbered fangs which a storm-torn land thrust far out into the Pacific for its own protection?

He was quite sheltered from the wind and spray in the chart-house, and, all at once, he became aware of a burning thirst. There was water in a decanter close at hand, so he indulged in a long drink. That was wonderfully vivifying. Then his mind turned longingly to tobacco. For the first time in his life he broke the strict rule of the service in which he had been trained--and smoked a cigar while on duty.

Now and again he spoke cheerily to the dog. It would be:

"Well, Joey, here we are; still got a bark in us!" . . . Or, "You and I must have our names on the Admiralty chart, Joey:--'Channel surveyed by Captain Courtenay and pup; details uncertain.' How does that sound, old chap?" And again, "I suppose your friend, Miss Maxwell, is asleep by this time. If she calls you 'Joey,' do you call her 'Elsie'? I rather fancy Elsie as a name. What do you think?"

To all of which the dog, who had found a dry corner, would respond with a smile and a tail-wag. What? Joey couldn't smile! Make a friend of a fox-terrier and learn what a genuine, whole-hearted, delighted-to-see-you grin he will favor you with: he can smile as unmistakably as he can yawn.

If deeper emotions peeped up in Courtenay's soul, he crushed them resolutely. Men of the sea do not cultivate heroics. They leave sentiment to those imaginative people who evolve eery visions of a storm in the smug comfort of suburban villas. When the **Kansas** lay on the shoal Courtenay was certain that the ship was lost, or he would never have dispatched some of his passengers and crew in the only boat available. He acted to the best of his judgment then; he was acting similarly now in abandoning the last resource of a raft in order to keep the vessel on her present course. But, then or now, he paid no heed whatever to the obvious fact that he and the second engineer, and at least one of the male passengers, must be the last to quit the ship. That was the code of all true sailor-men--the women first, then the male passengers and crew followed by the officers, beginning at the junior in rank. There could be room for no hesitancy or dispute--it was just a sailor-like way of doing one's duty, in the simple faith that the recording angel would enter up the log.

The long wait in the darkness would have broken many a man's nerve, but Courtenay was not cast in a mold to be either bent or broken by fear. When his cigar was not in his mouth he whistled, he hummed snatches of songs, and delivered short lectures to Joey on the absurdity of things in general, and the special ridiculousness of such a mighty combination of circumstances centering on one poor ship as had fore-gathered to crush the **Kansas**. Ever since he was aroused from sleep by the stopping of the screw, his mind had dwelt on the unprecedented nature of the break-down. Even before he discovered its cause he was wondering what evil chance bad contrived to cripple the engine at such a moment--in the worst possible place on the map.

"Joey!" he said suddenly, his thoughts reverting to a chance remark made to him in Valparaiso by Isobel's father, "what did Mr. Baring mean by saying there was a difficulty about the insurance?"

Joey gave it up, but he cocked his ears and looked towards the door. Christobal entered.

"Boyle will recover," he said, when he had wiped the spray off his face. "He had a narrow escape; the knife just grazed the spinal cord. The shock to the dorsal nerves induced temporary paralysis, and that rather misled me. He is much better now. Under ordinary conditions he would be able to get about in a few days. As it is, he will probably live as long as any of us."

Christobal waved a hand towards the external void. He was not sailor enough to realize the change in the weather.

"That is good news," said Courtenay.

"I thought you would like to know. How are things up here?"

"Better. The barometer has risen an inch in less than two hours. Possibly, nearness to the land has some effect, but wind and sea are subsiding."

"You surprise me; yet that is nothing. I have had several surprises to-night. What is the position? Of course, we must hit the South American continent sooner or later; can you fix an approximate time?"

"We are making about six knots, I fancy. If we are lucky, and avoid any stray rocks, we should see daylight before we reach the coast. That is our sole hope. The ship is in a powerful tidal current, and it is high-water at 5.30 A.M. At a rough estimate, Hanover Island is twenty knots distant. Now you know all. The outcome is mere guesswork."

"Why did the furnaces blow up?"

"I was cross-examining Joey on that point when you came in. He reserved his opinion. My own view is that, by accident or design, some explosive substance found its way into the coal."

"Shem, Ham and Japheth! Explosive substance! Do you mean dynamite, or gunpowder, or that sort of thing?"

"Something of the kind. That is only a supposition, but when I whispered it to Walker he agreed."

"Walker! Is he the man who speaks so queerly?"

"If ever you go to Newcastle, don't put it that way. I told him to take Miss Maxwell to her cabin. Did he do so?"

"Yes. I have not seen her since, so I assume that the bromide, plus the wine, was effective. Well, I must return to my patients. Can I get you anything? I am store-keeper, you know."

"No, thanks."

"Nothing to eat, or drink?"

"Nothing. I shall be ready for a square meal when I am able to come below-- not before."

Christobal smiled. Though he was a brave man, he thought such persistent optimism was out of place. Nevertheless, he could emulate Courtenay's coolness.

"Let me know when you are ready. I am an excellent cook," he said.

Then the captain of the **Kansas** resumed his smoking and humming, with occasional glances at the clock, and the compass, and the barometer. At two o'clock he felt the ship slipping from under the wheel. The compass showed that she was heading a couple of points eastward. He helped her, and telephoned instantly to Walker:

"Go forward and try if you can make out anything. Report to me here."

"Ay, ay, sir," came the reply, and anon Walker appeared.

"It's main thick ahead, sir, but I think we-aw passin' an island to port," said he.

"I thought so. You had better remain here, Walker. We have not long to wait now for the dawn, and four eyes are better than two."

Walker imagined that the skipper was ready for a chat.

"Things are in a dweadful mess below, sir. I can't make head or tail of the smash."

"Well, that must wait. Don't talk. Keep a sharp lookout."

The engineer could not guess that the captain's pulse was beating a trifle more rapidly with a certain elation. They were undoubtedly passing White Horse Island. It revealed its presence by deflecting the tremendous sea-river which ferried the *Kansas* onward at such a rate. In fifteen or twenty minutes Courtenay expected to find indications of a more northerly set of the tide, and he watched the compass intently for the first sign of this return to the former course. If the ship crossed the current one way or the other she would certainly be driven ashore on some outlying spur of the island or detached sunken reef. Hence, he must actually guess his way, with something of the acquired sense of the blind, because the slight chance of ultimate escape for the ship and her occupants rested wholly on the assumption that some ocean by-way was leading her to a deep-water inlet, where it might be possible to drop the anchor.

In eighteen minutes, or thereabouts, the needle moved slightly. Courtenay once more assisted the ship with the helm. She steadied herself, and the compass pointed due northeast again.

Walker, though an engineer, knew enough of navigation to recognize the apparent impossibility of the captain's being able to steer with any real knowledge of his surroundings. The wheel-twisting, therefore, savored of magic; but his orders were to look ahead, and he obeyed.

Soon he thought he could discern an irregular pink crescent, with the concave side downwards, somewhere in the blackness beyond the bows. He rubbed his eyes, and said nothing, believing that the unaccustomed strain of gazing into the dark had affected his sight. But the pink crescent brightened and deepened, and speedily it was joined by two others, equally irregular and somewhat lower. Then he could bear the suspense no longer.

"Captain, d'ye see yon?" he asked, in a voice tremulous with awe.

"Yes. That is the sun just catching the summits of snow-topped hills. It not only foretells the dawn, but is a sign of fine weather. There are no clouds over the land, or we should not see the peaks."

Walker began to have a respect for the captain which he had hitherto extended only to the superintending engineer, an eminent personage who never goes to sea, but inspects the ship when in port, and draws a fat salary and various commissions.

Ere long a silver gray light began to dispel the gloom. The two silent watchers first saw it overhead, and the vast dome of day swiftly widened over the vexed sea. The aftermath of the storm spread a low, dense cloak of vapor all round. The wind had fallen so greatly that they could hear the song of the rigging. Soon they could distinguish the outlines of the heavy rollers near at hand, and Courtenay believed that the ship, in her passage, encountered in the water several narrow bands of a bright red color. If this were so, he knew that the phenomenon was caused by the prawn-like Crustacea which sailors call "Whale-food," a sure sign of deep water close to land, and, further, an indication that the current was still flowing strongly, while the force of the sea must have been broken many miles to westward.

Suddenly he turned to Walker.

"Do you think you could shin up to the masthead?" he asked.

"I used to be able to climb a bit, sir."

"Well, try the foremast. Up there I am fairly certain you can see over this bank of mist. Don't get into trouble. Come back if you feel you can't manage it. If you succeed, take the best observations possible and report."

Courtenay was becoming anxious now. If he dared let go the wheel he would have climbed the mast himself. Walker set about his mission in a business-like manner. He threw off his thick coat and boots, and went forward. Half-way up the mast there was a rope ladder for the use of the sailors when adjusting pulleys.

The rest of the journey was not difficult for an athletic man, and Walker was quickly an indistinct figure in the fog. He gained the truck all right, and instantly yelled something. Courtenay fancied he said:

"My God! We-ah on the wocks!"

Whatever it was, Walker did not wait, but slid downward with such speed that it was fortunate the rigging barred his progress.

And then, even while Courtenay was shouting for some explanation, a great black wall rose out of the deep on the port bow. It was a pinnacle rock, high as the ship's masts, but only a few feet wide at sea level, and the *Kansas* sped past this ugly monitor as though it were a buoy in a well-marked channel.

Courtenay heard the sea breaking against it. The ship could not have been more than sixty feet distant, a little more than her own beam, and he fully expected that she would grind against some outlier in the next instant. But the *Kansas* had a charmed life. She ran on unscathed, and seemed to be traveling in smoother water after this escape.

Walker's dark skin was the color of parchment when he reached the chart-house.

"Captain," he said, weakly, "I 'll do owt wi' engines, but I'm no good at this game. That thing fairly banged me. Did ye see it?"

"Did *you* see land?" demanded Courtenay, imperatively. His spirits rose with each of these thrills. He felt that it was ordained that his ship should live.

"Yes, sir. The-aw 's hills, and big ones, a long way ahead, but I 'm no' goin' up that mast again. It would be suicide. I'm done. I'll nev-ah fo-get yon stone ghost, no, not if I live to be ninety."

Then Joey, sniffing the morning, uncurled himself, stretched, yawned loudly, and thought of breakfast, for he had passed a rather disturbed night, the second in one week. To cope with such excitement, a dog needed sustenance.

CHAPTER VIII
IN A WILD HAVEN

Fortune has her cycles, whether for good or ill. The *Kansas*, having run the gauntlet of many dangers, seemed to have earned an approving smile from the fickle goddess. A slight but perceptible veering of the wind, combined with the increasing power of the sun's rays, swept the ocean clear of its storm-wraiths. Soon after passing the pillar rock, Courtenay thought he could make out the unwavering outline of mountainous land amid the gray mists. A few minutes later the waves racing alongside changed their leaden hue to a steely glitter which told him the fog was dispersing. The nearer blue of the ocean carpet spread an ever-widening circle until it merged into a vivid green. Then, with startling suddenness, the curtain was drawn aside on a panorama at once magnificent and amazing.

Almost without warning, the ship was found to be entering the estuary of a narrow fiord. Gaunt headlands, carved on Titanic scale out of the solid rock, guarded the entrance, and already shut out the more distant coast-line. Behind these first massive walls, everywhere unscalable, and rising in separate promontories to altitudes of, perhaps, four hundred feet, an inner fortification of precipitous mountains flung their glacier-clad peaks heavenward to immense heights,--heights which, in that region, soared far above the snow-line. The sun was reflected with dazzling brilliancy from their icy summits, and wonderful lights sparkled in rainbow tints on their slopes. Delicate pink deepened to rose crimson; pale greens softened into the beryl blue of stupendous glaciers, vast frozen cataracts which flowed down deep and broad clefts almost to the water's edge.

Above these color-bands, the dead-white mantle of everlasting snow spread its folds, with here and there a black ridge of granite thrusting wind-cleared fangs high above the far-flung shroud. But, if the crests of peak upon peak were thus clothed in white, their bases wore a garment of different texture. Save on the seaward terraces of stark rock, with their tide-marked base of weed-covered boulders, the densest vegetation known to mankind imposed everywhere a first barrier to human progress far more unconquerable than the awesome regions beyond. Pine forests of extraordinary density crammed each available yard of space, until the tree-growth yielded perforce to hardier Alpine moss and lichens. This lower belt of deepest green ranged from five hundred to one thousand feet in height, as conditions were adverse or favorable; waterfalls abounded; each tiny glen held its foaming rivulet, rushing madly down the steep, or leaping in fine cascades from one rocky escarpment to another. Courtenay, after an astounded glance at the magnitude and solemn grandeur of the spectacle, had eyes for naught save the conformation of the channel. The change in the wind was caused, he found, by the northerly headland thrusting its giant mass a mile, or more, westward of its twin; but he quickly discovered, from the conformation of the land, that the latter was really the protecting cape of the inner water-way. He reasoned, therefore, that the deep-water channel flowed close to the northern shore until it was flung off by the relentless rocks to seek the easier inlet behind the opposite point.

He did not know yet whether the ship was entering some unknown straits or the mouth of a narrow land-locked bay. If the latter, the presence of the distant glaciers and the nearer torrents warned him of a possible bar, on which the *Kansas* might be lost within sight of safe anchorage. Not inspired guesswork now, but the skill of the pilot, was needed; this crossing the bar in broad daylight was as great a trial of nerve in its way as the earlier onward rush in the dark.

Wind and sea had abated so sensibly that the Pacific rollers raced on unbroken, and it was no longer a super-human task to make one's voice heard along the deck.

So the captain aroused Walker with a sharp order:

"Go and see if the donkey-boiler has a good head of steam. We may have to drop the stream anchor quick, and both bowers as well. If Tollemache is doing his work properly, go forward, and keep a sharp lookout for broken water. Clear off the tarpaulins, and be ready to lower away the instant I sing out."

Walker, who had been gazing spellbound at the majestic haven opening up before the ship, hurried on his errand. He found Tollemache seated on an upturned bucket, in which the taciturn one had just washed his face and hands.

"Have you seen it?" demanded Walker, gleefully, while his practised eyes took in the state of the gages and he overran a number of oil taps with nimble fingers.

"Seen what?" asked Tollemache, without removing his pipe.

"The land, my bonnie lad. We-ah wunnin' wight in now."

"We've been doing that for hours."

"Yes, but this is diff'went. The'aw's a fine wiv-ah ahead. Have ye ev-ah seen the Tyne? Well, just shove Sooth Sheels an' Tynemouth a few hundwed feet high-ah, an' you've got it. Now, don't twy to talk, or you might cwack yo' face."

With this Parthian shaft of humor he vanished towards the forecastle, whence the ubiquitous donkey-boiler, through one of its long arms, would shoot forth the stockless anchors at the touch of a lever. Tollemache, who had already glimpsed the coast, strolled out on deck and bent well over the side in order to look more directly ahead. He could see one half only of the view, but that sufficed.

"A respite!" he growled to himself. "Penal servitude instead of sudden death."

And, indeed, this was the true aspect of things, as Courtenay discovered when he had successfully brought the ship past three ugly reefs and dropped anchor in the backwater of a small sheltered bay. He speedily abandoned the half-formed hope that the **Kansas** might have run into an ocean water-way which communicated with Smyth Channel. The rampart of snow-clad hills had no break, while a hasty scrutiny of the chart showed him that the eastern coast of Hanover Island had been thoroughly surveyed. Yet it was not in human nature that he should not experience a rush of joy at the thought that, by his own efforts, he had saved his ship and some, at least, of the lives entrusted to his care. He was alone when the music of the chains in the hawse-pipes sounded in his ears. The **Kansas** had plenty of room to swing, but he thought it best to moor her. Believing implicitly now that he would yet bring his vessel into the Thames, he allowed her to be carried round by the fast-flowing tide until her nose pointed seaward, and she lay in the comparatively still water inshore. Then he dropped the second anchor and stepped forth from the chart-house. His long vigil was ended. Some of the cloud of care lifted from his face, and he called cheerily to Joey.

"Come along, pup," he said. "Let us sample Dr. Christobal's cookery. You have shared my watch; now you shall share my breakfast. We have both earned it."

It was in his mind to knock loudly on Elsie's door and awaken her; therefore he was dimly conscious of a feeling of disappointment when he saw her, in company with Christobal, leaning over the rail of the promenade deck, and evidently discussing the weird beauty of the scene spread before her wondering eyes.

The ship was now so sheltered by the shoulder of the southern cape that the keen breeze yet rushing in from the sea passed hundreds of feet above her masts. There was nothing more than a tidal swell on the surface of the water, in which the heavy-laden vessel rested as in a dock. In the new and extraordinary quietude the light thud of the donkey-engine sounded with a strange distinctness, and Elsie and her companion heard Courtenay's approaching footsteps almost as soon as he gained the deck.

Instantly she ran towards him, with hands out-stretched.

"Let me be the first to congratulate you," she cried, her cheeks mantling with a rush of color and her lips quivering with excitement. "How wonderful of you to bring the ship through all those awful reefs and things! No; you must not say you have done nothing marvelous. Dr. Christobal has told me everything. Next to Providence, Captain Courtenay, we owe our lives to you."

Courtenay felt it would hurt her were he to smile at her earnestness. But he did say:

"Surely it is not so very remarkable that I should do my best to safeguard the ship and such of her passengers and crew as survive last night's ordeal."

"I know that quite well. Even I would have striven to help when my life was at stake. But the really wonderful thing is that you should have guessed an unknown track in the dark; that you should actually be able to guide a helpless ship through waters so full of dangers that it would be folly to venture in their midst in broad daylight and with full steam-power."

Then Courtenay took off his sou'wester, and bowed.

"I had no idea I had such expert critics on board. Is it you, Christobal, who has followed the ship's course so closely?"

"Not I, my dear fellow. Miss Maxwell is only saying what I feel, indeed, but could not have expressed as admirably. Our silent friend, Tollemache, is the man who observes. I was so amazed when I came on deck half an hour ago that I sought him out, and he told me something of the night's later happenings. So I took the liberty of arousing Miss Maxwell from a very sound sleep, but we thought it best not to disturb you by appearing on the bridge until you had done everything you had planned."

"I shall never understand how I came to fall asleep," said Elsie. "I remember feeling very tired; I sat down for a moment, and that ended it. The next thing I heard was a rapping on my door, and Dr. Christobal's voice bidding me hurry if I would see the entrance to the harbor."

The two men exchanged glances. Courtenay laughed, so pleasantly that it was good to hear.

"Yet there was I up aloft, maneuvering the ship in the firm faith that Dr. Christobal was busy in the cook's galley," said he.

"Ah, we have news for you," cried Elsie. "One of the poor fellows who was knocked on the head during that terrible fight for the boats was the master cook himself. He is better now, and breakfast can be ready in five minutes. I'll go and tell him."

She ran off, and Joey scampered by her side, for he knew quite well where the kitchen lay.

"Bromide is useful at times," murmured Christobal, watching Elsie until she had disappeared. Then he turned to Courtenay.

"I suppose you have seen nothing of the boats?"

"No sign whatever. And I could hardly have missed them if they were here. They may have escaped, but I doubt it. The sea ran very high for a time, and the **Kansas** scraped past so many reefs that it was almost impossible for each of the three boats to have done the same."

"Even if one or more of them reached land, there is small likelihood that they would turn up in this particular bay?"

"That is true, especially if they used their sails. The Chileans who got away in the life-boats would know sufficient of the coast to endeavor to make a northerly course, while my parting instructions to Malcolm were to keep to the north all the time."

"I wish now that poor Isobel Baring and the others had not left us," said Christobal sadly.

Courtenay was about to say something, but checked himself. He was not blind to the aspect of affairs which Tollemache had summarized so pithily. It might yet be that those who remained had more to endure. Then Elsie summoned them to breakfast, which was served on deck, as the saloon had been temporarily converted into a hospital.

Before sitting down, Courtenay paid a brief visit to Mr. Boyle. Christobal told him not to allow the wounded man to talk too much, complete rest for a few hours being essential. But Boyle's pallid face lit up so brightly when the captain stood by his side that it was hard not to indulge him to some extent.

"Huh," he said, his gruff voice strong as ever. "Christobal was not humbugging me when he assured me you were all right. Where are we?"

"In a small bay on the east of Hanover Island. I have not taken any observations yet, and there is no hurry, old chap. You 'll be out and about long before we move again."

"Huh. D'ye think so? I know the beggar who knifed me. I 'll take it out of him when I see him."

"You are better off than he, Boyle. Unless he is here with you, I guess he is rolling on the floor of the Pacific by this time."

Boyle tried to turn and survey his fellow-sufferers; there was the fire of battle in his eye. Courtenay restrained him with a laugh.

"A nice thing I am doing," he cried, "permitting you to talk, and getting you excited. I believe you would punch the scoundrel now if he were in the next berth. You must lie quiet, old man; doctor's orders; he says you 're on the royal road if you keep on the easy list for a day or so.'"

Boyle smiled, and closed his eyes.

"I heard the anchors go, and then I knew that all was well. You 're the luckiest skipper afloat. Huh, the bloomin' **Kansas** was lost not once but twenty times."

"Are you in pain, Boyle?" asked Courtenay, placing a gentle hand on his friend's forehead.

"Not much. More stiff than sore. It was a knock-out blow of its kind. I can just recall you hauling me out of the scrimmage, and--"

"It will be your turn to do as much for me next time. Try to go to sleep; we'll have you on deck tomorrow."

Courtenay noticed that there were only four other sufferers in the saloon:

Three were firemen injured by the explosion. He had a pleasant word for each of them. The fourth was a sailor, either asleep or unconscious, and Courtenay thought he recognized a severe bruise on the man's left temple where the butt of his revolver had struck hard.

When he returned on deck he learned that two other members of the crew, in addition to the cook, were able to work. Walker had set one to clear up the stokehold; his companion, a fireman, had relieved Mr. Tollemache. Indeed, the latter had gone to his cabin, and was the last to arrive at the feast, finally putting in an appearance in a new suit and spotless linen.

Christobal protested loudly.

"I thought this was to be a workers' meal," he said. "Tollemache has stolen a march on us. He is quite a Bond-street lounger in appearance."

"Dirty job, stoking," said Tollemache.

"I seem to have been the only lazy person on board during the night," cried Elsie.

"Do you know what time it is?" asked Courtenay.

"No; about ten o'clock, I fancy."

"It is not yet half-past four."

The blue eyes opened wide. "Are you in earnest?" she demanded.

He showed her his watch. Then she perceived that the sun had not yet risen high enough to illumine the wooded crest of the opposite cliff. The snow-clad hills, the blue glaciers, the wonderful clearness of atmosphere, led her to believe that the day was much more advanced. Land and sea shone in a strange crystal light. None could tell whence it came. It seemed to her, in that solemn hour, to be the reflection of heaven itself. By quick transition, her thoughts flew back to the previous night. Scarce four hours had elapsed since she had waited in the captain's cabin, amidst the drenching spray and tearing wind, while he took Isobel, and Mrs. Somerville, and the shrieking maid to the boat. The corners of her mouth drooped and tears trembled on her eyelashes. She sought furtively for a handkerchief. Knowing exactly what troubled her, Courtenay turned to Christobal.

"This island ought to be inhabited," he said. "Can you tell me what sort of Indians one finds in this locality?"

Christobal frowned perplexedly. During many previous voyages to Europe he had invariably traveled on the mail steamers of smaller draft which use the sheltered sea canal formed by the Smyth, Sarmiento, and Messier channels, the protected water-way running for hundreds of miles to the north from the western end of the Straits of Tierra del Fuego, and, in some of its aspects, reminding sailors of the Clyde and the Caledonian Canal.

"I fear I do not know much about them," he said. "Behind those hills there one sees a few Canoe Indians; I have heard that they are somewhat lower in the social scale than the aborigines of Australia."

"Are they?" said Courtenay. He looked Christobal straight in the eyes, and the doctor returned his gaze as steadily.

"That is their repute. They live mostly on shellfish. They do not congregate in communities. A few families keep together, and move constantly from place to place. They have a quaint belief that if they remain on a camping-ground more than a night or two the devil will stick his head out of the ground and bite them. Obviously, the real devil that plagues them is the continuous wandering demanded by their search for food."

Christobal would have aired such a scrap of interesting knowledge at the foot of the scaffold, and expected the executioner to listen attentively.

"They are called the Alaculof. They use bows and arrows, with heads chipped out of stone or bottle-glass," put in Tollemache.

"Oh, you have been in these parts before?" cried Courtenay, regarding his compatriot with some interest, while the Spaniard surveyed his rival doubtfully.

"Yes--was on the *Emu*--wrecked in Cockburn Channel."

Now, the story of the *Emu* is one of those fierce tragedies which the sea first puts on the stage of life with dire skill, and then proceeds to destroy the slightest vestige of their brief existence. But such things leave abiding memories in men's souls, and Courtenay had heard how twenty-seven survivors, out of a muster-roll of thirty who escaped from the wreck, had been shot down by Indians ambushed in the forest. Elsie, whose tears were dispelled by the doctor's amusing summary of the Canoe Indians' theological views, was listening to the conversation, so the captain did not carry it further, contenting himself with the remark:

"That will be useful, if we are compelled to go ashore. You will have some acquaintance with the ways of our hosts."

Tollemache, having nothing to say, was not given to the use of unnecessary words. Elsie was conscious of a certain constraint in their talk.

"Please don't mind me," she said quietly. "I know all about the loss of the *Emu*. If we fall into the hands of the Alaculof tribe, we shall be not only killed but eaten."

She was pouring out a second cup of tea for Walker when she made this remarkable statement. Her eyes were intent on exact quantities of tea, milk, and sugar, and she passed the cup to the engineer with a smile. Each of the men admired her coolness, but Tollemache, who had been quietly scrutinizing the nearer hills, gave painful emphasis to this gruesome topic by exclaiming:

"There they are now: smoke signals."

Sure enough, thin columns of smoke were rising from several points on the land. It could not be doubted that these were caused by human agency. They were not visible when the party sat down to breakfast. The appearance of the ship was their obvious explanation, but not a canoe or a solitary figure could be seen, though Courtenay and others, at various times during the day, searched every part of the neighboring shore with field glasses and powerful telescopes.

After an all too brief burst of sunshine, the Land of Storms again justified its name. Giant clouds came rolling in from seaward. The mountains were lost in mist; the glaciers became sullen, rock-strewn masses of white-brown ice; the fresh greenery of the forests faded into somber belts of blackness. Though it was high summer in this desolate region, heavy showers of hail and sleet alternated with drenching rain. At low-water, though the *Kansas* floated securely in a depth of twenty fathoms, a yellow current sweeping past her starboard quarter showed how accurately Courtenay had read the tokens of the inlet. Many a swollen torrent, and, perhaps, one or two fair-sized streams at the head of the bay, contributed this flood of fresh water.

And, with the evening tide, there were not wanting indications that the gale without had developed a new fury. A solitary albatross, driven landward by stress of weather, rode in vast circles above the ship. There was no wealth of bird life in that place of gloom. Though fitted to rear untold millions of gulls and other sea birds, this secluded nook was almost deserted; generations of men had devoured all the eggs they could lay hands on.

To Elsie and the doctor were entrusted the daylight watch on deck and the

care of the sick. For the latter there was not much to be done. The cook undertook to feed them, and Frascuelo, the wounded stevedore who had been discovered
in a state of collapse, soon revived, and was practically able to look after himself.
The others, under Walker's directions, were hard at work in the engine-room and
stoke-hold, for there alone lay the chance of ultimate escape.

The two sentinels conversed but little. The outer war of the elements was disturbing, and Christobal, though unfailingly optimistic in his speech, was nevertheless a prey to dark forebodings. Once, they were startled by the fall of an avalanche,
which thundered down a mountain side on the farther shore, and tore a great gap
in the belt of trees until it crashed into the water. It sent a four-foot wave across
the bay, and the *Kansas* rocked so violently that the men toiling below raced up on
deck to ascertain the cause of the disturbance.

This was the only exciting incident of a day that seemed to be unending. Elsie,
worn out by the strain of the preceding twenty-four hours, and, notwithstanding
her brief sleep in the morning, thoroughly exhausted for want of rest, was persuaded to retire early to her cabin. She lay down almost fully dressed. Somehow, it was
impossible to think of a state of unpreparedness for any emergency.

She was soon sound asleep. She awoke with a start, with all her nerves a-
quiver. Joey was tearing along the deck, barking furiously. She heard two men run
past her door with ominous haste. Then, after a heart-breaking pause, there was
some shooting. Some one, she thought it was Courtenay, roared down the saloon
companion:

"On deck, all hands, to repel boarders!"

With a confused rush, men mounted the stairs and raced forward. She knew
that nearly all of those not on watch were sleeping with the injured men in the saloon, and now she understood the reason. The ship was being attacked by Indians,
and not altogether unexpectedly. The savages had stolen alongside in their canoes
under the cloak of night. Perhaps they were already on board in overwhelming
numbers. Poor girl, she murmured a prayer while she hurriedly drew on her boots
and ulster.

There seemed to be no end to the evils which assailed the *Kansas*, and she
dreaded this new terror more than the mad fury of the seas. But, if the men were
fighting for their lives and her's, she must help, too. That was clear. She had a

weapon, a loaded revolver, which she had picked up from beneath a boat's tarpaulin lying on the spar deck. She opened her door and peered out. She could not see any one, and the rattle of a hail-storm overhead effectually dulled any other noise. But several shots fired again in the fore part of the ship were audible above the din of the pelting hail. So she ran that way, with the fine courage of one who fears yet goes on, and her eyes pierced the shadows with a tense despair in them. For what could so few men do against the unseen watchers who sent up the thirty-four smoke columns she had counted?

Ah, trust a woman to read the unspoken thought! Courtenay and Christobal and Tollemache need not have striven to couch their warnings in ambiguous words. Elsie could have told them all that was left unsaid at breakfast. The ship had fought her own enemies; now the human beings she had saved must defend themselves from a foe against whom the ship was helpless.

CHAPTER IX
A PROFESSOR OF WITCHCRAFT

Quickly as Elsie had reached the deck, the warlike sounds which disturbed her rest had ceased. Save for the footsteps of men whom she could not see, the prevalent noises were caused only by wind and sleet. While she was hurrying forward as rapidly as the darkness permitted, the lights were switched on with a suddenness that made her gasp. The dog began to bark again, but it was easy to distinguish his sharp yelps of excitement and defiance from the earlier notes of alarmed suspicion. In fact, Joey himself was the first to discover the stealthy approach of the Indians. Courtenay and Tollemache, who took the middle watch, from midnight to 4 A.M., had failed to note the presence of several canoes on the ink-black surface of the bay until the dog warned them by growling, and ruffling the bristles on his back. The night was pitch dark; the rising moon was not only hidden by the hills of the island, but frequent storms of rain and hail rendered it impossible while they raged to see or hear beyond the distance of a few feet. In all probability, as the canoes bore down from windward, Joey had scented them. He also gave the highly important information as to the quarter from which attack might be expected. Three men, at least, had gained the deck, but the prompt use of a revolver had caused them to retreat as silently and speedily as they had appeared. That was all. There was no actual fight. The phantoms vanished as silently as they came. The only external lights on the ship were the masthead and sidelights, hoisted by Courtenay to reveal the steamer's whereabouts in case one of the boats chanced to be driven into the bay during the dark hours. There was an electric lamp turned on in the donkey-engine room, and another in the main saloon, but means were taken to exclude them from showing without; if the Indians meant to be actively hostile, lights on board would be more helpful to the assailants than to the assailed.

When the captain and Tollemache followed Joey's lead, they discerned three demoniac figures, vaguely outlined by the ruddy glare of the port light, in the very act of climbing the rails. They fired instantly, and the naked forms vanished; both men thought they heard the splashing caused by the leaping or falling of the Indians into the sea. By the same subdued radiance Courtenay made out the top of a pole or mast sticking up close to the ship's side. He leaned over, fired a couple of shots downwards at random, seized the pole, and lashed it to a stanchion with a loose rope end, a remnant of one of the awnings. A small craft, even an Indian canoe, would be most useful, and its capture might tend to scare the attackers.

Telling Tollemache to mount guard, he raced back to the saloon hatch and summoned assistance. The others searched the ship in small detachments, but the Indians were gone; it was manifest that none beyond those driven off at the first onset had secured a footing on deck. Then, taking the risk of being shot at, Courtenay ordered the lights to be turned on, and the first person he saw clearly was Elsie. He was almost genuinely angry with her.

"What are you doing here?" he demanded.

She was learning not to fear his brusque ways. He was no carpet knight, and men who carry their lives in their hands do not pick and choose their words.

"I thought you were in danger, so I came to help," she said calmly.

"You must go back to your cabin at once."

"Why? Of what avail is the safety of my cabin if you are killed?"

A woman's logic is apt to be irritating when one expects a flight of arrows, or, it may be, a gunshot, out of the blackness a few feet away.

"For goodness' sake, stand here, then," he cried, seizing her arm, and compelling her to shelter behind the heavy molding which carried the bridge.

She did not object to his roughness. In the midst of actual peril, impressions are apt to be cameo-cut in their preciseness, and she liked him all the more because he treated her quite roughly. Of course, the mere presence of a woman at such a time was a hindrance. But she was determined not to return to her stateroom, and, indeed, her obstinacy was reasonable enough, seeing the condition of affairs on board the *Kansas*.

The captain quitted her for a moment in order to dispatch a Chilean sailor for a lantern and a long cord. He wished to investigate the captured canoe.

Christobal, who had made the round of the promenade deck, came up.

"Oh, were you here, too?" he asked, on seeing the girl.

"I **am** here, if that is what you mean," she cried. "I heard Joey barking, and the shots that followed. Naturally, I wished to find out what had happened."

"Sorry. I imagined you were sleepless, like myself, and had joined Courtenay during his watch. That explanation must have sufficed. In any case, we have other things to trouble us at present."

Elsie had never before heard the Spaniard speaking so offhandedly. She gave small heed to his petulance; aroused from sound slumber by the alarm of an Indian attack--thrilled by the horror of the thought that she might fall into the clutches of the callous man-apes which infest the islands of southwest America--she was in no mood to disentangle subtleties of speech.

"Do you think they have left us?" she murmured, shrinking nearer to the iron shield which Courtenay seemed to think would protect her.

"Personally, I have seen no reason whatever for such a hubbub," was the flippant answer.

It was evident that Dr. Christobal was annoyed. Notwithstanding his conventional polish, he was not a man to conceal his feelings when deeply stirred. Yet Elsie failed to catch his intent, other than that he was adopting his usual nonchalant tone.

"But something must have caused Captain Courtenay and Mr. Tollemache to fire their revolvers so frequently. And, if they were mistaken, the dog would not have shared their error. Besides, one of the canoes did not get away. See! Its mast is fastened there."

"Ah! I had forgotten Tollemache. He was selected to join the captain's watch, of course."

"Yes, I was present when the watches were formed. Have you seen Mr. Tollemache? Is he safe?"

"He is among those making the round of the ship. I hope you will forgive me."

"Forgive you! What have you done that calls for forgiveness?"

"There are errors of speech which equal those of conduct, Miss Maxwell."

"Oh, what nonsense--at one in the morning--when we are threatened by savages!"

Christobal was relieved that she took this view of his abrupt utterances. He thought the incident was ended. He was mistaken; Elsie was able to recall each word subsequently. At the moment she was recording impressions with uncomprehending accuracy, but her mind was quite incapable of analyzing them; that would come later.

The lantern was brought. Courtenay stood on the lowermost rail, and carefully paid out a rope to which the light was slung. He was far too brave a man to take undue risks. He was ready to shoot instantly if need be, and, by his instructions, Tollemache and Walker kept watch as best they could in case other canoes were lying close to the ship.

Any doubt in this regard was dispelled in a singular manner. The flickering rays of the lantern had barely revealed the primitive craft lying alongside when a voice came from the depths, crying in broken Spanish:

"Don't shoot, senors--spare me, for the love of heaven! I am a white man from Argentina."

Christobal and Elsie alone understood the exact significance of the words. Courtenay, of course, knew what language was being spoken, and it was easy to guess the nature of the appeal. But the lantern showed that the canoe was empty. In the center lay the Fuegian fire, its embers covered with a small hide. The pole, fastened to a cross-piece in the thwarts, was not a mast, but had evidently been shipped in order to give speedy access to the deck by climbing.

Then Courtenay caught sight of two hands clinging to the stern of the canoe. He swung the lantern in that direction, and an extraordinary, and even an affrighting, object became visible. A caricature of a human head was raised slightly above the level of the water. It was crowned by a shock of coarse, black, knotted hair, tied back from the brows by a fillet of white feathers. An intensely black face, crossed by two bars of red and white pigment, reaching from ear to ear, and covering eyelids, nose, and lips, was upturned to the watchers from the deck. The colors were vivid enough, notwithstanding the sheets of rain which blew in gusts against the ship's side, dimming the dull light of a storm-proof lamp, to convey a most uncanny effect; nor did Courtenay remove either his eyes or the revolver while he said to Christobal:

"Ask him who he is, and what he wants."

The answer was intelligible enough.

"I am a miner from Argentina. I have been among these Indians five years. When their attack failed, I thought there was a chance of escape. For pity's sake, senor, help me instantly, or I shall die from the cold."

"Have the Indians gone?" asked Christobal.

"Yes. They thought to surprise you. When they come again it will be by daylight, as they are afraid of the dark. But be quick, I implore you. My hands are numb."

There was no resisting the man's appeal. A rope ladder was lowered, and a Chilean sailor went down in obedience to the captain's order, though he disliked the job, and crossed himself before descending. He passed a rope under the fugitive's armpits, and, with aid from the deck, hoisted him aboard. The unfortunate miner gave proof of his wretched state by promptly collapsing in a faint, with a sigh of "Madre de Dios!"

His only garments were a species of waistcoat and rough trousers of untanned guanaco hide. The white skin of his breast and legs, though darkened by exposure, showed that he had told the truth as to his descent, notwithstanding the amazing daubs on his face. His hair, stiffened with black grease, stood out all around his head, and the same oily composition had been used to blacken his forehead, neck, and hands.

Some brandy and hot water, combined with the warmth of the saloon, soon revived him. He ate a quantity of bread with the eagerness of a man suffering from starvation; but he could not endure the heated atmosphere, although the temperature was barely sufficient to guard the injured occupants from the outer cold. When offered an overcoat, he refused it at first, saying:

"I do not need so much clothing. It will make me ill. I only felt cold in the water because it is mostly melted ice."

He was so grateful to his rescuers, however, that he took the garment to oblige them when he saw they were incredulous. Christobal brought him to the chart-house, where most of the others were assembled, and there questioned him.

It was a most astonishing story which Francisco Suarez, gold-miner and prospector, laid before an exceedingly attentive audience. As the man spoke, so did he recover the freer usage of a civilized tongue. At first his words had a hoarse, guttural sound, but Dr. Christobal's questions seemed to awaken dormant memories, and every one noticed, not least those who had small knowledge of Spanish, that he had practically recovered command of the language at the end of half an hour.

And this was what he told them. He, with three partners and a few Indians from the Pampas, had set out on a gold-prospecting expedition on the head waters of the Gallegos River. They were disappointed in their search until they crossed the Cordillera, and sighted the gloomy shores of Last Hope Inlet, leading into Smyth Channel. They there found alluvial sand and gold-bearing quartz, yielding but poor results. Unfortunately, some natives assured them that the metal they sought abounded in Hanover Island. They obtained canoes, voyaged down the long inlet, crossed the straits, and struck inland towards the unknown mountains beyond the swamps of Ellen Bay.

After enduring all the hardships entailed by life in such a wild country, they blundered into a gully where a brief analysis of the detritus gave a result per ton which was not to be measured by ounces but by pounds.

"Virgin! What a place that was!" exclaimed Suarez, his dark eyes sparkling even yet with the recollection of it. "In one day we secured more gold than we could carry. We threw away food to make room for it, and then threw away gold to secure the food again. We called it the Golden Valley. When weary of digging, we would spin coins to see who drew corner lots in the town we had mapped out on a level piece of land."

White men and Indians alike caught the fever. They accumulated a useless hoard, having no means of transport other than their own backs, and then, all precautions being relaxed, the nomad Indians, whom they despised, rushed the camp when they were sleeping. They were nearly all killed by stones shot from slings. Suarez was only stunned, and he and a Spaniard, with two Indians, were reserved for future slaughter.

"The others were eaten," he said, "and their bones were used for making fires. I saw my friend, Giacomo, felled like a bullock, and the Indians as well. By chance, I was the last. I had no hope of escape. I was too downcast even to make a fight of it, when, at the eleventh hour, the mad idea seized me that I might please and astonish my captors by performing a few sleight-of-hand tricks. I began by throwing stones in the air, pretending to swallow them and causing them to disappear otherwise, but finding them again in the heel of my boot or hidden beneath any object which happened to be near. When the Indians saw what I was doing, they gathered in a circle. I ate some fire, and took a small toad out of a woman's ear. Dios! How they gaped. They had never seen the like. All the tribe was summoned to watch me."

Then the poor fellow began to cry.

"Holy Mother! Think of me playing the fool before those brutes! I became their medicine man. I fought and killed my only rival, and, since then, I have doctored a few of the chief men among them, so they took me into the tribe, and always managed to procure me such food as I could eat. They gave me roots and dried meat when they themselves were living on putrid blubber, or worse, because they kill all the old women as soon as famine threatens. The women are devoured long before the dogs; dogs catch otters, but old women cannot. In winter, when a long storm renders it impossible to obtain shell-fish, any woman who is feeble will steal off and hide in the mountains. But the men track her and bring her back. They hold her over the smoke of a fire until she is choked. Ah! God in heaven! I have seen such sights during those five years!"

Elsie, of course, understood all of this. When Christobal put it into literal English, Courtenay looked at her. She smiled at his unspoken thought.

"I am already aware of most of what he is telling us," she said. "It is very dreadful that such people should exist, but one does not fall in a faint merely because they cumber the earth. Perhaps you will not send me away next time, if they try to board the ship again. I can use a revolver quite well enough to count as one for the defense."

"You are henceforth enrolled as maid-at-arms, Miss Maxwell," said the captain, lightly. He was by no means surprised at the coolness she displayed in the face of the new terror. She had given so many proofs of her natural courage that it must be equal to even so affrighting a test as the near presence of the Alaculof Indians. But he broke in on the Spaniard's recital with a question of direct interest.

"Ask him, Christobal, why he said those devils would come again by daylight."

"Because they have guns, and can use them," was the appalling answer given by Suarez. "They secured the rifles belonging to my party, and one of them, who had often seen ship's officers shooting wild geese, understood the method of loading and aiming. They will not waste the cartridges on game, but keep them for tribal warfare, and they think a gun cannot shoot in the dark. To-night they only attempted a surprise, and made off the moment they were discovered. To-morrow, or next day, they will swarm round the ship in hundreds, and fire at us with rifles, bows, and slings. They do most harm with the slings and arrows, as they hold the gun away from the shoulder, but they can cast a heavy pebble from a sling quite as far and almost as straight as a revolver can shoot."

"How do they know the ship will not sail at once?" demanded Courtenay.

Suarez laughed hysterically, with the mirth which is akin to tears, when the query was explained to him. He looked bizarre enough under ordinary conditions, but laughter converted him into a fair semblance of one of those blood-curdling demons which a Japanese artist loves to depict. Evidently, he depended on make-up to supplement his powers as a conjurer.

"It is as much as a canoe can manage in fine weather to reach the island out there, which they call Seal Island," he cried, pointing towards the locality of White Horse Island. "Even the Indians were astonished to see so big a ship anchored here safely. They have watched plenty of wrecks outside, and hardly anything comes ashore. At any rate, they are quite sure you cannot go back."

It would be idle to deny that the Spaniard's words sent a chill of apprehension down the spine of some of those present; but the captain said quietly:

"Where a ship is concerned, if she can enter on the flood she can go out on the ebb. How came you to escape to-night?"

Tears stood again in Suarez's eyes as he replied:

"When I heard their plan, I imagined they would be driven off, provided a watch were kept. I resolved to risk all in the attempt to reach the company of civilized men once more. I do not care what the outcome may be. If I can help you to overcome them I am ready to do so; if not, I will die by your side. To-night I followed in a canoe unseen. When I heard the shooting, I leaped overboard and swam to the ship. It was lucky for me some one seized the canoe which I found there. The men in her had to swim to other canoes, and two were wounded, I heard them say; this caused some confusion, and I had something to grasp when I reached the ship; otherwise I must have been drowned, as the water was very cold."

"Yet you refused an overcoat a little while ago," interjected Christobal.

"Ah, yes. For many years I have lived altogether in Indian fashion. My skin is hard. Wind or rain cannot harm me. But melted ice mixed with salt water drives even the seals out to sea."

"Can you speak the Alaculof language?"

"Is that what you call them? Their own name for the tribe is 'The Feathered People,' because all their chief men and heads of families wear these things," and he touched his head-dress. "Yes, I know nearly all their words. They don't use a great many. One word may have several meanings, according to the pitch of the voice."

"They captured you on the Smyth Channel side of the island. Have they deserted it? Why are they on this side now?" asked Courtenay.

"I believe they brought me here at first because they wished to keep me on account of my magic, and they knew I would endeavor to escape to a passing ship. We came over the mountains by a terrible road. I have been told that landslips and avalanches have closed the pass ever since. I do not know whether that is true or not, but if I had tried to get away in that direction they would have caught me in a few hours. No man can elude them. They can see twice as far as any European, and they are wonderful trackers."

Suddenly his voice failed him. Though the words came fluently, his long-disused vocal chords were unequal to the strain of measured speech. He asked hoarsely for some hot water. When Courtenay next came across him in the saloon he was asleep, and changed so greatly by the removal of pigments from his face that it was difficult to regard him as the same being.

His story was unquestionably true. Tollemache, who had fought an offshoot tribe of these same Indians, Christobal, who vouched for the Argentine accent, and Elsie, who seemed to have read such rare books of travel as dealt with that little known part of the world, bore out the reasonableness of his statements. The only individual on board who regarded him with suspicion was Joey, and even Joey was satisfied when Suarez had washed himself.

It was daylight again, a dawn of dense mist, without wind or hail, ere any member of the ship's company thought of sleep. Then Elsie went to her cabin and dreamed of a river of molten gold, down which she was compelled to sail in a cockle-shell boat, while fantastic monsters swam round, and eyed her suspiciously.

When, at last, she awoke after a few hours of less exciting slumber, she came out on deck to find the sun shining on a fairy-land of green and blue and diamond white, with gaunt gray rocks and groves of copper beeches to frame the picture. There was no pillar of smoke on the lower hills to bear silent testimony to the presence of the Indians; but the canoe lying alongside told her that the previous night's events were no part of her dreams, and a man whom she did not recognize--a man with closely cropped gray hair and a deeply lined, weather-tanned face, from which a pair of sunken, flashing eyes looked kindly at her--said in Spanish:

"Good morning, senorita. I hope I did not startle you when I came aboard. And I said things I should not have said in the presence of a lady. But believe me, senorita, I was drunk with delight."

CHAPTER X
"MISSING AT LLOYD'S"

Elsie had slept long and soundly: she found herself in a new world of sunshine and calm. When she looked over the side to examine the crudely fashioned canoe, she was astonished by the limpid purity of the water. She could see white pebbles and vegetation at a vast depth. It seemed to be impossible that a few hours should have worked such a change, but Suarez assured her that the streams which tumbled down the precipitous gorges of the hills ran clear quickly after rain, owing to the sifting of the surface drainage by the phenomenal tree-growth.

"Wherever timber can lodge on the hillsides," he told her, "fallen trunks lie in layers of fifteen or twenty feet. They rot there, and young saplings push their way through to the light and air, while creepers bind them in an impenetrable mass; in many places small trees and shrubs of dense foliage take root amidst the decaying stumps beneath, so that even the Indians cannot pass from one point to another, but are compelled to climb the rocky watercourses or follow the slopes of glaciers. When you see what appears to be a smooth green space above the lower brown-colored belt of copper beech, that is not a moss-covered stretch of open land, but the closely packed tops of young trees, where a new tract has been bared by an avalanche."

She was in no mood this morning to assimilate the marvels of Hanover Island. Her brain had been cleared, restored to the normal, by refreshing sleep. With a more active perception of the curious difficulties which beset the *Kansas* came a feeling akin to despair. The brightness of nature served rather to convert the ship into a prison. Storm and stress, whether of the elements or of the less candid foes who lurked unseen on the neighboring shores, made the *Kansas* a veritable fortress, a steel refuge seemingly impregnable. But the knowledge of the vessel's help-lessness, and of the equally desperate hazard which beset her inmates, was rendered only more poignant by the smiling aspect of land and sea.

Elsie was not a philosopher. She was just a healthy, clean-minded English-woman, imbued with a love of art for art's sake, a girl whose wholesome, cou-rageous temperament probably unfitted her to achieve distinction in the artistic career which she had mapped out for herself. So the super-Alpine glories sur-rounding that inland sea, and the prismatic hues flashing from many a glacier and rainbow of cataract mist, left her unmoved, solely because the rough-hewn Indian craft bobbing by the side of the great ship called to mind the extraordinary condi-tions under which she and all on board existed.

But she was hungry, and that was a saving sign. She guessed that many of the men, after mounting watch until broad daylight, were asleep. Others were at work below, as was testified by a subdued sound of hammering, with the sharp clink of metal against metal. Walker was tinkering at the engines. With him, in all likeli-hood, were the captain and Tollemache. She and Suarez were the drones of the ship, and Suarez, poor fellow, had earned an idle hour if only on account of the scrubbing he had given himself to wash away the tokens of five years of slavery.

Before going in search of the cook, she walked a few steps towards the bridge. At the top of the companion she saw Joey, sitting disconsolately on his tail, a sure indication that Courtenay was occupied in depths approachable only by steep iron ladders whither the dog could not follow.

She whistled softly to her little friend, knowing that Christobal, and perhaps Mr. Boyle, would be on the bridge, keeping the lookout, and she was not inclined for talk at the moment. The doctor would have understood at once that the girl was below par, owing to the strain of the preceding days, and the lethargic rest which exhaustion had imposed on her. Yet, there are times when science does not satisfy.
. . .

But Joey, who recked naught of philosophy, and to whom the alarms and excur-sions of fights on deck came as a touch of mother earth to the sole of Antaeos--Joey, then, sprang down the stairs, barking joyously, and leaped into her outstretched arms.

He honored no other person on board, except his master, with such extravagant friendship, and, as the girl carried him aft to the cook's galley, she asked herself why the dog had taken such a liking to her.

She blushed a little as she thought:

"It may be that I resemble the lady whom Captain Courtenay is going to marry. I wonder why he did not show us her photograph that day when Isobel and I visited his cabin and looked at the pictures of his mother and sister. I should like to see her, but how can I manage it? I simply dare not tell him I read that scrap of a letter, even by chance."

The dog, apparently, found her an excellent substitute; he licked her ear contentedly. That tickled her, and she laughed.

"I fear you are a fickle lover, Joey," she said aloud. "But you will simply be compelled to remain constant to me while we are in this horrid place, and that may be for the remainder of our lives, dear."

Joey tried to lick her again to show that he didn't care. What could any reasonable dog want more than fine weather, enough to eat, and the prospect of an occasional scrimmage?

When Elsie did ultimately climb to the chart-house, the fit of despondency had fled. Boyle was there, having been carried up in a deck chair early in the day. He was alone.

"Huh!" he growled pleasantly. "You 're lookin' as bright as a new pin, Miss Maxwell. Now, if I had been among the pirates, I'd have taken you with me."

"Do you mean to say that you are actually paying me compliments?" said she.

"Am I? Huh; didn't mean to. I'm an old married man. But pirates, especially Spanish ones, are supposed to be very handy with knives and other fellows' girls."

"You see they did not consider me a prize."

"The rascals! Good job you missed that boat. Christobal has been tellin' me all about it. They've gone under."

"Do you really think so?"

"Can't see any chance for them, Miss Maxwell."

"But we are almost as badly situated here?"

"Huh, not a bit of it. Lucky chap, Courtenay. He couldn't lose a ship if he tried. She 'd follow him 'cross country like that pup. Look at me: lost three, all brand new from the builders. One foundered, one burnt, an' one stuck on the Goodwins. I'm careful, steady as any man can be, but no owner would trust me with a ship now, unless she was a back number, an' over-insured. Even then my luck would follow me. I 'd bring that sort of crazy old tub through the Northwest passage. So I'm first mate, an' first mate I'll remain till my ticket gives out."

A good deal of this was Greek to Elsie. But she knew that Boyle was a man of curt speech, unless deck hands required the stimulus of a tongue lashing. Such a string of connected sentences was a rare occurrence. It argued that the "chief" was not unwilling to indulge in reminiscence.

"Why do you consider Captain Courtenay so fortunate?" she asked, flushing somewhat at the guile which lay behind the question.

"Huh," snorted Boyle, amazed that even a slip of a girl should need informing on so obvious a fact. "Don't you call it luck to be given command of a ship like the *Kansas* at his age? An' to get five hundred pounds an' a gold chronometer because the skipper of the *Florida* was too full to hold on to the bridge? You mark my words. He'll be made commodore of the fleet after he pulls the *Kansas* out of this mess."

"What happened to the *Florida*?"

"Haven't you heard that yarn? Bless my soul, she was our crack ship. She broke her shaft in a gale, an' the skipper was washed overboard--you always tell lies about deaders, you know--so A. C. just waded in an' saved the whole outfit, passengers an' all."

"But he has had reverses, too. He was in the Royal Navy, I have been told, and he had to give it up because his people--"

"More luck. The Royal Navy! Huh, all gold braid, an' buy your own vittals. There's no money in that game."

"Money is not everything in the world. A man's career may be more to him than the mere monetary aspect of it."

"If ever you meet my missus, you 'll hear the other side of the question, Miss Maxwell. S'posin' Courtenay was in the Navy, an' had a wife an' family to keep. Could he do it on his pay? Not he. As it is, he's sure to marry a girl with a pile, and wind up a managing owner."

"Perhaps he is engaged to some such young lady already?"

"Haven't heard so. You may be sure there's one waitin' for him somewhere. *I* know. There's no dodgin' luck, good or bad. I thought it was goin' to be that friend of yours, but she's off the register, poor lass. There! I didn't mean that. I 'm an idiot, for sure. You see, I don't talk much as a rule, Miss Maxwell, or I should know better than to chin-wag like a blazin'--huh, like a babblin' fool."

Elsie turned her face aside when he mentioned Isobel. It seemed to her sensitive soul an almost unfair thing that she should be gossiping about trivialities when the girl who had commenced this unlucky voyage in such high spirits was lying beneath that grim sea behind the smiling headland. Yet she knew that Boyle meant no harm by his chatter. He was weak from his wound, and perhaps a trifle light-headed as the result of being brought from the stuffy saloon to the airy and sunlit chart-room. So she crushed a sorrow that was unavailing, and strove to put the sailor at his ease again.

"I do not find any harm in your remark," she said resolutely. "Were it possible, I should have been very pleased to see Miss Baring married to a man of strong character like Captain Courtenay. By the way, who is keeping watch on deck?"

"The doctor was here with me until a few minutes ago. Then the skipper telephoned him. I guess there is some one on the lookout, but you might just cast an eye shorewards. I'm not supposed to move yet."

He wriggled uneasily in his chair, for the spirit was willing; but Elsie made him lie quiet; she rearranged his pillow, and stepped on to the bridge. By walking from port to starboard, and traversing the short length of the spar deck, she could command a view of the bay and of most parts of the ship. She heard the dog scuttling down the companion; on reaching the after-rail, she saw the captain engaged in earnest, low-toned conversation with Tollemache and Walker. They were standing on the main deck near the engine-room door, and examining something which resembled a lump of coal; she saw the engineer take three similar lumps from a pocket.

Christobal appeared, carrying a bucket of water, into which the lumps were placed by Walker, who handled them very gingerly. After a slight delay, he began to crumble one in his fingers, still keeping it in the water, until finally he drew forth what Elsie recognized at once as a stick of dynamite. Though it was blackened by contact with the coal, she was certain of its real nature. She had visited a great many mines, and the officials always scared the ladies of the party by telling them what would happen if the explosives' shed were to blow up. She had even seen dynamite placed in the sun to dry, as it is very susceptible to moisture, and she wondered, naturally enough, why such a dangerous agent should be hidden in, or disguised as, a piece of coal.

She thought that the men should be made aware of her presence, so she leaned over and said:

"May I ask what you four are plotting?"

They looked at her in surprise. They were so engrossed in their discovery that they had eyes for nothing else. Walker straightway plunged the sausage-shaped gray stick into the water again.

"What are you doing with that dynamite?" she demanded. "Do you intend to visit the Valley of the Golden Sands? If so, please take me. I am very poor."

It was Courtenay who answered.

"Are you alone?" he asked.

"Mr. Boyle is in the chart-house."

"I know; but is any one else up there?"

"No."

"Then we shall join you at once."

Notwithstanding the serious demeanor of the men, Elsie was far from guessing what had happened. But she was soon enlightened.

"In which bunker was the coal placed which we shipped at Valparaiso?" Courtenay asked Boyle.

"In the forrard cross bunker," was the instant answer.

"And that was the first coal used in the furnaces?"

"Yes, sir."

The captain's tone was official, exceedingly so, and the chief officer took the cue from his superior in rank.

"Did we get up steam with it?"

"There might have been a hundred-weight or two lying loose in the stoke-hold, but, for all practical purposes, we have used nothing but the Valparaiso bunker since we left port."

"The rest of our coal was shipped at Coronel?"

"Yes, sir."

"You hear? It is exactly as I have told you," said Courtenay, glancing at the others. "I must explain to you, Mr. Boyle, that I wished you to state the facts in front of witnesses before I gave you my reasons for cross-examining you on the matter. Mr. Walker and I have been certain, all along, that the furnaces were blown up wilfully. Now our suspicions are proved. This morning, after a careful scrutiny, we came across a number of lumps of coal cleverly constructed out of small pieces glued together. In the center of each lump was a stick of dynamite, protected by an asbestos wrapper. It was undoubtedly the intent of some miscreant that a number of these lumps should be fed into the furnaces. This actually occurred, as we know, but, by the mercy of Providence, the ship did not experience the full power of the explosion, or she must have sunk like a stone."

"Huh," grunted Boyle. "Who holds the insurance?"

"The shippers of the cargo, of course--Messrs. Baring, Thompson & Miguel."

"Worth a quarter of a million sterling, ain't it?"

"Yes."

"Huh, it's a lot of money."

There was a momentary silence. Elsie's eyes grew larger, and she became rather pale. As was her habit when puzzled, she placed a finger on her lips. Christobal noted her action. Indeed, he missed few of her characteristic habits or expressions. He laughed quietly.

"I think you are quite right, Miss Maxwell," he said. "This is one of the many instances in which silence is golden."

Taken by surprise, she blushed and dropped her hand. But Courtenay said promptly:

"There are some instances in which silence may be misinterpreted. Let me state at once that the shippers of the valuable cargo on board the *Kansas* will suffer a serious financial reverse if the ship is lost. Two thousand tons of copper may be worth a considerable fixed sum, but the lack of the metal on the London market at the end of January will have far-reaching consequences in a fight against the bull clique in Paris, and that is why Mr. Baring made this heavy shipment."

"Those consequences could be foreseen and discounted," put in Tollemache, dryly.

"Exactly. But by whom? By the man who sent his only daughter as a passenger on this vessel?"

Every one scouted that notion. But Tollemache, though disavowing any thought of Mr. Baring as a party to the scheme, stuck to his guns.

"Somebody will make a pile when the *Kansas* is reported missing," he said.

"The insurance money would not be paid for a long time," Courtenay explained.

"No, but the copper market will respond instantly."

"Then the process has commenced already. The *Kansas* should have been reported yesterday from Sandy Point. The news that she has not arrived will soon reach the nearest cable station. There will be terrific excitement at Lloyd's when that becomes known."

"It is distinctly odd that Suarez should turn up last night, and tell us how gold slipped through his fingers five years ago. Let us hope the parallel will hold good for the gentleman who so amiably endeavored to send the *Kansas* to the bottom of the Pacific," said Christobal.

"It is rather a rotten trick," broke in Tollemache, "just a bit of Spanish roguery-- Well, I'm sorry, Christobal, but I can't regard you as quite a Spaniard, you see."

"Nevertheless, I am one," and the doctor stiffened visibly.

"What Tollemache means is that he would expect you to take the English and straightforward view of a piece of rascality, doctor." Then Courtenay paused in his turn. "By the way," he continued, with the frowning dubiety of one whose thoughts outstrip his words, "does any one here know a man named Ventana?"

"It is a name common enough in Chile," said Christobal.

"If you mean Senor Pedro Ventana, who is associated with Mr. Baring in mining matters, I am acquainted with him," said Elsie. The men seemed to have forgotten her presence. They were wrapped up in the remarkable discovery which Courtenay himself had made by diligent search among the coal ready for use in the furnaces when the explosion took place.

For no reason in particular, save the unexpectedness of it, Elsie's statement was received with surprise. They all looked at her, and some of them wondered, perhaps, why her smiling eyes had lost their mirth. Yet there was nothing unreasonable in the mere fact that a certain Chilean named Ventana, who had business relations with Mr. Baring, should make the acquaintance of Isobel Baring's friend. As quickly as it had arisen, the feeling of strangeness passed.

Courtenay even laughed. Elsie as the Jonah of the ship was a quaint conceit.

"I mentioned Ventana because I was told he took some part of the insurance on his own account," he explained. "But he was a member of Baring's copper syndicate, and, indeed, was spoken of as a mining engineer of high repute. Believe me, I was not jumping to conclusions on that account."

"I know him to be a very bad man," said Elsie, slowly. Her face was white and her eyes downcast. It was evident that the sudden introduction of Ventana's personality was distressing to her, but Courtenay, preoccupied with the dastardly attempt made to sink his ship, did not observe this feature of a peculiar discussion.

"Bad! In what sense, Miss Maxwell?" he asked unguardedly.

"In the most loathsome sense. He is evil-minded, vicious, altogether detestable. If Mr. Baring knew his character as I know it, Ventana would not be allowed to enter his office."

"Pedro Ventana?" interrupted Christobal. "Is he a half-caste, a tall, brown-skinned man, who affects an American drawl when he speaks English--a man prominent in Santiago society and in mining circles generally?"

"Yes," said Elsie.

"That is odd, exceedingly so. I once heard a rumor--but perhaps it is unfair to mention it in this connection. Yet it cannot hurt any one if I state that Isobel Baring and he were--well--how shall I put it?--at any rate, there was a lively summer-hotel sort of attachment between them."

"Isobel has never told me that," said Elsie, nerving herself for a personal disclosure which was obviously disagreeable. "I own a small ranch near Quillota, and, as there was a chance of copper being located there, Mr. Baring advised me to employ Ventana as an expert prospector. Indeed, Mr. Baring himself sent Ventana to examine the property and report on it. He came to see me. He told me there were no minerals of value on my land, but I could never free myself from him afterwards. Indeed, I am running away from him now."

She uttered the concluding words with a genuine indignation which forthwith evaporated in its unconscious humor. Everybody laughed, even the girl herself, and Boyle grunted:

"Huh, shows the beggar's good taste, anyhow."

Courtenay, perhaps, thought that if he encountered Ventana again he would take the opportunity to reason with him in the approved manner of the high seas. And, as there was no need to prolong a topic which caused Elsie any sort of embarrassment, he hastened to say:

"I have brought names into the discussion largely to show what a doubtful field is opened once we begin to suspect without real cause. The only witness of any value we have on board is Frascuelo, and his evidence merely goes to prove a secret design to interfere with, or control, the trimming of the bunker. That particular hatch must be sealed, and the specimens we have secured put away under lock and key. I feel assured that the remainder of our coal is above suspicion. We can carry the inquiry no further while we remain here. Now, Mr. Walker, you have something of a more cheering nature to communicate, I think."

The engineer grinned genially.

"I don't wish to bind myself to a day or so, Miss Maxwell and gentlemen," he said, "but I've had a good look at the damage, an' I feel pwitty shu-aw I'll get up steam in one boil-aw within ten days or a fawt-night. It'll be a makeshift job at the best, because I have so few spa-aw fittin's, an' no chance of makin' a castin', but I'll bet a ye'aw's scwew the *Kansas* gets a move on her undaw her own steam soon aftaw New Ye-aw's Day."

New Year's Day! What a lump in the throat the words brought. In three days it would be Christmas, in seven more the New Year! Though, from the beginning of the voyage, they were prepared to pass both festivals at sea, there was all the difference in the world between a steady progress towards home and friends and the present plight of the *Kansas*. Death, too, had thrown its shadow over them. Some there were to whom the passing of the years would mean no more in this world. Others, the great majority of the ship's company, were probably hidden by the same eternal silence; the last sight they had of them was a dim vision of boats rushing into a chaos of angry seas and sheeted spray.

But Courtenay would have none of these mournful memories. He had solved the mystery of the ship's breakdown, and an expert mechanical engineer had just pledged his reputation to restore wings to the *Kansas*--somewhat clipped wings, it is true, but sufficient, given fair weather and reasonable good fortune, to bring her to a civilized settlement in the Straits. Why, then, should they yield to gloom?

"Isn't that glorious news?" he cried. "Now, Christobal, that motor trip in June through the Pyrenees looks feasible once more. And you, Miss Maxwell, though you have never quailed for an instant, can hope to be in England in the spring. As for you, Tollemache, surely you will say that our prospects are 'fair,' at the least."

"I would say more than that if it were not for these poisonous Indians," replied Tollemache. "Here they come now, a whole canoe load of 'em. I have never seen such rotters."

And, indeed, Francisco Suarez, detailed to keep watch and ward over the ship until noon, ran up the companion and cried excitedly:

"Four head men have just put off from Otter Creek. They have missed me, I expect. They will want me to go back. I beseech you, senor captain, not to give me up to them, but rather to send a bullet through my miserable heart."

"Tell him to calm himself," said Courtenay, coolly, when Christobal had translated this flow of guttural Spanish. "He has no cause to fear them now; let him nerve himself, and show a bold front. A palaver is the best thing that can happen. We must display all the arms we possess. Bid any of your invalids who can stand upright show themselves, Christobal. We must lift you outside, Boyle. Bring your camera, Miss Maxwell. If we could give these fellows a good picture of themselves it would scare them to death."

The captain of the *Kansas* was not to be repressed that day. He refused to look at the dark side of things. He even found cause for congratulation in the threatened visit of cannibals whom Suarez feared so greatly that he preferred death to the chance of returning to them, although they had spared his life.

And Courtenay infected them all with his splendid optimism. It was with curiosity rather than dread that they watched the rapid approach of the canoe and its almost naked occupants.

CHAPTER XI
CONFIDENCES

Courtenay was mistaken in thinking that the savages sought a parley. The canoe was paddled by two women; they changed its course with a dexterous twist of the blades when within a cable's length of the ship, and then circled slowly round her. The four men jabbered in astonishingly loud voices. Suarez, who gathered the purport of their talk, explained that they were discussing the best method of attack.

"The three younger men belong to the tribe which I lived with," he said. "The old man sitting between the women is a stranger. I think he must have come from the north of the island with some of his friends, attracted by the smoke signals."

"From the north? Is there a road?" asked Courtenay, when he learnt what Suarez was saying.

"He would arrive in a canoe," was the answer. "The Indians venture out to sea in very bad weather. He probably passed the ship late last night, and, now I come to think of it, the canoe which you captured is not familiar to me, whereas I know by sight every craft owned by the Feathered People."

"How many do they possess?"

"Twenty-three."

These statements were disconcerting. Not only was it possible for the natives to surround the *Kansas* with a whole swarm of men, but the mere number of their boats would render it exceedingly difficult to repel a combined assault. And nothing could be more truculent than the demeanor of the semi-nude warriors. They pointed at each person they saw on the decks, and made a tremendous row when they passed the canoe fastened alongside. Despite their keen sight, they evidently did not recognize Suarez, who now wore a cap and a suit of clothes taken from the locker of one of the missing stewards, while his appearance was so altered otherwise that even the people on board found it difficult to regard him as the monstrous-looking wizard whom they had dragged out of the water some twelve hours earlier.

The impudence of the Indians exasperated Courtenay. The sheer size of the *Kansas* should have awed them, he thought.

"I wish they had left their women behind," he muttered. "If the men were alone, an ounce or two of buck-shot would soon teach them to keep their distance."

"Perhaps they are aware of the danger of boarding a ship which stands so high above the sea as the *Kansas*," said Christobal. "Why not fire a couple of rounds of blank cartridge at them?"

"Worst thing you can do," said Tollemache.

"But why?"

"They would be sure, then, you could not hurt them. If you shoot, shoot straight, with the heaviest shot you possess."

At that moment the rowers permitted the canoe to swing round with the tide. One of the men stood up, and Elsie, who seized the chance of snap-shotting the party, ran to the upper deck, so she did not overhear Courtenay's smothered ejaculation. He was scrutinizing the savages through his glasses, and he had distinctly seen the ship's name painted on a small water-cask on which the Indian had been sitting. Tollemache made the same dramatic discovery.

"Out of one of the ship's life-boats, I suppose?" he said in a low tone to the captain.

"Yes. Did you see the number?"

"Number 3, I think."

"I agree with you. That was the first life-boat which got away."

Christobal, startled out of his wonted sang-froid, whispered in his turn:

"Do you mean to say that one of the boats has fallen into the hands of these fiends?"

"I am afraid so," replied Courtenay. "Of course, that particular keg may have drifted ashore. In any case, it tells the fate of one section of the mutineers. Either the boat is swamped, or the crew are now on the island, and we know what that signifies."

"Is there no chance of bribing these people into friendliness, or, at least, into a temporary truce?"

"It is hard to decide. Tollemache and Suarez are best able to form an opinion. What do you say, Tollemache?"

"Not a bit of use; they are insatiable. The more you give the more they want. The only way to deal with those rotters is to stir them up with a Gatling or a twelve-pounder."

Suarez, when appealed to, shook his head.

"Last winter," he said, "the man sitting aft, he with the single albatross feather sticking in his hair, seized his own son, aged six, and dashed his brains out on the rocks because the little fellow dropped a basket of sea-eggs he was carrying. The woman nearest to him is his wife, and she raised no protest. You might as well try to fondle a hungry puma. I am the only man they have ever spared, and they spared me solely because they thought I gave them power over their enemies. If you had a cannon, you might drive them off. As it is, we shall be compelled to fight for our lives; they are brave enough in their own way."

The experience of the miner from Argentina was not to be gainsaid. The predicament of the giant ***Kansas***--inert, immovable, lying in that peaceful bay at the mercy of a horde of painted savages--was one of the strange facts almost beyond credence which men encounter at times in the byways of life. It reminded Courtenay of a visit he paid to the crocodile tank at Karachi when he was a midshipman on the ***Boadicea***. He noticed that some of the huge saurians, eighteen feet in length and covered with scale armor off which a bullet would glance, were squirming uneasily, and the Hindu attendant told him that they had been bitten by mosquitoes!

He laughed quietly, but his mirth had a curious ring in it which boded ill for certain unknown members of the Alaculof tribe when the threatened tussle came to close quarters. Elsie heard him. Leaning over the rails of the spar deck, she asked cheerfully:

"What is the joke, Captain Courtenay? And why don't the Indians come nearer? Are they timid? They don't look it."

He glanced up at her. If aught were needed to complete the contrast between civilization and savagery it was given by the comparison which the girl offered to the women in the canoe. The hot sun and the absence of wind had changed the temperature from winter to summer. After breakfast, Elsie had donned a muslin dress, and a broad-brimmed straw hat. Exposure to the weather had bronzed her skin to a delightful tint. Her nut-brown hair framed a sweetly pretty face, and her clear blue eyes and red lips, slightly parted, smiled bewitchingly at the men beneath. The camera in her hands added a holiday aspect to her appearance, an aspect which was unutterably disquieting in its relation to the muttered forebodings she had broken in on.

But Courtenay's voice gave no hint of the tumult in his breast, though some malign spirit seemed to whisper the agonizing question: "Will you permit her to fall into the hands of the ghouls waiting without?"

"I find the get-up of our visitors distinctly humorous," he said, "and I hope they are a bit scared of us. We would prefer their room to their company."

"I thought that Senor Suarez would hail them, as he can speak their language. Perhaps he does not wish them to know he is on board?"

Now, Elsie had heard the man's impassioned appeal when the Indians were first sighted, so Courtenay felt that she, too, was acting.

"You look nice and cool up there," he answered, "and your words do not belie your looks."

"Please, what does that mean exactly?"

"Need I tell you? You treat our troubles airily."

"Shall one 'wear a rough garment to deceive'?" she quoted with a laugh. "Don't you remember the next verse? You ought to retort: 'I am no prophet, I am an husbandman!' But that would not be quite right, for you are a sailor."

She blushed a little at the chance turn of the phrase. Neither the girl nor her hearers recalled the succeeding verses, wherein the destruction of Jerusalem is foretold: "And I will bring the third part through the fire, and will refine them as silver is refined, and will try them as gold is tried."

Indeed, a new direction was given to Elsie's thoughts by the somewhat scowling aspect of Christobal's face. He was looking at Courtenay in a manner which betokened a certain displeasure. The Spaniard's cultivated cynicism was subjugated by a more powerful sentiment. It seemed to Elsie that he envied Courtenay his youth and high spirits, for, in very truth, the mere exchange of those harmless pleasantries had tuned the younger man's soul to the transcendental pitch of the knight errant. In his heart he was vowing to rescue this fair lady from the dangers which beset her, though he said jokingly with his lips:

"If a husbandman has to do with a tiller I may claim some expert knowledge, Miss Maxwell."

Elsie dared not meet his eyes; a flood of understanding had suddenly poured its miraculous waters over her. Incidents unimportant in themselves, utterances which seemed to have no veiled intent at the time, rushed in upon her with overwhelming conviction. Christobal suspected her of flirting with Courtenay, and disapproved of it as strongly as she herself had condemned Isobel's admitted efforts in the same direction. Though not a little dismayed, she resolved to carry the war into the enemy's territory.

"Why are you looking so glum, Dr. Christobal?" she demanded. "Has the captain's quip given you a shock, or is it that you are surprised at my levity?"

"I am neither shocked nor surprised, Miss Maxwell. I have not lived fifty years in this Vale of Tears without being prepared for the unexpected."

"Does that imply that you are disillusioned?"

"By no means. My heart is amazingly young. 'There is no fool like an old fool,' you know."

"Oh, please don't speak of age in that way. You are far from being an antiquity. Why, within the past twenty-four hours I have come to look on you as a sort of elder brother, who can be indulgent even while he chides."

Courtenay found himself wondering what had caused this flash of rapiers. But, so far as he was concerned, the proceedings of the Indians put a stop to any further share in the conversation. The canoe had drifted closer to the ship. It was about eighty yards distant when the Indian who was on his feet suddenly whirled a sling, and sent a stone crashing through the window of the music-room. The heavy missile, which, when picked up, was found to weigh nearly half a pound, just missed Tollemache, who was the first to take note of the sharp warning given by Suarez, but failed, nevertheless, to dodge quickly enough.

The captain raised a double-barreled fowling-piece, the only gun on board, and fired point blank at the savages. But the women were paddling away vigorously, and the shot splashed in the water on all sides of the canoe, though a howl and a series of violent contortions showed that one, at least, of the pellets had stung the wizened Indian whom Suarez believed to be a newcomer.

There was no second shot--cartridges were too precious to be wasted at an impossible range--but the undeniable fact remained that the Indians meant to be aggressive. For a little time no one spoke. They heard the echoes of the gunshot faintly thrown back by the nearest wall of rock; the regular plash of the paddles as the canoe sped shorewards was distinctly audible. They watched the tiny craft until it vanished round the wooded point which concealed Otter Creek. Then, to add to the sense of loneliness and peace conveyed by the placid bay and the green slopes beyond, a big whale rolled into view in the middle distance, and blew a column of water high in air.

The muffled clang of a hammer broke the silence which had fallen on the watchers from the ship. Walker had slipped back to his beloved engines. Had he not vowed that the massive pistons should again thrust forth their willing arms on or about New Year's day? He had forgotten the cannibals and their threats ere he was at the foot of the engine-room ladder. Courtenay and Tollemache joined him; Christobal went to the saloon to visit his patients; Elsie was left with Mr. Boyle, who forthwith fell into a doze, being worn out by the fresh air and the excitement.

Joey, having followed Courtenay to the one doorway in the ship which he could not enter, trotted back to find Elsie. She greeted him with enthusiasm.

"Hail, friend," she said. "You, at least, are not jealous if I speak to your master, wherein you show your exceeding wisdom. Now, since you and I are persons of leisure, tell me, Joey, what we shall do to make ourselves useful?"

The dog was accustomed to being spoken to. He awaited developments.

"It seems to me, Joey," she continued, "that Gulielmo Frascuelo is the one person on board who claims our attention. There is a mystery to be solved. Bound up in it are my poor Isobel, that beast, Ventana, and a drunken coal-trimmer. An odd assortment to rub shoulders, don't you think?"

Joey still reserved his opinion. When the girl went to the forecastle by climbing down the sailors' ladder to the lower deck, he thought she was making a mistake; but she held her arms for his spring, and all was well. She had not previously visited the quarters set apart for the crew. Puzzled by the large number of small cabins with names of subordinate officers painted on them, she paused and cried loudly:

"Are you there, Frascuelo? May I speak to you?"

An exclamation of surprise, a somewhat forcible exclamation, too, answered her from an inner berth. Frascuelo had heard from the Chilean who brought his meals that there was an Englishwoman on board, but he did not know that she spoke Spanish fluently. He answered her question politely enough in the next breath, and the dog indicated the right door by hopping inside.

Frascuelo was reclining on a lower bunk. His injured leg was well on the way towards recovery, but the wound and its resultant confinement had chastened him; he had lost the brigandish swagger which was his most cherished asset.

After acknowledging inquiries as to his progress, he showed such eagerness for news that Elsie told him briefly what had caused the latest uproar. She cheered him, too, with the announcement made by the engineer, and then led him to the topic on which she sought information.

"In some ways, I regard you as most unfortunate," she said. "I have been told you are here by accident--that you never meant to take the voyage at all. Is that true?"

Frascuelo, delighted to have secured a sympathetic listener, poured forth his sorrows volubly. He bore no ill-will against the captain he said. He knew it was wrong to draw a knife on the chief officer, as his tale was an unlikely one, and he ought to have trusted to a more orderly recital of the facts to obtain credence.

"But I was that mad, senorita, I just saw red, and the drink was yet surging up in me. I felt I must fight somebody, whatever the consequences."

"Can you tell me why any one had such a grievance against you that you should be thrown into the hold and nearly killed? That was a strange thing to do, especially as you came aboard too late for your work."

"Ah, that is the point, senorita. You see, we trimmers work in gangs, and the man who flung me through the hatch was the man who had taken my place. I see no reason to doubt that it was he who made me drunk the previous evening, and I know who did that."

"What was his name?"

"Jose Anacleto--'Jose the Wine-bag' we call him on the Plaza. I ought to have smelt mischief when Jose paid. Never before had I seen him do such a thing. And a good liquor, too. Dios, it must have cost him dollars."

"What object had he in coming on board instead of you?"

"Ah, there you beat me, senorita. I have twisted my poor brain with thinking of that. We only earned a dollar a head, and bunkering a ship from a flat is hard work while it lasts, whereas one would expect Jose to ride twenty miles the other way to escape such a task. But he was in the plot, and he shall tell me why, or--"

By force of habit, Frascuelo put his right hand to his belt, but his sheath knife had been taken from him. He smiled sheepishly; yet his black eyes twinkled.

"Plot! Why do you speak of a plot?" asked the girl, hoping that the word betokened some more promising clue than she could discern thus far.

"Why did the furnaces blow up? Tell me that, and I can answer you. Good, honest coal isn't made of gunpowder. Jose, or some one behind him, meant to sink the ship, and, as I might have proved awkward, they were willing that I should go down with her. Maybe I shall meet Jose if we get out of this rat-trap; then we shall have a little talk."

Again his hand wandered towards his waist, but he bethought himself, and bent in pretense that the bandage on his leg needed readjusting.

Despite the man's shrewd guess as to the cause of the accident in the stokehold, Elsie was at a loss to connect the freak of some Valparaiso loafer with the deep-laid scheme which contemplated the destruction of the *Kansas*. She had followed the discussion in the chart-room with full appreciation of its significance. Valuable as the ship and cargo were, there was far more at stake in the effect of the loss on the copper markets of the world. The most important copper-exporting firm in Chile would practically be ruined, while the Paris "ring," of which she had read in the newspapers, would have matters its own way. Financial interests of such magnitude would hardly be bound up with the carousals and quarrels of Frascuelo and Jose the Wine-bag. Yet--

"Have you ever heard of a Senor Pedro Ventana?" she asked suddenly.

"Has he to do with mines?" inquired the Chilean, tentatively.

"Yes."

"I know him by sight, senorita."

"Would he be acquainted with this man, Anacleto, do you think?"

"Can't say. Jose would know anybody whom he could touch for a few pesetas."

She left him, promising to visit him daily in the future. As she walked back towards the bridge companion, she met Dr. Christobal. His fit of ill-humor had gone: he was all smiles; but Elsie, having extracted such information as Frascuelo possessed, was bent on adding to her store of knowledge. Incidentally, she meant to widen the doctor's views.

"Why have you taken to lecturing me?" she asked, with a simple directness which Christobal was not slow to profit by.

"Because, though old enough to be your father, or your elder brother, as you were kind enough to put it, I have not yet reached years of discretion."

If candor were needed, he would be candid. Sophistry was worse than useless with a woman of Elsie's type. The only way to win her was to be transparently honest. To Christobal, after an experience of a generation of Chileans, this came as a refreshing novelty.

"You mean, I suppose, that if every one attended to their own affairs it would be a less spiteful world? I am inclined to agree with you. Unhappily, life is largely made up of these minor evils. Yet I should have thought that the desperate conditions under which we exist at this hour might protect me from uncharitableness."

"You are pleased to be severe."

"No; it is the last privilege of danger that shams should vanish. Yet we plumb the depths of absurdity when we contest the right of any woman, even a young and unmarried one, to appreciate all that a brave man has done and is doing to save her life."

Here was candor undiluted. Elsie was speaking without heat. She might have been reasoning some disputed point in ethics. The Spaniard was obviously thrown off his guard.

"You seem to demand an explanation," he said with some warmth. "Well, you shall have it. I am not a man to flinch from the disagreeable. I admit a sort of impression, I might almost describe it as a conviction, that Captain Courtenay's manner towards you betokens a growing admiration."

"This is the wildest folly," cried Elsie in bewilderment. "I--I cannot imagine what put such a notion into your head."

"Let me at least lay claim to a species of altruism," he replied. "I can see fifty excellent reasons why our young and good-looking commander should be drawn to you, nor can I urge one against it."

"But he is already engaged to another woman, so my one reason is worth more than all your fifty."

"Ah, can that really be so?"

The tense eagerness in his voice might have warned her, were it not that she was shocked by the bitterness which welled up in her heart. She was amazed by this introspective glimpse; it alarmed her; she must convince herself, at all costs, that she had spoken truly.

Although the evidence she tendered was of dubious value, she strove to advance her argument further.

"I have prized our friendship greatly, Dr. Christobal," she said, speaking with a calm deliberateness that rang hollow in her own ears, "so greatly that I am compelled to utter this protest. Now, to end a distasteful controversy, let me tell you what I know to be true. When the ship was stranded, and we all thought our only chance of safety was to take to the boats, by a fluke, the accident of the moment, I was left alone in the captain's cabin. The sea was breaking in through the doorway, and it brought an odd relief to my over-burthened mind when I endeavored to rescue the contents of a locker which, for some reason, had been scattered on the floor previously. Among them I found some letters. I think you will believe me when I say that I would not consciously read another person's private correspondence. Just then, I was hardly responsible for my actions, and I did happen to see and grasp the meaning of a passage in a letter from Captain Courtenay's sister which alluded to his affianced wife. It is not such a tragic admission, is it? I would scarce have given it another thought were it not for your manner this morning and your words last night. I paid no heed at the time to the innuendo that I had come on deck to find him--to waylay him, as I have heard men say when speaking of a type of woman I despise. So I resolved to straighten out a stupid little tangle. It would be ridiculous, in our present state of suspended animation, to let such a slight thing mar our friendship."

Elsie, was indulging in that most delusive thing, self-persuasion. It was not surprising, therefore, that she failed to note the unmixed satisfaction with which Christobal listened.

"Am I forgiven, then?" he asked, with a new tenderness in his voice.

"Oh, yes, let us laugh at it."

"But--"

"Please let us talk of something more useful. I have a little plan, and you might ask the captain if he approves of it. We have plenty of strong canvas; what do you say if I set to work and cover in the promenade deck, fore and aft as well as on both sides? Then, if the Indians try to seize the ship, they would not be able to gain a lodgment at so many points simultaneously. It would simplify the defense, so to speak."

"Admirable! I am sure Courtenay will agree. Indeed, I am ashamed that we superior males failed to hit on the idea earlier. Before I go, let me be certain that my forgiveness is complete?"

"Shall we quarrel about a degree of blessedness? I assure you I like you more than ever. When all is said and done, you thought I was flinging myself at our excellent captain's head, so you tried to spare me the pangs of unrequited love." The words hurt, but she did not flinch. Christobal, anxious to deceive himself, was radiant.

"Your charity goes too far," he cried. "That was not the exact reason. No, my dear Miss Maxwell, I begin to exercise a new-born discretion. I shall not elucidate that cryptic remark until after New Year's Day. But I don't mind telling you why I have hit on a definite date. If all goes well with us--and we have had so many escapes that Providence may well send us a few more--the *Kansas* should steam out of our little bay of Good Hope about that period. Then I shall remind you of our discussion, and keep my promise."

With that he left her. After a gasp or two of surprise, for Elsie could read only one meaning into his words, she hurried up the bridge companion to arouse Mr. Boyle and ask what he would like for luncheon.

"Thank goodness, Joey," she murmured to the dog, whom she picked up in her arms, "thank goodness, Mr. Boyle is neither an engaged man nor a widower. I do believe our excellent doctor is more concerned on his own account than on mine. And he said that your master's manner 'betokened a growing admiration.' I wish--no, Joey, I mean nothing of the sort, and if you dare to hint at such a thing I shall be very angry with you--very--angry--indeed."

"Huh," muttered Boyle, wide awake and watching her through the open door, "some one has been worryin' that girl. It's a sure sign of trouble when a woman whispers in the ear of a dog or cat. Now, who can it be? That doctor chap? He cocked his eye at her this mornin' when she spoke about Ventana. He's a pretty tough old bird to think about settin' up house with a nice young jenny wren. Damn his eyes! he may be as rich as a Jew, but if she doesn't want him, an' is too skeered to say so, I 'll tell him, in the right sort of Spanish, an' all. Now, had it been the skipper--"

Boyle hardly knew what to think--"had it been the skipper."

CHAPTER XII
ENLIGHTENMENT

The captain was enthusiastic when he heard of Elsie's idea for the protection of the main deck--"an excellent notion," he termed it, but he scouted the suggestion that she should undertake the work herself.

"You little know what hauling taut heavy canvas means," he said when they met at lunch. "It would tear the skin off your hands. No, Miss Maxwell, we can put our Chileans on to that job. I have something better for you to do. Can you map?"

"I have copied heaps of plans for my father," she told him.

"Excellent! At noon to-day I took an observation, so I intend to devote an hour to revising the chart. Will you help? Joey is in the scheme already. Then the Admiralty will gracefully acknowledge the survey supplied by Miss Elsie Maxwell, Captain Arthur Courtenay, and Joey, otherwise known as 'the pup.'"

His allusion to the dog by name recalled "Jose the Wine-bag," but Elsie thought she would retain that tiny scrap of detective information for the present. So she simply said:

"You will explain to me my part of the undertaking, of course?"

"Certainly. You must first correct the Index Error. Then you subtract the Dip and the Refraction in Altitude, take the sun's semi-diameter from the Nautical Almanac, and add the Parallax. Do you follow me?"

"Perfectly; it sounds the easiest thing. But I don't wish to hear the remarks of the Admiralty when they see the result."

"I am interested in navigation, to the slight extent possible to a mere yachtsman: may I join you?" interposed Christobal.

"Oh, yes," said the captain off-handedly.

Elsie repressed the smile on her lips. Did the worthy doctor fear developments if this harmless map-making progressed in his absence? She imagined, too, that Courtenay's acquiesence in Christobal's desire to be present was not wholly in accordance with his innermost wish. She promptly crushed that dangerous fancy. The captain was only seeking for some excuse to take her away from the rough work of rigging the extra awnings. How odd that the other thought should have cropped up first!

"You still think the **Kansas** will win clear of her difficulties?" she said rather hurriedly. "I am sorry to bring King Charles's head into the conversation, but, after all, the ship's safety is essential to your survey."

"Every hour strengthens my opinion," was the confident reply. "Suarez says that there is a reasonable chance of occasional brief spells of fine weather at this period of the year. At any rate, the gale may not be absolutely continuous, and Walker is assured that he can patch up the engines for half speed. Given a calm day, a day like this, for instance, we can reach the Straits in a few hours."

"And the Indians?"

"I leave them out of my reckoning. What else can I do?"

"Kill 'em," said Tollemache.

Courtenay glanced sharply at his fellow-countryman. He disliked these references to the Alaculof bogy in Elsie's presence. It was enough that it should exist without being constantly paraded. Though the girl herself was the culprit, Tollemache should have left the topic alone.

But Tollemache was a man of fixed ideas. The device of canvas shields to repel boarders had set him thinking how much more effective it would be if the savages were kept at a distance. He well knew that they would not be deterred by a shotgun and a few revolvers, once they had made up their minds to carry the ship by assault. To explain himself, he was compelled to speak at some length, and his swarthy face flushed under the unusual strain.

"We have dynamite aboard," he said. "Why not construct a couple of infernal machines which could be fired by pulling a string, and let them drift towards the canoes when the Indians are near enough?"

"It is worth trying," was Courtenay's brief comment, though he saw later that Tollemache's suggestion was a very useful one.

Elsie's first task was to prepare a large-scale drawing of the southern part of Hanover Island, as set forth in Admiralty Chart No. 1837 (Sheet 2, Patagonia), which is the only trustworthy record available for shipmasters using the outer passage between the Gulf of Penas and the Straits of Magellan. It was a simple matter to fill in the few contours given. The neighboring small islands were shown in reasonable detail, but the whole western coast of Hanover Island itself consisted of a dotted line and a solitary peak, Stokes Mountain, the height of which could be estimated and its position triangulated from the sea. Even Concepcion Straits on the north and the San Blas Channel on the south were marked in those significant dotted lines. The coast was practically unknown to civilized man. One of the last fortresses of the world, grim, inhospitable, it guarded its secret recesses with crag and glacier and reef-strewn sea.

It was borne in on the girl, while she worked, that the chiefest marvel in her present condition was the triumph of science over nature in its most hostile mood. The *Kansas* boasted all the comforts and luxuries of a well-equipped hotel. Seated at the same table as herself was a skilful sailor, using logarithms, secants and cosecants, polar distances and hour angles, as if he were in some university class-room. Near the door, enjoying the warm sun, Boyle was stretched on a deck-chair, while Christobal was offering a half-hearted protest against his patient's manifest enjoyment of the first cigar he had been able to smoke since a Chilean knife disturbed certain sensory nerves between his shoulder-blades. The every sociableness of the gathering was a paradox: the truth lay with the ice-capped hills and the ape-like nomads who infested the humid forests of the lower slopes.

She stole a glance at Courtenay. He was so keenly engaged on the business in hand, so bent on achieving accuracy in his figures, that she chided herself for her morbid reverie. Then she wondered if he ever gave a thought to that promised wife of his, who must soon suffer the agony of knowing that the *Kansas* was overdue.

Elsie was sufficiently well acquainted with shipping to realize the sensation that would be created by the first cablegram from Coronel anouncing the nonappearance of the steamer in the Straits. The Valparaiso newspapers would be full of surmises as to the vessel's fate. They would publish full details of the valuable cargo--and give a list of the passengers and officers. Ah! Ventana would learn then, if he had not heard of it earlier, that she was on board. And he alone would understand the true reason of her flight from Chile. Her cheeks flushed, and she applied herself more closely to the chart she was copying. She had left a good deal unsaid in her brief statement that morning. How strange, how utterly unexpected it was, that Ventana's name should fall from Courtenay's lips--Courtenay, of all men living! And what did Isobel mean, during that last dreadful scene ere she was carried away to the boat, by screaming in her frenzy that Ventana had taken "an ample vengeance." Vengeance for what? Had the half-breed dared to make the same proposal to the rich and highly placed Isobel Baring that he did not scruple to put before the needy governess? Surely that was impossible. There were limits even to his audacity--

"Well, how is my chief hydrographer progressing?"

Courtenay's cheery voice banished the unwelcome specter of Ventana. Elsie started.

"I do believe you were day-dreaming," said the captain with a surprised smile. "A penny for your thoughts?"

"I don't think you can pay me," she retorted, hoping to cover her confusion.

"Won't you accept Chilean currency?"

"Not on the high seas."

"But you are on dry land. Please make a dot on your map at 51 degrees 14 minutes 9 seconds South, and 74 degrees 59 minutes 3 seconds West. That is the present position of the ship. Are you listening, Boyle? According to the chart, the ship is high and dry, four miles inland."

"Huh!" grunted Boyle. "Reminds me of a skipper I once sailed with, bound from Rotterdam to Hull in ballast. There was a Scotch mist best part of the trip, an' the old man loaded with schnapps to keep out the damp. First time he got a squint of the sun he went as yaller as a Swede turnip. 'It's all up with us, boys,' he said. 'My missus is forty fathoms below. We've just sailed over York.' You see, he'd made a mistake of a few degrees."

"Boyle," said Courtenay, severely, "what has come to you? Are you actually making a joke?"

"I think I must have bin tongue-tied before, captain."

"Before what?"

"Before that lame duck in the fo'c'sle stuck his tobacco-cutter into my jaw. I can talk like a prize parrot now--can't I, Miss Maxwell?"

Elsie was laughing, but she remembered the subject on which Boyle had displayed his new-found power of speech; and human parrots are apt to say too much.

"Please don't tell any more funny little stories," she cried, "or I shall be putting dots in the wrong places."

"And causing us to waste time scandalously. Are you ready, Miss Maxwell? Let me pin this compass card on the table. Use the parallel ruler; regard each inch as a mile, and I'll do the rest by guesswork."

Courtenay took his binoculars, and went on to the bridge. He called out the apparent distance of each landmark he could distinguish, described it, and gave its true bearing. In the result, Elsie found she had prepared a clear and fairly accurate chart of the bay and its headlands, while the position of the distant range of mountains was marked with tolerable precision. But Courtenay was far from being satisfied.

"If I had a base line, or even a fresh set of points taken higher up the inlet, I could improve on my part of the survey," he said. "Yours is admirable, Miss Maxwell. Of course, I know you are an artist; but mapping is a thing apart. That is first-rate."

"Perhaps you may be able to secure fresh data when the *Kansas* puts to sea again," said Christobal.

"If I am conning the wheel, I must leave the chart-making entirely to my assistant," replied the captain, lightly. "But I do mean to peep a little further into our estuary. Before the ship sails I may have another spare hour to devote to it."

"In what way?" asked Elsie.

"By utilizing the canoe. A mile or so higher up the channel I should be clear of the bluff which hides Otter Creek. I imagine it will be possible then to see the full extent of the bay. I must get you to sound Suarez as to the lie of the land."

"I hope you will do nothing of the sort," protested Elsie, earnestly.

"Why? Do you think the canoe unsafe?"

"No, no; not that. But those waiting Indians. They might see you."

"Oh, the Indians again! I shall run no risk of that sort. It would indeed be the irony of fate if the *Kansas* slipped her cable and left the skipper behind."

"Huh! No fear! She'd follow you like Joey. I was tellin' Miss Maxwell what a lucky fellow you were. Besides, if you went, I 'd be in command, and you know what would happen then. By gad, if all else failed, the bloomin' tub would turn turtle in the Pool."

To emphasize his remarks, Boyle blew a big smoke ring, and shot several smaller rings through it.

Elsie felt Christobal's critical eye on her; she was shading the outlines of the map, and trusted that her head was bent sufficiently to hide the tell-tale color which leapt to her face. But Courtenay wished to hear more of this.

"I hope you do not credit everything my chief officer says about me," he said, glancing over her shoulder at the drawing. "Nor about himself," he added, as she was too busy to look up. "To my knowledge, he has refused the command of two ships since we both joined the **Kansas**."

"Home orders!" cried Boyle, who was certainly beyond himself. Probably he missed his regular vocal exercise owing to lack of a crew. "My missus says to me, 'You just stick to Captain Courtenay, young feller-me-lad. He's one of the get-rich-quick sort. P'raps you 'll learn from him how to dodge Board of Trade inquiries.' You stand on what I told you, Miss Maxwell. You remember? Commodore! Huh!"

Something must be done to stem the long-pent flood of Mr. Boyle's gossip. Elsie turned on him desperately.

"How do you expect me to listen to you, and work at the same time?" she said.

"Sorry," he answered, composing himself to sleep.

Courtenay glanced at the chronometer.

"I must be off," he announced. "Tollemache may need some help with his bombs, and those Chileans require looking after."

Christobal, too, quitted the chart-room to visit his patients. He had said very little while he sat there, and Elsie did not know whether to laugh or cry at the tragic-comedy of her environment. She was only certain of one thing--she would like to box Boyle's ears. She was completely at a loss to account for his persistent efforts to drag in references to their prior conversation. She dared not catechize him. That would be piling up more difficulties for the future. But what possessed him to blurt out such embarrassing details in the presence of the two men whom she most wished to remain in ignorance of them?

She peeped at Boyle sideways. His eyes were closed, the cigar was between his teeth, and he had a broad grin on his face. She could not guess that the once taciturn chief officer of the **Kansas** was saying to himself:

"My godfather, how Pills glared! There will be trouble on this ship about a woman before long, or I'm a Dutchman. An' didn't the skipper rise at the fly, too! Huh!"

He uttered the concluding monosyllable aloud.

"Did you speak?" inquired Elsie, severely.

"Eh? No, Miss Maxwell."

"Oh, I thought you wanted to say something."

"Not a word. Too much talking makes my back stiff."

"Your physical peculiarities are amazing, Mr. Boyle."

"Huh, it's odd how things take some people. I once knew a chap, skipper of the **Flower of the Ocean**, who could drink a hogshead of beer an' be as sober as a judge except in one leg, an' that was a wooden one."

She laughed. It was impossible to be vexed with him.

"You have met some very remarkable shipmasters, if all you say be true," she cried.

"Sailors are queer folk, believe me. That same brig, **Flower of the Ocean**, an' a pretty flower she was, too--all tar an' coal-dust, with a perfume that would poison a rat--put into Grimsby one day, an' the crowd went ashore. They kicked up a shindy with some bar-loungers, an' the fur flew. When the police came, old Peg-leg, the skipper, you know, was the only man left in the place, havin' unshipped his crutch for the fight. 'What have you bin a-doin' of here--throwin' grapes about?' asked the peeler, gazin' at the floor, suspicious-like. 'Grapes,' said Dot-an'-carry-one, 'them ain't grapes. Them's eyeballs!' Another time--"

"Mr. Boyle!" shrieked Elsie, and fled.

"Huh!" he grunted. "Off before the wind when she hears a Sunday-school yarn like that. Wonder what she 'd say if I told her about the plum-duff with beetles for Sultanas. Girls are brought up nowadays like orchids. They shouldn't be let loose in this wicked world."

As Elsie passed along the promenade deck she saw Courtenay, Tollemache, and Walker deep in consultation. They were arranging a percussion fuse of fulminating mercury. While she was watching them, Walker dropped a broken furnace bar on top of a small package placed on an iron block. Instantly there was a sharp report, and Joey, who was an interested observer, jumped several feet. The men laughed, and she heard Courtenay say:

"That is the right proportion of fulminate. Now, Tollemache, I'll help you to fix them. We do not know the moment those reptiles may choose to attack."

So the captain did not leave the Alaculof menace altogether out of count. Something rose in her throat, some wave of emotion which threatened her splendid serenity. She ran rather than walked to her cabin, flung herself on the bed, and sobbed piteously. It had to come, this tempest of tears. When desperate odds demanded unflinching courage, she faced them dry-eyed, with steadfast heart. But to-day, in the bright sunshine and apparent security of the ship, sinister death-shadows tortured her into rebellion. She did not stop to ask herself why she wept; being a woman, she yielded to the gust, and when it had ended, with the suddenness of a summer shower, she smiled through the vanishing tears. Her first concern was that none should be aware of her weakness.

"How stupid of me," she murmured. "What would the men think if they knew I broke down in this fashion."

She looked in a mirror. In the clear light without, any one could see she had been crying, and there was so much work to be done that she did not wish to remain in her stateroom until all tokens of the storm had passed. She searched for a powder-puff, and was at a loss to discover its whereabouts until she recollected that the doctor had borrowed it for the use of a man slightly scalded when his own supply of antiseptic powder was exhausted. So she went into Isobel's room, entering it for the first time since the *Kansas* struck on the shoal. The two cabins communicated, as Mr. Baring had gone to the expense of having a door broken through the partition for the girls' use during the voyage. If Elsie had not already given way to tears she must have faltered now at the sight of her friend's belongings strewed in confusion over the floor, chairs, dressing-table, and bed. Isobel possessed a gold-mounted dressing-case the size of an ordinary portmanteau. It held an assortment of pretty, and mostly useless, knick-knacks, and they had all been tumbled out in a frantic hurry. At first Elsie flinched from further scrutiny, but common sense told her that this despondent mood must be fought. She dropped to her knees, found a mother-o'-pearl *poudrier*, and picked up other scattered articles and replaced them in the dressing-case. To accomplish this it was necessary to rearrange various trays and drawers. Portraits of girl friends, including her own, and of men unknown to her, letters, memoranda, and other documents, were thrown about in disorder. All these she put back in their receptacles, wondering the while what motive had led Isobel to make such a frenzied search for some special object that she cared not a jot what became of the remaining articles.

Yet, who could account for the frenzy of that terrible hour when the captain announced the ship's danger? Even Courtenay himself, she remembered, had emptied a locker in a rapid hunt for the dog's coat; but he had laughingly explained his haste later when some chance reference was made to his soaked garments.

Anything was explicable in the light of panic. She gathered up a skirt and some blouses, locked the dressing-case, put the key in her purse, and quitted the room with a heavy heart, for the handling of her friend's treasures had brought sad memories.

Passing into the deck corridor, she heard the captain's voice, apparently at a considerable distance. Two hundred yards away from the ship, Courtenay and Tollemache were anchoring a flat framework, built of spare hatches and secured by wooden cross-pieces. On it stood the first of the infernal machines. The raft floated level with the water, so its only conspicuous fitting was a small spar and a block, to which a line and an iron bar were attached. The men looked strange in her eyes at that distance. In the marvellously clear light she could see their features distinctly, and, when Courtenay shouted to a sailor to haul in the slack of the line, she caught a trumpet-like ring that recalled the scene in the saloon when he held back the mob of stewards. His athletic figure, silhouetted against the shimmering green of the water, was instinct with graceful strength. He looked a born leader of men, and, as though to mark his quickness of observation, no sooner had Elsie glanced over the side of the ship than he waved a hand to her.

She sighed. A bitter thought peeped up in her that he was perhaps a trifle careless in showing her these little attentions. She wished he would speak to her of that other girl who awaited him in England. A pleasant state of confidence would be established then; these secret twitches of sentiment were irritating.

Some women, in her place, would pay no heed to that aspect of their enforced relations; not so Elsie, whose virginal breast was unduly fluttered by the discovery that a young man is the most natural thing in the world for a young woman to think about.

She walked aft to obtain a nearer view of the operations. The sailors had already shut in a large portion of the promenade deck with canvas, and she noticed that loopholes were provided, every ten feet or so, to permit the effective use of the defenders' firearms. Thus, at each step, she was reminded of the precarious hold she had on life, and she was positively frightened when some mad impulse surged through her whole being, bidding her imperiously to abandon her ultra-conscientious loyalty to a woman she had never seen. Why struggle against circumstance? If death were so near, what did she gain by prudery?

For an instant she stood aghast at the revelation which had come to her. She was in love with Courtenay. She was ready to die by his side, fearless and joyous, if only he would put his arms around her and tell her that she was dear to him. Ah, the fierce delight of that first silent surrender! Her heart beat as it had never pulsed before, even under the stress of the storm or the sudden terror of the night attack. Her eyes shone, and her breath came laboriously between parted lips. Golden dreams coursed through her brain. She was thrilled with an unutterable longing.

Then her swimming eyes rested on a group of men standing on the poop. Among them was Christobal, interested, like the rest, in the floating of the mine. And forthwith Elsie fell from the clouds, and was brought back, shuddering, to cold reason again. She was sick at heart; she hated herself for her self-abasement. She must gird her with sackcloth and mourn; and the fight must be fought now, without parley or hesitation, unless the sweetness were to go forth from life for ever, and all things should turn to ashes in her mouth.

So, marshaling the best qualities of her womanhood, she quelled the turmoil in her breast, forced herself to join the men on the after deck, and said, when the smiling Spaniard turned to receive her:

"Why am I denied the mild excitement of mine-laying, Dr. Christobal? Is it that you dread the effect on my nerves of these murderous preparations?"

"No," he answered, making room for her at the railing by his side. "I had missed you, of course, but I thought you were resting."

"Resting, indeed! I have been quite busy. Where do they mean to put the second contrivance?"

"About there," he said, indicating a point on the surface of the bay eastward of the canoe. His right arm was extended, and he placed his left hand on her shoulder. Courtenay, hailing Walker, saw the two leaning over the rails in that attitude. Perhaps one of the two hoped that Courtenay would see them. Elsie, as part of her punishment, did not shrink away, though the touch of Christobal's hand made her flesh creep. But Joey, whose mind was singularly free from complexities, leaped up at her. He wanted Elsie to tell him what Courtenay was doing out there, so far away from the ship. She stooped and picked him up. Christobal had no excuse for a second caress.

"Bark, Joey," she whispered, "bark and call your master. If anything happens to him, you and I shall never see England again. And I am longing for home to-day."

CHAPTER XIII
THE FIGHT

Christmas Day arrived, and maintained its kindly repute by finding affairs on board the *Kansas* changed for the better. Mr. Boyle was so far recovered that he could walk; he even took command of two watches in the twenty-four hours, but was forbidden to exert himself, lest the wound in his back should reopen. Several injured sailors and firemen were convalescent; the two most serious cases were out of danger; Frascuelo, hardy as a weed, dared the risk of using his damaged leg, and survived, though his progress along the deck was painful. Nevertheless, on Christmas morning he presented himself before the captain, and asked leave to abandon his present quarters. He felt lonely in the forecastle, and wished to berth with the other Chileans in the neighborhood of the saloon. Although his luck was bad in some respects, the coal-trimmer was endowed with the nine lives of a cat, for there could be no manner of doubt that he dragged himself aft just in time to avoid being killed.

Yet, never was day less ominous in appearance. The breezy, sunlit morning brought no hint of coming tragedy. The fine weather which had prevailed since the *Kansas* drifted into the estuary seemed to become more settled as the month wore. Suarez said it was unprecedented. Not only had he not witnessed in five years three consecutive days without rain, snow, or hail, but the Indians had a proverb: "Who so-ever sees fire-in-the-sky (the sun) for seven days shall see the leaf red a hundred times." In effect, centenarians were needed to bear testimony to a week's fine weather; whereas no man--most certainly no woman--among the Alaculofs ever succeeded in reaching the threescore years and ten regarded by the psalmist as the span of life.

But the miner from Argentina never wavered in his belief that the Indians would soon muster every adult for an assault on the ship. The elements might waver, but not the hate of the savage. From the rising of the sun to the going down thereof Suarez was ever on the alert. He ate his meals with his eyes fixed on the low point of land which hid Otter Creek. He saw thin columns of smoke rising when no other eye on board could discern them. Once he made out the forms of a number of women searching for shellfish on some distant rocks at low water, and on Christmas morning he reported the presence of three canoes among the trees near Otter Creek, when Courtenay could scarce be sure of their character after scrutinizing them through his glasses.

Every other person on the ship held the opinion that the Alaculofs would attack by night, if they were not afraid to attempt the enterprise at all. So Suarez slept soundly, while his companions were on the *qui vive* for a call to repel boarders. Were it not for the strain induced by the silent menace of their savage neighbors, the small company suffered no ill from their prolonged stay in this peaceful anchorage. There was work in plenty for all hands. Walker was re-enforced by a trio of firemen, whose technical knowledge, slight as it was, proved useful when he began to fit and connect the disabled machinery. For the rest, the promenade deck was walled with strong canvas, while Courtenay and Tollemache gave undivided attention to the fashioning of several other floating bombs which could be exploded from the ship. They also provided flexible steam-pipes in places where a rush might be made if the Indians once secured a footing on the deck, fore or aft. Steam was kept up constantly in the donkey-boiler, not alone for the electric light and the daily working of the pumps--as the *Kansas* had not blundered over the shoal without straining some of her plates--but for use against the naked bodies of their possible assailants.

When day followed day without any sign of hostility, not a man on board, save Suarez and Tollemache, paid much real heed to the shoreward peril. Walker, with his hammers and cold chisels, his screw-jacks and wrenches, was the center of interest. And Walker's swarthy visage wore a permanent grin, which presaged well for the fulfilment of his promise. Elsie devoted herself to the hospital. She was thus brought more in contact with Christobal than with any of the others. Nor did he make this close acquaintance irksome to her. Always suave and charming in manner, he exerted himself to be entertaining. Though she knew full well that if the *Kansas* reached the open sea again he would ask her to marry him, he was evidently content to deny himself the privileges of courtship until a proper time and season.

She was far too wise to appear to avoid Courtenay. Indeed, she was studiously agreeable to him when they met. She adopted the safe role of good-fellowship, flattering herself that her own folly would shrink to nothingness under the hourly castigation thus inflicted. During this period, Mr. Boyle's changeable characteristics puzzled and amused her. As he grew stronger, and took part in the active life of the ship, so did his sudden excess of talkativeness disappear. Once she happened to overhear his remarks to a couple of Chileans who were told to swab off the decks. Obviously, they had scamped their work, and Boyle expostulated. Then she grasped the essential element in Boyle's composition. He was capable only of a single idea. When he was chief officer he ceased to be an ordinary man; the corollary was, of course, that he ceased to use ordinary language.

She was in her cabin, and dared not come out while the tornado raged. She did not know that Tollemache was listening, too, until she heard him ask:

"Did you ever meet any fellow who could swear harder than you, Boyle?"

"Yes, once," was the curt answer.

"He must have been a rotter. What did he say?"

"Huh! just the regulation patter, but he used a megaphone, so I gave him best. . . ."

But, so far as Elsie was concerned, Boyle's fund of reminiscence had dried up.

After the midday meal on Christmas day--a sumptuous repast, for the due preparation of which Elsie had come to the Chilean cook's assistance in the matter of the plum-pudding--Suarez suddenly reported that a new column of smoke was rising from Guanaco Hill, a crag dominating the eastern side of the bay. The hill owed its name, he explained, to a large cave, in which a legendary herd of llama was said to have its abode. Probably there had never been any llama on the island, but the Indians were frightened of the cave, with its galloping ghosts, and would not enter it. He was unable to attribute any special significance to the signal on that particular place. During the five years with the Alaculof tribe he had never seen a fire lit there before. That, in itself, was a fact sinister and alarming.

Suarez had sufficient tact not to make this statement publicly. He told Christobal, and the doctor passed on the information to the captain. Both men went to the poop with their glasses, and carefully examined the coast line.

Courtenay was the first to break an oppressive silence, and his low pitched voice announced stirring tidings.

"Do you see those canoes yonder?" he said.

"There were three under the trees before Suarez discovered the smoke on Guanaco. Now I fancy I can make out nearly a dozen. Though they are not launched, they have been put there for some purpose. Would you mind going forrard and asking Mr. Boyle to summon all hands on deck? He knows exactly what to do. Remember that I regard you and Miss Maxwell as non-combatants, and expect you both to remain in the saloon. If these painted devils really mean to attack, some of us will get hurt, and then your services will be of greater value than in the fighting line. And, if I do not see Miss Maxwell before the trouble begins, please tell her she need fear no alarm. We shall be able to beat off our assailants with comparative ease."

When the captain of the *Kansas* spoke like that there was no gainsaying him. Even Christobal, whose jealous suspicions were ever ready to burst into flame, was roused to enthusiasm by his cool gallantry.

But, ere the Spaniard turned to go, a disturbing thought forced its way to his lips.

"We have every confidence in you," he said, "and I admit that it should be a simple matter to prevent the savages from gaining the upper hand. Yet, accidents happen. Suppose they manage to rush your defense?"

"They will not do that while I and every other man on deck are alive. If the worst comes to the worst, you have a revolver--"

"Yes," said Christobal.

"It will suffice for two, but not for a hundred." The two men, united by the very bond which threatened to bring them into antagonism, looked into each other's eyes.

"Is that your last word?" asked Christobal.

"It is."

"I feel sure that you are right. Good-by!"

They shook hands. They were nearer a real friendship then than either of them thought possible, and the bond which held them was love for the same woman.

Courtenay, using his glasses again, saw that a number of Indians were launching the canoes simultaneously. He counted nine small craft, each holding five or six men, or men and women--at the distance, nearly three miles, he could not be certain whether or not they all wore the distinguishing head-dress of feathers. Against wind and current they could not possibly reach the ship under half an hour, and the smallness of the fleet surprised him.

He stooped and patted Joey, who was at peace with the world after a good dinner.

"We are in luck's way, pup," he said. "These rascals might get the better of us by sheer force of numbers, but there are not fifty of them, all told. Poor devils! They are coming to the slaughter!"

The news that the Indians were advancing ran through the ship like wildfire. Including Mr. Boyle, Frascuelo, and those among the Chileans whose wounds were not serious, there were fourteen men available for the defense. Unfortunately, the supply of firearms was inadequate. A shot-gun and five revolvers constituted the armory, and one of the pistols was in Christobal's pocket. The supply of ammunition was so small that the revolvers could not be reloaded more than three times; but Courtenay had two hundred shot cartridges, and, against naked men, an ounce of shot is far more effective than a bullet.

The captain hoped to terrify the Indians before they attempted to scale the ship's sides. If various ruses failed, and the attack was pressed, he had decided not to split up his small force in the effort to repel boarders. A scattered resistance would surely break down at one point or another: there would be a rush of savages along the decks, a panic among the Chileans, and all would be ended. On the other hand, when fighting collectively under European leadership, and well aware that the Indians would kill and spare not, the half-breeds might be trusted to acquit themselves like men.

The canvas awning constituted a flimsy citadel in the center of the vessel. Six men were stationed on the starboard side of the promenade deck, and six on the port side. Tollemache and a Chilean, who said he could shoot well, were told to frustrate any attempt to climb the after part of the ship, while Courtenay, with his fowling-piece, would have the lion's share of this work from the spar deck, as he undertook to keep the rails clear forward and help the revolver practise if necessary. With him was Suarez, who knew what was expected of him, so the language difficulty offered no apparent hindrance once the fight began. Finally, if the Indians made good their footing, the defenders were to rally towards the saloon companion where steam jets were ready to spurt withering blasts along the corridors.

It was a good plan, and might have kept at bay an enemy of higher valor than the Alaculofs, provided they were not armed with rifles. Against modern weapons of long range nothing could be done. If Suarez did not exaggerate, therein lay the real danger. Courtenay wished to make sure at the outset of the number of guns carried by the savages; it was also important to know whether their marksmen were distributed, or crowded together in one or two canoes. If the latter, he would give those warriors his special attention.

His binocular glasses were not strong enough so he walked back towards the chart-house to procure a telescope. Catching Joey under his left arm, he climbed the short ladder leading to the spar deck, and pulled it up after him, the bolts having been already removed to permit of that being done. Walker was screwing tight the door of the engine-room, in order to safeguard the fireman in attendance on the donkey-boiler. Now that the screw-driving was actually in operation, it very unpleasantly reminded Courtenay of the fastening of a coffin lid. Neither Walker nor the man inside could guess the gruesome notion which held the captain in its chilly grip for an instant; indeed, the engineer looked up with a grin.

"I suppose it's twue, sir, the-aw's goin' to be a fight?" he asked.

"There's a fair chance of one, Walker."

Walker winked suggestively.

"That chap inside thinks he's out of it," he said, "so that's all wight." An energetic turn of the screwdriver signified that the man from Newcastle held the opposite view. Much as he loved his engines, he preferred to be on deck when the trouble came.

It happened that during this slight delay Courtenay glanced at the northern headland, which Elsie had christened Cape Templar, owing to the somewhat remarkable profile of a knight in armor offered by its seaward crags. Possibly, had he gone straight to the chart-house, he might not have noticed a signal fire which was in full blast on the summit of the cliff. It had not been many minutes in existence, and it struck him at once that it was a vehicle of communication between the savages in the approaching canoes and others, yet invisible, who were expected to share in the attack.

He was quick to perceive how seriously this new peril affected his calculations. By the time the nine canoes he had counted were alongside the ship, there might be dozens of others ready to help them. He leaned over the rail.

"Did you test those flexible pipes this morning?" he inquired.

"Yes, sir, they-aw in fine condition," said Walker.

"Try them again, will you? I want to make sure. Our lives may depend on them very soon."

He saw Suarez watching the oncoming canoes. By a touch on the shoulder he called the man's attention to the smoke signal on Cape Templar. A voluble and perfervid explanation in Spanish was useless. Here arose the unforeseen need of an interpreter. Without troubling to analyze his feelings, Courtenay was glad of the excuse which presented itself of obtaining a momentary glimpse of Elsie.

"Bring the senorita," he said, and Elsie, wondering why she had been summoned from the saloon, ran up the bridge companion. Her face was aglow with excitement, her heart going pit-a-pat. She hoped that Courtenay meant to keep her near him during the fight; she almost doubted Christobal's statement that the captain had given specific orders that she was to remain in the saloon. It was one thing that she should wish to avoid him, but why should he wish to avoid her?

The joy in her eyes died away when she found that the captain merely required a translator. The restraint she imposed on herself made her tongue trip. She had to ask Suarez to repeat his statement twice before she was able to put it into English.

"He says that the Indians only kindle a fire on that point when they want the signal to be seen from the sea," she explained at last. "They used it once, to his knowledge, when some of them had gone to the island out there to kill seals. He cannot guess what it portends to-day, but he is quite sure that they have many more canoes at command than those which you now see up the bay."

Courtenay could not fail to notice her agitation. His quick intent was to soothe her.

"I am afraid my sending for you in such a hurry rather alarmed you. Suarez strikes me as a person of nerves; he overrates the enemy, Miss Maxwell. I think you know me well enough to believe that I would not mislead you, and I am quite in earnest when I tell you that we shall drive off these unfortunate wretches with comparative ease. Why, I had it in my heart to pity them a moment ago."

She was glad he misunderstood the cause of her agitation.

"Suarez is certainly rather dramatic," she said, smiling wistfully. "I ought to have discounted his Spanish mode of address. But is it really necessary that I should remain below?"

"It is. If shots are fired, or stones slung at us, the chart-house will probably be hit. Ah, yes, I am sure you would risk that, and more. But we may sustain casualties. And Christobal ought to have help. You see, I am asking you to act the braver part."

He caught her hand and looked into her eyes. There are so many messages that can be given in that silent language; for a blissful moment, Elsie forgot the other woman. Not until she had left the bridge did she realize that Courtenay, too, must have been equally forgetful. And that was very distressing, both for her and the unknown. But here she was, face to face with him, and in such close proximity that she was unaccountably timid. While her heart leaped in tumult, she forced her lips to answer:

"You are right. You are always right. I was selfish in thinking that--that I--might--"

There was a pitiful quivering in the corners of her mouth. Courtenay felt her hand tremble.

"Be a brave girl, Elsie," he murmured. "You must go now. Have no fear. We are in God's care. May His angels watch over you!"

"But you, you will not risk your life? What shall we do if anything happens to you?"

She was strung to that tense pitch when unguarded speech bubbles forth the soul's secrets. All she knew was that Courtenay was looking at her as a man looks at the woman he loves. And that suffced. The mere sound of her name on his lips was music. He told her to go, yet held her hand a willing prisoner. His words had the sound of a prayer, but it was the orison of a knight to his lady. He bade her fear not, while he trembled a little himself, though she well knew it was not fear which shook him. Neither of them paid heed to the presence of Suarez. For an instant they had a glimpse of heaven, but the curiously harsh voice of the Spanish miner fell on their ears, and they came back to earth with a sudden drop.

"The Feathered People are singing their war chant," he said, and his gesture seemed to ask them to listen. They started apart, and it was not Elsie alone who blushed. Courtenay crimsoned beneath the tan on his face, and pretended a mighty interest in the doings of the savages. The girl recovered her self-control more rapidly. She half whispered the meaning of the miner's cry, whereon Courtenay tried to laugh.

"They will be singing a dirge next," said he with a jaunty confidence. "Now, Elsie, off with you! Be sure I shall come and tell you when you may appear on deck."

She hurried away. She recked naught of the Alaculof challenge. Though the raucous notes of the tuneless lay could be heard plainly enough, they did not reach her ears. When she raced down the saloon companion she found Christobal bending over the small case of instruments he always carried. He straightened himself in his peculiarly stiff way.

"What did the captain want?" he asked, with a suspicious peevishness which, for once, detracted from his habitual courtesy. The note of distrust jarred Elsie back into her senses.

"He wished me to translate Senor Suarez's explanation of another smoke signal," she answered.

"Oh, was that all?"

"Practically all."

"He told you himself, I suppose, that he wished you to stay here."

"He did more. He drove me away."

"Against your will?"

"No. Am I not one of the ship's company? Is he not the centurion? He says to this woman, Go, and she goeth, nor does she stand upon the order of her going. Oh, please don't look at me as if I were cracked. Surely one may mingle the Bible and Shakespeare in an emergency?"

"One may also tear linen sheets into strips," said Christobal, gravely. Elsie's quip had saved the situation. He attributed her flushed cheeks and sparkling eyes to the fever of the threatened fight.

She applied herself eagerly to the task. Already the fume and agony of vain regret were striving to conquer the ecstasy which had flooded her whole being. She remembered that passionate longing to be clasped in Courtenay's arms which she experienced when she saw him in the canoe, and now, after draining to the dregs the cup of bitterness she had forced on herself during these later days, here she was, ready as ever to quaff the love potion. Poor Elsie! She longed for the waters of Lethe; haply they are denied to young women with live blood in their veins.

Courtenay, meanwhile, was examining the advancing flotilla. His brain was conning each detail of the Alaculof array, but his heart was whispering gladly:

"In another moment you would have kissed her and told her you loved her. You know you would, so don't deny it! Ah! kissed her, and held her to your breast!"

So Suarez spoiled a pretty bit of romance by his ruffling agitation over some bawl of savage frenzy, for Courtenay, of course, would have laughed away the girl's protests that she was usurping another woman's place. It was really a pity that the man from Argentina had not found something else to occupy his mind at that precise juncture in the affairs of two young people who were obviously mated by the discriminating gods. A good deal of suffering and heartburning would then have been avoided; but perhaps it was just the whim of fate that the captain's love affair should follow the irregular course mapped out for his ship, and the **Kansas** was not yet re-launched on the ocean high-road to London, no, not by any manner of means.

In fact, if the confident demeanor of the paddling warriors in the canoes were destined to be justified, the big steamer was in parlous state. Her vast bulk and sheer walls of steel did not daunt them. They came on steadily against the rapid current, and spread out into a crescent when within a few hundred yards of the ship. Then three men, crouching in the bows of different canoes, produced rifles hitherto invisible and began to shoot. The bullets ricochetted across the ripples, and Courtenay saw that the savages did not understand the sighting appliances. They were aiming point-blank at the vessel, in so far as they could be said to aim at anything, and the low trajectory caused the first straight shot to rebound from the surface of the water and strike a plate amidships. The loud clang of the metal was hailed by the Alaculofs with shouts of delight. Probably they had no fixed idea of the distance the tiny projectiles would carry. Joey began to bark furiously, and the Indians imitated him. The hammer-like blow of the bullet, the defiance of the dog, and the curiously accurate yelping of the men in the canoes, mixed in wild medley with the volleyed echoes of the firing now rolled back from the opposing cliffs. In such wise did the battle open. Courtenay, more amused than anxious, did not silence the terrier, and Joey's barking speedily rose to a shrill and breathless hysteria. Some savage, more skilled than his fellows, reproduced this falsetto with marvelous exactness. There never was a death struggle heralded by such grotesque humor; it might have been a tragedy of marionettes, a Dutch concert on the verge of the pit.

The long-range firing was kept up for several minutes, much to Courtenay's relief, as Suarez was certain that the Indians' stock of cartridges did not amount to more than four hundred at the utmost. The canoes crept gradually nearer, and bullets began to strike the ship frequently. One glanced off a davit and shattered a couple of windows in the chart-house. This incident aroused even greater enthusiasm than the first blow of the attack. There was renewed activity among the paddle wielders. Two canoes were not fifty yards from the most southerly floating mine. Courtenay commenced to haul in the slack of one among the half-dozen thin cords: he turned to tell Suarez to be ready for the duty which had been entrusted to him, when his glance happened to travel towards the mouth of the bay.

Then he learnt the significance of that column of smoke on the northern point. A fleet of at least forty canoes was advancing on the ship from the sea. Tide and paddles were swinging the small craft along at a spanking pace. They were already much nearer the vessel than the first batch of Indians, who had very cleverly contrived to enlist the attention of the defenders while the real attack was developing without let or hindrance. It was a smart ruse, worthy of a race of higher attainments than the tribe which is ranked lowest in the human scale. During long days of patient watching, they had probably estimated to a nicety the number of men on board. They reasoned that a show of force to the south would draw all eyes from the north, and the stronger squadron of canoes might be enabled to run under the bows of the ship so speedily and quietly that the occupants of the leading craft, men who could climb like monkeys, stood some chance of gaining the deck unobserved. That this was their design was proved by the abstention of the newcomers from firing or stone-slinging. They were gathering with the speed and silence of vultures.

Two mines protected the front of the *Kansas*, and several canoes had passed them. Indeed, Courtenay soon found that some of the assailants were already screened by the ship's bows, but the larger number were clustered thickly round Tollemache's infernal machines. It was well that a cool-headed sailor was called on to deal with this emergency. The captain of the **Kansas** even smiled as he appreciated the full meaning of the trick which his adversaries had tried to play on him, and the man who smiles in the face of danger is one to be depended on.

The six cords were numbered. He dropped No. 2, which he was holding, and seized Nos. 4 and 5. He drew them in, hand over hand, as rapidly as possible, but careful not to sacrifice a smooth tension to undue hurry. In a few seconds two deafening reports split the air, the glass front of the chart-house shook, pieces of the broken panes rattled on the floor, several scraps of iron, bolts, nuts and heavy nails fell on the decks and hatches, and a tremendous hubbub of yells came from the main body of Indians. A couple of heavily charged dynamite bombs had burst in their midst, dealing death and destruction over a wide area. Several canoes near the floating platforms were torn asunder and sank, while men were killed or wounded out of all proportion to the number of craft disabled.

Courtenay at once picked up the governing cord of the mine which he was about to fire in the first instance. He felt that the Alaculof flotilla would act in future on the "once bitten twice shy" principle where those innocent-looking little poles showed above sea level, and he must strike fierce blows while the opportunity served. The nine canoes on the south were not clustered around the bomb in the same manner as the others, but they were near enough to sustain heavy loss, and their affrighted crews had ceased to ply their paddles. So he fired that shell also, and had the satisfaction of seeing two more of the frail craft capsize.

He heard the crash of bullets against the ship's sides; a volley of stones smashed several more panes of stout glass; many arrows were embedded in the woodwork: but he calmly pulled another cord, and blew a single loud blast on the siren. That was the agreed signal to warn those below that they must expect to be attacked from the fore part of the vessel. His shot-gun was lying on the table. He took it up, and faced forward again; several canoes were scurrying past and away from the ship as fast as the current and many arms could propel them. He fired both barrels at those within range on the port side. He reloaded, and the sharp snapping of revolver-shots told him that Tollemache and the Chilean were busy.

But the Indians were demoralized by the complete failure of their scheme.

They had ceased firing and stone-slinging; they were flying for their lives. Courtenay wheeled round on Suarez.

"Now!" he cried, pointing to a speaking-trumpet. Suarez ran out on deck, put the megaphone to his mouth, and roared after the discomfited enemy a threat of worse things in store if they dared to come near the ship again. As he used the Alaculof language, the sounds he uttered were the most extraordinary that Courtenay had ever heard from a human throat--a compound of hoarse, guttural vowels, and consonants ending in a series of clicks--and the stentorian power of his lungs must have amazed the Indians.

Courtenay saw that the two fleets were combining forces about five hundred yards to westward. They were close inshore, but none of the savages landed, nor did they head for the more remote Otter Creek. As he was anxious to keep them on the run, he resolved to try the siren again. He judged rightly, as it transpired, that they would fear the bellow of the fog-horn even more than the flying missiles which had dealt death and serious wounds so lavishly.

He knew sufficient Spanish, eked out by signs, to bid Suarez hold the siren cord taut for a minute. While the **Kansas** was still trumpeting forth her loud blare of defiance, he ran down the bridge companion. Mr. Boyle and the tiny garrison of the port promenade deck received him jubilantly; they had escaped without a bruise, and, owing to their position, were able to witness the Indians' retreat.

He raced across to starboard, and found that, by unfortunate mischance, a Chilean fireman in Tollemache's detachment had been shot through the brain. The poor fellow was prone on the deck; it was only too evident that a doctor's skill could avail him naught, so Tollemache had decided that he should not be taken below. The incident marred an easily won victory. Courtenay was assured in his own mind that none of the men had been injured, seeing that he and Suarez, who occupied the most dangerous position, were untouched. This fatality was a mere blunder of fate, and it grieved him sorely.

Even while he bent reverently over the unlucky Chilean's body, the deafening vibration of the fog-horn ceased, and he heard Elsie's glad cry from the saloon:

"Oh my, here comes Joey! That means that Captain Courtenay has left the bridge."

The girl's joyous exclamation, her prelude to a paean of thanks that the dreadful necessary slaying of men had ceased, was a strange commentary on the shattered form stretched at the commander's feet. Among the small company on board, it had been decreed that one, at least, after surviving so many perils, should never see home and kin again.

He gave orders that the dead man should be carried to the poop to await a sailor's burial; then he turned, and with less sprightly step descended the main companion. In the saloon he found Elsie and Christobal watching the stairs expectantly. The girl had the dog in her arms, and Courtenay perceived, for the first time, that Joey's off fore paw had been cut by the broken glass which littered the floor of the chart-house.

"Then the attack has really failed?" was Elsie's greeting. "I saw some of the canoes turn and scurry away. That was the first good sign. And then Joey came."

"You saw them?" repeated Courtenay, his bent brows emphasizing the question.

"Yes. I was looking through one of the ports. Was that wrong?"

"Which one?"

She pointed. "That one," said she, wondering that he had never a smile for her.

"Then you must obey orders more faithfully next time. A man was shot dead by a stray bullet not three feet above your head."

She paled, and her eyes fell before his stern gaze, which did not deceive her at all, for she read the unspoken agony of his thought.

"I am sorry," she murmured, "not so much on my own account, though I shall be more careful in future, but because some one has suffered. Who is it? Not one of our own people, I hope?"

"A fireman; I think his name is Gama. You have hardly seen him, I fancy, but I regret his loss exceedingly. It must have been the merest accident."

The captain of the *Kansas* was certainly preoccupied, or he would never have failed to inquire the extent of Joey's injury. Nor would either he or Elsie have forgotten that Christobal was not "one of our own people," though the girl might protest hotly against any invidious twisting of the phrase.

The Spaniard missed nothing of Courtenay's solicitude for Elsie's well-being, nor of her shy confusion. By operation of the occult law which governs static electricity, it was possible that the magnetism flowing between those two communicated itself to a third person. However that might be, Christobal was under no sort of doubt that, unless another "accident" intervened, he had lost all chance of winning this woman's love.

But he swallowed the bitter knowledge and said:

"If you undertake to hold the dog, Miss Maxwell, I will bind his paw."

"Oh, my ducky darling little pet! Did I actually forget all about his dear wounded little foot? And he came hopping in so bravely, too, carrying himself with such a grand air. Come, then, Joey dear! Let us see what has happened. Yes, this is the doctor, but he won't hurt you. He is so good and kind to little dogs; he will wrap up the bleedy part until it is quite nice and comfy."

"Your only patient, doctor," said the captain, cheerily, when Elsie had done fondling the dog. "Even crediting our poor fireman to the enemy's score, we have had the best of the first round."

"Is there any likelihood of a second attack?"

"I hope not. Indeed, I shall be very much surprised if they show up again."

"Ah, that is excellent. Our young lady here does not thrive on excitement, especially of the murderous variety. She is on the verge of a high fever."

"Then she can calm down now; there will be no more fighting to-day," said Courtenay, with a smiling glance at Elsie which told her quite plainly that Christobal did not really know what he was talking about. Which goes to prove that even a prudent man may say mistaken things, with both his tongue and his eyes.

CHAPTER XIV
THE FIRST WATCH

On his way back to the deck, the captain encountered Suarez. The man's gestures, and the satisfaction which lit up his wrinkled face, would have told the news he wished to convey if Courtenay were not able to catch the words "Indianos" and "van." In his excitement the Spaniard pulled the Englishman towards one of the peep-holes in the canvas screen. Sure enough, the canoes were making off towards Otter Creek. In the marvelously clear light it was easy to see the threatening arms held out towards the ship by a few men who stood upright. Even their raucous cries were yet audible. Courtenay was glad he had not missed this demonstration of hatred. It argued the necessity of continued watchfulness.

The general attitude of the crew was one of real annoyance that the fight had not been carried on at close quarters. They had heard a good deal of noise and yelling, the starboard squad had experienced the thrill of having a man fall dead in their midst, but, with the exception of Tollemache and the Chilean marksman, the main body of the defenders took no part in the fray and saw but little of it. And it is one of human nature's queer proclivities that it seeks rather than shirks a combat when the loins are girt for the smiting.

Walker, though eager to return to his lathe, was no exception to the rule. He looked a trifle discontented when the captain found him unscrewing the engine-room hatch.

"That was a pwetty poo-aw scwap, sir," said he. "I did expect to have a smack at some of those magpies, if only for the sake of washin' the paint an' feath-ahs off 'em with a jet of steam."

"They came quite near enough to be pleasant, Walker. Their flank march was almost a surprise; if a swarm of vicious savages had succeeded in reaching the decks--well, we might have beaten them off, but it would have been touch and go."

"Mebbe you-aw wight, cap'n. 'Best look at a bull ov-ah a fence,' as they say in the Canny Toon. Eh, but I'll have a fine tale to tell when next I meet my butties on the Quay-side. Did ye ev-ah see such faces as yon, all daubed wi' black an' white! Talk about Chirgwin--"

Courtenay smiled and passed on. He was in no mood for jesting: the death of the Chilean fireman had damped his high spirits. The *Kansas* bore tokens in plenty of the battle. Many bullets and arrows had struck the ship; the canvas was torn in several places; a number of port lights were broken, and the open decks fore and aft, as well as the spar deck, were littered with stones. He picked up some of these missiles, man's earliest and latest projectile. They were round and heavy; a few bore the red streaks of oxidized iron; some appeared to be veritable lumps of ore, though the action of water had made them "smooth stones out of the brook." He showed one to Tollemache, who seemed to possess a good deal of out-of-the-way knowledge, and the latter instantly pronounced the specimen to be almost pure copper veined with silver.

"Queer thing!" he commented. "You find the worst rotters in any country squatted over the richest minerals."

At the time, Courtenay gave slight heed to this bit of crude philosophy. It was not until he called to mind the Kaffir, the Australian black, the Alaskan Indian, the primeval nomads of California, Colorado, and Northern Siberia, that he saw how extraordinarily true was his friend's dictum. Then he looked on the shores of Good Hope Inlet with a new interest. Would a city ever spring up in that desolate land, a city builded of those pebbles which had clattered against the solid walls of the *Kansas*? Who could tell? The long romance of gold contained stranger chapters.

But the captain had more important things with which to bother his brains than the fanciful laying out of corner lots on the comparatively level bluff overlooking Otter Creek. He saw to the reverent burial of poor Pietro Gama, entered full details of the fight in the ship's log, and helped Walker to search the suspected coal for a further supply of dynamite, as the utility of the surface mines had been demonstrated beyond a doubt. He thought it possible, given the necessary time, to rig a device which would be practically invisible. A fresh set of dummy poles, which the Indians would probably avoid in the event of a second attack, might deflect the canoes into the area of new mines laid at sea level.

Their utmost diligence brought to light no further supply of the explosive. Evidently, the prepared lumps of coal, each containing a stick of dynamite, which were placed among the bunker at Valparaiso, had been conveyed on board by one man, so it was more than likely there was not another ounce of the stuff on the ship except the three specimens first discovered. These, water-soaked and useless, were locked in a drawer in the chart-house.

While scrutinizing the bunker, Courtenay found a grimy piece of paper, crushed into a ball and amalgamated with coaldust by means of the glue, or other substance, which had been used for making the bombs intended for the destruction of the furnaces. He examined it carefully, believing it had the appearance and texture of cartridge paper. He placed it in his pocket, and, while changing his clothes before joining the others at supper, came on it again with a certain surprise. He plunged it into a basin of hot water, and it yielded its secret. It was the outer wrapper of a stick of dynamite; it bore the circular stamp of the manufacturers, the "Sociedad Anonyma de las Costas del Pacifico." This, in itself, meant nothing. The same company probably supplied hundreds of mines with the five-pound boxes in which dynamite is packed, and, if the stamp were the only clue, none could possibly say when or where it had been issued for use.

But miners are apt to be careless; men accustomed to dynamite will handle it with an astounding disregard for danger. And here was a case in point. Some Spanish overseer, evidently at a loss for a memorandum tablet, had scribbled hieroglyphics with an indelible pencil on this particular wrapper. It was clear that the figures and abbreviated words referred to the development of a cross-heading and the position of certain lodes, but Courtenay was quick to see that the official who made those notes would recognize them. Hence, the mine or store from which the package had been stolen or bought could be identified. Such evidence was of high circumstantial value. Courtenay put the wrapper in the same drawer as the cartridges, entered in the log the time and manner of its discovery, and forthwith dismissed it from his mind.

It was almost dark when he went on deck. The wind was keen and chilly. It whistled through the broken windows of the wheel-house, and seemed to have in it a promise of bad weather. But a glance aloft and at the sky beyond the southern headland--Point *Kansas*, as it was called on board--reassured him. The far-flung arc overhead was cloudless. The stars of the southern hemisphere, vivid and bright, though less familiar than those of the north, were reflected in the black water. The ship was so still, the surroundings so peaceful, save for the plash of tiny waves created by the breeze, that he was almost startled when a soft voice came from the lower deck:

"Where in the world have you been, Captain Courtenay? Joey is fretting for you, and I have carried him all over the ship in vain search."

His heart jumped with gladness. Elsie was awaiting him at the foot of the companion. Be sure he was by her side without needless delay. The dog wriggled in her arms, so she said:

"I don't think he ought to run about. His dear little paw is rather badly cut, and there may be more broken glass on the deck."

"I hope not, for our Chileans' sake," laughed Courtenay. "I heard Mr. Boyle telling them to sweep it up, and they were hard at work when I went to my cabin."

"Oh, is that where you hid yourself? No wonder I could not find you. Of course, Joey knew where you were. How stupid of me!"

"Please don't call yourself names, Elsie. You don't deserve them. And, by the way, may I address you by your Christian name? It slipped out to-day unawares. Not that I feel like apologizing, because I don't. There are times when the heart speaks, not the guarded tongue."

Luckily, the darkness covered the hot blush which leaped to her cheeks. She gave a nervous little laugh, and strove desperately to parry this wholly unexpected assault.

"I shall be delighted if you always call me Elsie. It sounds friendly, and I think our circumstances warrant a true friendship."

"Excellent. I suppose you know that my name is Arthur?"

"Yes, but I had no notion of that sort of exchange. You are the captain, and a very serious sort of captain at times. I feel like a little girl when you look at me and tell me not to be naughty. So 'Elsie' sounds all right, but I simply dare not call you 'Arthur.' Just imagine what a sensation it would create in the saloon. I should feel creepy all over. And hadn't we better be--"

"Elsie," said he, with a tender note in his voice which thrilled her like a chord of exquisite music, "I want to tell you something. The knowledge is forced on me that there is another man on this ship who wishes to make you his wife. But I, too, love you, and I see no reason why I should stand aside for any man on God's earth until you tell me with your own lips that you prefer him to me."

"Oh!" gasped Elsie, and "Oh!" again, but not another word could she utter, she who had been so voluble a moment ago. The bitter-sweet pain of hearing this sudden avowal was almost overpowering. Her ideals of honor and truth were shocked; but she was a woman as well as an idealist, and she was stirred to the depths of her soul by the knowledge that she had won the man whose love she craved. Yet it must not be: she could never again hold her head high if she yielded to him. She must relinquish him, drive him away from her by an assumed coldness which would wring her very heart-strings. If he came nearer, if he took her in his arms, she would be unable to resist him. Her impulse was to fly, to lock herself in her room. But she could not drop the wounded dog on the deck, and Joey, satisfied by his master's presence, snuggled up close to her breast, and made the most of his comfortable quarters. And now, while Courtenay stroked Joey with one hand, he placed the other on Elsie's shoulder. What a plight for a frightened maid who wished to escape! Of course, because she wished that some one would come to her help, the deck was practically deserted. Certainly, Mr. Boyle did appear at the after end of the corridor; but he seemed to remember something strong and urgent which the crew ought to hear, and he turned back.

And here was Courtenay speaking again, speaking in the slow and definite way of a man who was determined that there should be no lingering doubt as to his meaning.

"I want you to listen to me, Elsie," he said, with a passionate intensity that stilled the rising storm in her bosom. "Doctor Christobal may have pleaded his own cause already. It is not for me to cavil at him for doing that. But I cannot lose you without a word. Whether you marry him or me, or neither of us, I shall love you for ever. I want you to know that. It is no new discovery to me. I think my heart went out to you when I carried you in my arms through the gale, and since that hour you and I have had experiences denied to most men and women ere they reach the conclusion that they are fit mates for the voyage of life. Do you feel that, sweetheart? Have we known each other ten days, or ten years?"

His face was very near to hers now. His arm had encroached so far that it was around her neck. It was quite dark where they stood in the shadow of the bridge. He could not see the tears in her eyes, but he heard her broken answer:

"Are you--quite--fair--in using such words to me?"

"Fair, Elsie! 'Fair' to whom?"

"Because--oh, how can I tell you? Are you free to--to speak to me in this way?"

"Elsie, I am pledged to no other woman, if that is what you mean. Who has been telling you otherwise?"

"No one. Indeed, indeed, I alone am to blame. You will be angry with me, but I could not help it."

She could say no more. If she had uttered another syllable just then she would have broken down completely. Joey did not seem to need any further fondling; hence, having a hand at liberty, so to speak, Courtenay placed it under her chin, and lifted her unresisting lips to his. He kissed her twice, and laughed softly, with a glad confidence that sent a wave of delight coursing through Elsie's veins.

"Sweetheart," he whispered, "I am sure you would not have allowed me to speak so plainly if you were going to send me away. Now, I don't want you to bind yourself irrevocably to-night. That would certainly not be fair. I don't know why I am to be angry, or what it was you couldn't help, and I don't care a red cent. All I want to know is this--if the **Kansas** brings us both back to the outer world once more, have I as good a chance of winning your love as any other man?"

"But I must tell you. I could not look you in the face again if you did not hear it. When I was left alone in your cabin, the second time, and the sea came in, a packet of letters fell out of some clothes which I picked up from the floor. There was one from your sister. I hardly knew what I was doing, but I saw her name, 'Madge,' and I read a few words on the half page above her signature."

His left arm was now so well established that his hand touched her cheek, and he found it wet with tears.

"What wild conceit has crept into your pretty little head?" he cried in amaze, unconsciously raising his voice somewhat. "A letter from my sister! She is the most straightforward woman breathing, I assure you. Never a line has she written to me which could bear any construction such as seems to trouble you. Why, on the contrary, Madge has often chaffed me for being so like herself in giving no thought to matrimony."

"It is horrid of me to persist, but I owe it to you to tell you what I saw. She alluded to your 'affianced wife,' and said that 'under no other circumstances,' whatever they were, would she receive her."

Then Courtenay laughed again, and Elsie found it was absolutely essential, if Joey were not to be crushed, that her head should bend a little forward, with the obvious result that it rested on Courtenay's shoulder.

"I must show you the whole of that letter," he cried, "and the others which are tied up in the same bundle. You will see me blush, I admit, but it will not be from a sense of perfidy. But there is one thing you have forgotten, Elsie--" and his voice dropped to a tense whisper again--"In telling me your secret, which is no secret, you have given me my answer. Your heart must have crept out a little way to meet mine, dear, or my sister's words would not have perplexed you. So that is why you have avoided me during the past few days! But there! Now, indeed, I am not acting quite fairly. It is unfair to ask you to confess when I want you to wait until we win clear of our present difficulties before you decide whether or not you can find it to your liking to make a poor sailor-man happy."

Joey was a highly accommodating dog under certain conditions. He had curled up so complacently that Elsie found she could hold him quite easily with one arm. So the other went out in the darkness until it rested timidly on her lover's disengaged shoulder.

"It is easy to confess that which is already known," she murmured. "Whether we are fated to live one day or fifty years, it will be all the same to me, dear."

She lifted her face again to his, and would have returned the kisses he gave her were it not that they lost their one-sided character this time. It was an odd place for love-making, this darkened nook on the deck of a disabled and beleaguered ship. But a man and a woman reck little of time or locality when the call of love's springtime sounds in their ears. That magic summons can be heard but once, and it is well with the world, for those two at least, while its ecstasy floods the soul.

There was a chance that Joey might have been partly suffocated--though, to all appearance, he meant to die a willing martyr--had not Suarez leaned over the upper rail, and asked, in his grating accents, if he heard the senor captain's voice below.

Elsie, all tremulous and rosy, and profoundly thankful for the darkness, withdrew herself from Courtenay's embrace and answered the Argentine.

"Ah," said Suarez, "I am glad you are there too, senorita. Will you tell him that I am very hungry, and that I have not been relieved at the proper time. I have been waiting half an hour or more."

"There!" cried the captain, squeezing Elsie's arm, "that comes of using so many unnecessary explanations. I ought to have adopted the recognized Jack Tar method and just grabbed you round the waist without ceremony. I wonder where Boyle is. He and Christobal take the first watch, and it must be two bells, or later. I will hunt them up. Good-by, sweetheart. Meet you at supper in ten minutes."

It was a strange and peculiar fact that Boyle had cornered Christobal in the saloon, and had insisted on telling him various remarkable anecdotes concerning the one-legged skipper of the *Flower of the Ocean* brig. It was still more odd that when Christobal yielded to a fit of unwonted and melancholy silence after learning from Suarez that the senor captain had been talking to the senorita for a very long time on the promenade deck, Boyle should feel inclined to sing.

The chief officer's musical attainments were not of the highest, and his repertory was archaic. But there must be some explanation of his unwonted and melancholy chanting. He always spoke of Elsie with the utmost admiration, and it was no secret that he rendered Courtenay a sort of hero-worship hidden under the guise of an exaggerated belief in the good luck which followed the captain of the *Kansas* in all his doings. And then, with a chilling inspiration, Christobal knew why the chief officer had caused him to miss the hour for relieving the watch. Boyle had seen those two together, and had planned to leave them undisturbed!

The Spaniard was a dignified man; he had inherited from his English mother a saving sense of humor. It was intolerable that the pleasant relations existing between the few survivors on board the Kansas should be disturbed by reason of any failure on his part to acquiesce in Elsie's right to bestow her affections where she listed. He wondered if the girl had come on deck after supper; her habit was to retire early, as she rose soon after the sun. He had seen her for a moment only in passing out of the saloon, and there was a suspicious brightness in her eyes for which solicitude on the dog's behalf would hardly account. Why not put his fortunes to the test that night and have done with it? Yes, that was the right course. He would cease this petty watchfulness, this campaign of planning and contriving lest others should monopolize more of her smiles and pleasant words than he. A simple question would determine his fate. Either she was heart-whole, or not; at any rate, he would receive a straight answer.

So it was on the cards that Elsie would be the amazed recipient of two proposals in one evening, which is a better average than most women are favored with in a lifetime. Christobal had entered the chart-house with the fixed intent of warning Boyle that he was going below for a moment to ask Miss Maxwell to come on deck, when a hurried step on the bridge companion caused the imminent words to be withheld.

It was Courtenay, who had run up from the saloon to procure those fateful letters which had so nearly parted Elsie and himself. He had laughingly refused to tell her their history. That would spoil their effect, he said. She must take them to her state-room and read them at her leisure. Then she would see their true inwardness, and his feelings would be spared, as he could not deny that the majority of them had been written by ladies.

On his way, he looked into the wheel-house. There was no light in the interior. Boyle, wrapped in a heavy coat, was seated in the most sheltered corner.

"All quiet?" asked the captain, in his brisk way.

"Nothin' doin', sir," answered Boyle.

"I expect you are both feeling pretty tired. Tollemache and I propose to relieve you at six bells."

"But why?" demanded Christobal. "It is you who have passed an exciting day. I am ready to mount guard until dawn. Tollemache can join me now if he likes, as Mr. Boyle ought to be in bed."

"I'm all right," said Boyle, gruffly. "I am only sitting here because my back is stiff."

Courtenay glanced at the somber shadow of Point *Kansas*, silhouetted against the deep blue of the seaward arc.

"Suarez has retired to roost," he said. "He seems to be quite assured that the Indians will never deliver a night attack."

"To-day's hammering should teach them to leave the *Kansas* alone in future," said Christobal.

"I hope so, but Suarez and Tollemache agree that they are most persistent wretches. Now, Boyle, you must obey the doctor. I am going back to the saloon to give Miss Maxwell some documents I wish her to see. Then, Tollemache and I will relieve the pair of you. All right, Christobal; I promise to take my share of the blankets in the morning. I shall be ready for a nap at four o'clock. At present I feel particularly wide-awake."

He went to the cabin. They heard him unlock the door and enter. At that instant a startling hail came from two sailors stationed on the poop.

"Indianos!" they yelled.

The three men were on the spar deck a second later, straining their eyes into the black vagueness of the water.

"Indianos!" shouted two other sailors on the forecastle, and from the spar deck it seemed to be possible to distinguish several black objects moving towards the ship.

"The siren, Boyle," cried Courtenay, striking a match. At once the swelling note of the fog-horn smote the air and thundered away in tremendous sound waves. Soon a hissing, fiery serpent ran up the port wall of the chart-house, and a fine star rocket soared into the sky. It illuminated a wide area of the bay, and revealed a number of crowded canoes darting in on the ship from all sides. Courtenay grasped the lines connected with the remaining mines and hauled for dear life. Already the Indian rifle fire was crackling with vivid spurts of flame, and stones and arrows were beginning to patter on the deck and bang against the steel plates. Two of the dynamite bombs exploded with the usual din, but it was impossible to ascertain their effect owing to the yelling of the Indians.

The loud summons of the siren brought all hands from below; arms were hastily secured, the fore and aft awnings closed, and Walker made shift to hammer the engine-room door tight. The increasing violence of the stone-slinging showed that the Alaculofs meant to press home this time. Whatever their dread of the fiends who roam the world in the dark, they had conquered it, and this latest phase in the stormy history of the ship threatened to be its most trying one.

Courtenay, who seemed to be everywhere at once, lighted torches which were fastened to the empty davits in readiness for a night alarm. He had used the last rocket on board, but the flares would burn for fifteen minutes at least. By their light the defenders were able to shoot or smash the skulls of several savages who climbed up roughly contrived grapnells fashioned out of bent sticks and thongs of hide. But there were only thirteen men to repel an attack which developed at fifty points simultaneously. Ere the torches flickered in their sockets the savages had swarmed over poop and bows. They were tearing at the canvas shields and sweeping the hurricane deck with showers of missiles. Tollemache was injured, and Walker. Courtenay had his forehead cut open. Suarez fell insensible while he was bellowing curses through the megaphone in the vain hope of frightening the determined enemy. Two Chileans were down, one struck with a stone and the other shot through the lungs.

So, at last, the ***Kansas*** was in the grip of a savage and implacable foe. Courtenay, while hauling a steam hose to the weakest point, the after part of the promenade deck, met Christobal. He clutched the Spaniard in a way there could be no mistaking.

"Go below!" he muttered in a terrible voice. "I cannot leave the deck. You must go. And, for God's sake, don't tell her! Let her die without knowing!"

CHAPTER XV
IN WHICH THE UNEXPECTED HAPPENS

When Christobal descended to the saloon he found Elsie holding the excited dog. It was instantly perceptible that she was not aware of the grave position of affairs on deck. She knew, of course, that the Alaculof menace had become active again, but the first attack had been beaten off so easily that she was sure this later effort would fail.

The dog was better informed. His alert ears told him that there were strange beings on board. He struggled so resolutely that Elsie freed him just as the Spaniard reached the foot of the stairs. Forgetting his wounded paw, and all a-quiver with the fine courage of his race, Joey galloped up the companion and disappeared. Elsie was much distressed by her four-footed friend's useless pugnacity.

"I could not keep him back," she said, "and I am afraid he runs some risk of being hit. Do you think he will go to the chart-house? That is so exposed--Captain Courtenay is not there, is he?"

"No. I left him a moment ago, close to the saloon entrance."

She listened intently. Her imagination led her astray, it was so hopelessly on the wrong tack.

"There does not appear to be so much stone-throwing now, but I suppose I ought not to go on deck?" she cried.

"It is not to be thought of, Miss Maxwell. Indeed, the captain asked me to come and bear you company."

"Just fancy those horrid Indians venturing to approach the ship to-night after the dreadful lesson they received this afternoon! And what will poor Senor Suarez say? He was so positive that they would never come near us after dark."

"I saw him, also, on the promenade deck," answered Christobal quietly. "He had very much the semblance of a false prophet."

The Spaniard meant to meet grim fate with a jest on his lips. He had seen Suarez lying dead or insensible close to the rails. In fact, the unlucky Argentine was only separated by the thickness of the ship's deck from the table near which Elsie was standing. Unless he were speedily rescued he would bleed to death.

"Ah, I heard Joey barking. He has gone aft," cried Elsie. "And what is that?" she added, moving suddenly towards the center of the saloon. She had caught the fierce hiss of steam, and she was well aware that steam would only be brought into use if the Indians were endeavoring to climb the ship's sides: not yet had it occurred that they could possibly be on board.

"Some of our friends the enemy have come near enough to be scalded," said the man, coolly. "That should soon drive them away. You are not frightened, I hope?"

"Not a bit. My only regret is that I am not permitted to help in the defense. It must be irksome for you, Dr. Christobal, to be stationed here when the ship is in danger. I am certain you would prefer to be up there with the others."

"Thank you for saying that. I wish you were able to read all my thoughts as accurately."

His right hand went to the pocket in which he had placed the revolver. The stock appeared to have a peculiar clamminess as his fingers closed around it. Though he was proud of the iron nerve which had won him repute in his profession, he almost prayed now that it might not fail him at the last. What a horror, to be compelled with his parting glance to see this bright and gracious woman crumple up on the deck!

"But I know you are a brave man," she said with a confidant smile. "It demanded a higher courage to pass undaunted through the ordeal of the storm than to face these ill-armed Indians. Please don't think I am a warlike person, but it makes my blood boil to find that there are wretches who regard our distress as their opportunity to murder us and pillage the ship. What have we done to them? If they are poor and hungry, and they would only come to us in a peaceful way, Captain Courtenay would give them all the stores he could spare."

Christobal heard ominous sounds from the fore part of the vessel. The revolver shooting had ceased, for the convincing reason there were no more cartridges. Courtenay's double barrelled gun was being fired as quickly as he could reload it, and the sharp snap of one of the rifles in the Indians' possession was recognizable as coming from the poop, the remaining marksmen having preferred to fire wildly from their canoes. But Christobal knew that a deadly struggle was in progress on the fore deck. Tollemache, Frascuelo, and three Chileans were engaged in a hand-to-hand fight with nearly a score of savages; the doctor could distinguish the cries of the combatants, the irregular stamping of boot-shod feet.

He wondered why the girl, with her acute senses, did not grasp the significance of the yells and trampling on the deck, until it occurred to him, with a quick pang, that she was listening for one voice alone; owing to her ignorance of the desperate nature of the conflict raging overhead she had ears for nothing further.

He placed a hand on her shoulder. She turned and looked at him. There was a gravity in his eyes, which startled her.

"Elsie," he said, "you believe in the efficacy of prayer, don't you? Well, then, pray now a little. I shall be glad to think, when this time of danger has passed, that we owed something to your invocation."

It was in his mind that he must shoot her within a few seconds, and the immeasurable agony of the thought reflected itself in his face. He had no notion that she would give his words a more direct significance than he intended them to bear. But a strange, hoarse yell of triumph, the war-cry of an Alaculof leader who had hauled himself to the bridge and found it undefended, warned her in the same moment that all was not well with the defense.

She sprang towards the saloon stairs.

"Do you hear that?" she cried in a ringing voice. "There are Indians on board. Come! We must not stay here when our friends are fighting for their lives."

Christobal knew that this active girl would readily outstrip him in a race to the deck. She was already several feet distant, but he must detain her, no matter what the cost; if she fell into the clutches of the ghouls then over-running the *Kansas*, she might not be killed, but only wounded, and her sufferings would be inconceivable ere the end came.

"You are wrong," he shouted with convincing vehemence. "But, if you wish to see for yourself, at least allow me to go first."

While he was speaking, he ran forward. She thought he meant what he said, and waited for him. Then he caught her right arm firmly in his left hand.

"Let us wait here a moment or two," he breathed.

"No, no; I am going now. You shall not hold me back. You don't understand. The man I love is up there, perhaps surrounded by savages. Let me go, I tell you! If he is dying I shall die by his side. Let me go! Would you have me strike you?" She turned on him like an angry goddess, and strove to wrest herself from his grip. At that instant Tollemache and Frascuelo, the only survivors of the deadly struggle forward, were driven back by a rush of Indians. They caught sight of others leaping down the bridge companion.

"To the saloon, Courtenay!" roared Tollemache, clearing a path for himself with an iron bar which he swung in both hands. Followed by Frascuelo, he jumped inside the saloon gangway. Four savages followed, two entering through the doorway behind him. One raised a hatchet-like implement, and would have brained the Englishman had not Christobal whipped out his revolver and shot him through the body, releasing the girl's wrist in his flurry. The Indian pitched headlong down the stairs, falling limply at Elsie's feet. She stooped over the terrifying figure and seized the man's weapon. Her eyes shone with a strange light. She felt her arms tingle. A wonderful power seemed to flow through her body, like a gush of strong wine. She was assured that she, unaided, could beat down all the puny, despicable creatures who barred the path to her lover. She vaulted over the writhing form of the Alaculof, and made to climb the stairs, but Christobal, admirably cool, fired again and brought another Indian to his knees. The second Indian's fall caused Frascuelo to trip; and the Chilean, locked rib to rib with a somewhat sturdy opponent, rolled into the saloon. Elsie drew back just in time, or the two men would have knocked her down. Even as they were turning over on the steep steps she saw Frascuelo's knife seek that favorite junction of neck and collar-bone which Christobal had said was so well understood by those of his ilk. At the foot of the stairs the Indian lay still, and Frascuelo tried to rise. She helped him gladly. The awfulness of this killing no longer appalled her. Each dead or disabled Indian was one less obstacle between her and Courtenay. A third time the revolver barked, but Christobal missed. It did not matter greatly, as Tollemache had shortened his bar, using it twice as a miner delves at a rock. But the doctor did not forget that he had only three cartridges left, two of which were bespoke long before the fight began.

At last, then, the way was clear. Elsie would have mounted the stairs but an appealing hand detained her.

"I cannot walk, senorita. My leg has given way. And we can do no good there. They are all down."

A death chill gripped her heart at Frascuelo's words.

"All down!" she repeated, white-lipped.

"I think so," said he, blankly. The man was dazed by the ordeal through which he had passed.

As if to answer and refute him, Joey's hysterical yelp sounded from a point close at hand, and they distinctly heard Courtenay's loud command:

"This way, Boyle! Rally to the bridge!"

"You are mistaken!" shrieked Elsie, wrenching herself free from the Chilean's grasp. Nothing short of violence would stop her now. Tollemache darted out into the darkness, and she mounted the steps two at a time. Christobal panted by her side. He was determined not to be parted from her: if necessary, he would drag her away from any doubtful encounter on the battle-field of the deck. But his blood was aflame now with the lust of combat. He wished to die fighting rather than by a suicide's bullet.

They were not yet clear of the doorway when an extraordinary burst of cheering and shouts in English and Spanish assailed their wondering ears. The sounds seemed to come from the sea, from some point very near to the ship. A loud hubbub arose among the Indians; Courtenay, clubbing his gun, rushed past, with the dog at his heels, and ran up the bridge companion. They could follow his progress as he raced towards the port side, and they heard his amazed cry:

"What boats are those?"

"Your own, captain," came the answering yell, plainly audible above the din.

"That is Mr. Gray," screamed Elsie, and she, too, ran towards the bridge, with the doctor close behind.

"Sink every canoe you can get alongside of, and knock those fellows on the head who are swimming," roared Courtenay, who was so carried away by the fierceness of the fight from which he had just emerged that he would have given the same directions to the archangel Michael had that warrior-spirit come to his aid.

He seemed to have eyes in the back of his head, he turned so suddenly when Elsie neared him.

"Ah, thank God you are safe!" he said, drawing her to him for an instant. "Stand there, dear heart!"

He placed her in the forward angle of the bridge rail, and leaned out over the side. She understood that she must not speak to him then, but a great joy overwhelmed her, and her eyes melted into tears.

Christobal, who had missed no word of Elsie's frenzied protest in the saloon, nor failed to note the manner of Courtenay's greeting, seemed to take the collapse of his own aspirations with the unmoved stoicism he had displayed in the face of danger.

"The ship's boats--" he began, but the captain raised his gun and fired twice aft along the side of the vessel. Cries of pain and a good deal of splashing in the sea proved that he had expedited the departure of several Indians who were perched on the rails beyond the reach of Walker's steam jet.

"The ship's boats," went on Christobal calmly, "have turned up in some mysterious manner, just in the nick of time. A few minutes more, and they would have been too late."

"But where have they come from? Where can they have been all these days?" whispered Elsie, whose eyes were so dimmed that she perforce abandoned the effort to make out what was going on in the sea near the ship.

"My brain reels under the wildest guesses. At present we are chiefly concerned in the fact that they are here. Yet people say that the age of miracles has passed: obviously a foolish remark."

Those who have been plucked from the precipice by a sleeve, as it were, are seldom able to concentrate their attention on the one thought which should apparently swamp all others. They either yield to the strain, and lapse into unconsciousness, or their minds become the arena of minor emotions, wherein trivialities play battledore and shuttlecock with the tremendous issues of the moment. When a more extended knowledge of all that had happened, joined to a nicer adjustment of the time-factor in events, enabled Elsie to realise the extraordinary deliverance from death which she had been vouchsafed that night, she began to appreciate the service which Christobal rendered her in discussing matters with such nonchalance.

Barely a minute had elapsed since they were in the throes of a struggle which promised to be the last act of a tragedy. The ship was then over-run by a horde of howling savages, maddened by the desperate resistance offered by the defenders, and ruthless as wolves in their lust for destruction. Now, the **Kansas** was clear of every bedaubed Alaculof, save the many who cumbered the decks, either dead or so seriously wounded that they could not move. These men were so near akin to animals, that this condition implied ultimate collapse save in a few instances of fractured skulls and broken limbs. From the final stage of a hopeless butchery the survivors of the ship's company were suddenly transferred to a position of reasonable security. It was not that the arrival of the ship's boats meant such an accession of fighting strength that the Alaculofs could not have made sure of victory. Gray and his companions were badly armed. The Indians remaining in the canoes could have pelted them to shreds in a few minutes. Even those on the ship had the power to resist any attempt by the newcomers to gain the decks. But the superstitious savages had already screwed themselves up to an act of unusual daring in delivering a night attack, and the appearance of boats filled with men of whose fighting qualities they had already such a lively experience quite demoralized them. They fled without attempting a counter assault. Just as negroes conjure up white demons, so did these nude Alaculofs regard with awe men who wore clothes. They were ready to kill and eat the strange beings of another race who, few in numbers and ill armed, wandered into their rock-pent fastness, but it was quite a different thing to face them in equal combat.

At last the sounds of conflict died away. The black waters closed over the dead; the last swimmer vanished into the silence. The spasmodic barking of the dog, the groaning of men lying on the decks and the shouts exchanged between Courtenay and Gray for the guidance of the boats, were the only remaining symbols of the fiercest crisis which had yet befallen the **Kansas**.

Elsie, wandering through a trance-like maze of vivid impressions, awoke with a start to the fact that Courtenay was giving directions for the lowering of the ship's gangway, meanwhile receiving information as to the identity of the boats beneath.

"Mr. Malcolm is in charge of the jolly-boat," Gray was saying. "Miss Baring and Mr. and Mrs. Somerville are with him. Miss Baring's maid is dead. Senor Jerrera is in my boat, Number 2. We have been on White Horse Island all this time, but we have seen nothing of the other life-boat."

That meant that two boats out of those which quitted the ship had arrived thus opportunely. Senor Jerrera was the Spanish mining engineer who had been hustled into one of the craft manned by the mutineers. And Isobel was actually sitting down there in the darkness a few feet away. How wonderful it all was! Elsie thought her heart would never cease its labored throbbing. Even yet her breath came in little gasps. How could the captain and Gray talk so coolly, as if some of the passengers and crew were returning on board the ship after an evening ashore? It was the bedizened savages who now assumed reality: the simple orders which dealt with the clearing of the falls and the lowering of a ladder became wildly fantastic.

And Christobal was saying:

"Well, Miss Maxwell, you and I can look forward to a busy night. The ship is littered with wounded men, and our newly arrived friends must be worn with fatigue."

His smooth, even sentences helped to dispel the stupor of amazement which had made her dumb. And the first reasoned thought which came to her was that the Spanish doctor had treated her with the kindness of an indulgent parent, for Elsie was far too unselfish not to be alive to the unselfishness of others.

"How good you have been to me!" she murmured. "I can never repay you. I remember now that I said dreadful things to you in the saloon. But you did not know what it meant to me when I realized that Captain Courtenay might be falling even then beneath the blows of those merciless savages. I have not had a chance to tell you that he has asked me to be his wife, and I have consented. I love him more than all the world. And you, Dr. Christobal, you who knew my father and mother, who have grown-up daughters of your own, you will wish me happiness?"

It was not easy to bear when it came, although he had guessed the truth already. But he choked back the wrath and despair which surged up in him, and said with his stately courtesy:

"I do wish you well, Elsie. No man can hope more earnestly than I that you have made the better choice."

Then he turned, with a certain abruptness which reminded her of the change in his manner she had noticed once or twice during recent days, and quitted the bridge. She sighed, and was sorry for him, knowing that he loved her.

Courtenay, who had been far too busy to pay heed to anything beyond the brief fight between the boats and the canoes, perceived now that the gangway was in position; lights were shining on both the upper and lower platforms.

He stretched out his hand, and drew Elsie to him.

"Are you alone, sweetheart?" he asked.

"Yes."

"Kiss me, then, and go to meet your friends. They will be aboard in less than a minute. Oh, Elsie, I thought I had seen the last of you."

"Was it so bad as that?" she murmured, a great content soothing her heart and brain at her lover's admission that he was thinking of her during the worst agony of the fray. He gave her a reassuring hug.

"You will never know how bad it was," he said. "I cannot understand how we escaped. One moment it all looks like blind chance; the next I feel like going on my knees in thankfulness for the direct intervention of Providence. Those brutes ought to have mastered us a dozen times. I almost lost faith when I heard Tollemache shout that the saloon was in danger, but I could not leave the after deck, where four of us were keeping fifty in check. The least sign of yielding would have caused an overwhelming rush. Well, all's well that ends well. And not a sailor living can squeeze his best girl and do his work at the same time. Off with you, or I shall never bring you on a voyage in my ship again."

With her soul singing a canticle of joy she passed from the bridge to the lower deck. Mr. Boyle was waiting there, holding a lantern.

"Huh!" he growled, when he saw her, "p'raps you'll believe what I tell you before your hair turns gray, if not sooner. Luck! Did any man ever have such luck as the skipper? Why, if he fell off Mong Blong he'd find a circus net rigged up to catch him."

"I agree with you so fully, Mr. Boyle," she whispered, "that I am going to marry him."

"I guessed as much," he answered. "At any rate I fancied it wouldn't be for want of axing on his part." He whirled off into a tempest of wrath because a sailor beneath had failed to keep a guide-rope taut. The occupants of the boats might have saved his life, but he would let them know that he was still chief officer for all that.

At last he stooped and gave his hand to some one who emerged from the darkness beneath.

"Glad to see you again, Miss Baring," he said gruffly. "And you, Mrs. Somerville. And you, sir," to the missionary. "We thought you'd gone under, an' good folks are scarce enough as it is."

It was a wan and broken-spirited Isobel whom Elsie led to her cabin, but notwithstanding her wretched state, her eyes quickly took in the orderly condition of the room.

"I left my clothes strewed all over the floor," she said, with a nervousness which Elsie attributed to the hardships she had undergone. "Why did you trouble to pack them away?"

Then Elsie told her of her hunt for the poudriere, and was so obviously unconcerned about any incident other than the adventures they had both experienced since they parted, that Isobel questioned her no further. A bath and a change of clothing worked marvels. Though thin and weak for want of proper food, neither Isobel nor Mrs. Somerville had suffered in health from the exposure and short fare involved by life on the island. It was broad daylight ere they could be persuaded to retire to rest, there was so much to tell and to hear.

Meanwhile, the meeting between Tollemache and Gray was full of racial subtleties.

Tollemache, stepping forward to grasp Gray's hand, felt it was incumbent on him to utter the first word.

"Had a pretty rotten time of it, I expect?" said he.

"Poisonous. And you?"

"Oh, fair. Beastly close squeak when you turned up."

Gray became more explicit when Courtenay met him in the chart-room, where the table had to be cleared of debris before some glasses and a couple of bottles of champagne could be staged.

"When those blackguards cast off from the ship," he said, "we scudded away in a sort of ocean mill-race which threatened to upset us at any moment. In fact, we gave up hope for a time, but, as the boat kept afloat, Mr. Malcolm and I managed to stir up the Chileans, and we got them to steady her with the oars. Some time before daybreak we ran into smooth water, and made out land on the port bow. In a few minutes we were ashore on a pebbly beach, in a place alive with seals. When the sun rose we found we were on a barren island, and, what was more, that one of the ship's life-boats had been upset on a reef which we just missed, and had lost all her stores, though the men had scrambled into safety. With the aid of our boat, and helped by fine weather, we raised the life-boat, and recovered some of her fittings. The water-casks and tins of food were hauled up by a chap who could dive well. We have been on that lump of rock until today, when I finally persuaded the others that unless we made for the land which we could see in the dim distance the weather would break and our food give out. The trouble with the Chileans was that they were afraid of the natives hereabouts, and preferred to wait on the off chance of a ship showing up. At last they saw that Malcolm and I were right, but we missed the full run of the tide, and were some miles from the mainland, or whatever it is, when night fell. We pushed along cautiously, found the entrance to the cove we had made out before the light failed, and were about to lay to until dawn, when we saw a rocket and heard the fog-horn. That woke us up, you bet. The Chileans pulled like mad, but when we came near enough to discover that the ship was being attacked by Indians, I had a fearful job to get my heroes to butt in. That fellow Gomez is a brick. He orated like a politician, and finally they got a move on. From what I have seen since I came aboard, I guess you were hustling about that time?"

"Yes," said Courtenay, filling a glass with wine as he heard Boyle's step without. He handed the glass to the chief when he entered.

"How many?" he asked.

"Huh! We've slung fifty-three Indians an' six of the crew overboard. There's fourteen wounded natives an' five of our men in the doctor's hands. Two Alaculofs died of funk when they set eyes on the nigger who turned up in the life-boat. They thought--well, here's chin chin to everybody. I'm thirsty."

CHAPTER XVI
CHRISTOBAL'S TEMPTATION

By the way, what of Monsieur de Poincilit?" said Courtenay. "I saw him come aboard with Malcolm, but he dived into the saloon, and has not re-appeared. Is he ill?"

Gray's mouth set like a steel trap; his eyes had a glint in them. He seemed to be unwilling to speak; when words came, they were cold and measured.

"I haven't any use for that fellow," he said. "I suppose the unpleasant story must be told sooner or later, so here goes. In the first place, Poincilit forgot that I understood Spanish, and I heard him yelping to the Chileans in the jolly-boat that if we took any more people on board we should be swamped. It was he who put the notion in their heads to cast off while you were lowering Miss Baring's maid into my arms. I tried to forget that, as he was blue-white with fear, and some fellows are not responsible for their actions when their liver melts. But I can never forget his action on the island. Yesterday morning I was just in time to stop him and four others from sneaking off in the life-boat with all our provisions."

Courtenay's face hardened too.

"Necessity may have no laws," said he; "but I fancy I should have found a code to meet his case."

"I have organized a Vigilance Committee in my time, and its articles kind of fit-ted in," was the American's quiet reply. "That is why I have a few recent knife-cuts distributed about my skin; I began to shoot and we were two short on the muster roll next day. De Poincilit ran, and fell on his knees. So did a skunk of an Italian, and I did not want to waste cartridges. They were tied back to back until we sailed to-day."

"And the fifth?"

"The fifth was a woman."

"Huh!" Boyle reached out for a bottle of wine and refilled his glass. For a little while there was silence. Then Courtenay muttered:

"Poor devil of a Count! 'She gave me of the tree and I did eat.' Did he blame the woman?"

"Well, yes. But it was a mean business, any how."

"Better sponge it off the slate, eh?"

"I agree heartily. Drink up, Boyle, and pass the buck. I have a five years' thirst."

They talked until day-break; then Courtenay turned in. He did not appear on deck again until noon. By that time the *Kansas* had lost all marks of the fight excepting the smashed windows, and a sailor who understood the glazier's art was replacing the broken glass. Making the round of the ship, the captain found Elsie sitting with Isobel and Mrs. Somerville on the promenade deck. She was binding Joey's foot, and he knew then why the dog had scampered off on three legs as soon as the cabin door was opened.

The girl colored very prettily the moment she set eyes on her lover. Memories of the previous night became exceedingly vivid. She was adorably shy, Courtenay thought. As he approached, he debated the manner of his greeting; being a sailor, he did not hesitate.

Lifting his cap with a smile and a general "Good morning," he bent over Elsie.

"Well," he said, "surely you owe me at least one kiss?"

If her cheeks were red before they became scarlet now. But his kindling glance had warned her that he would adopt no pretence, so she lifted her face to his, though she did not dare to look at her amazed companions. Courtenay explained matters quite coolly.

"If Elsie has not told you already, it is my privilege to announce that she and I have signed articles," he said with a smile. "That is, we intend to get married as soon as the ship reaches England."

"Indeed, I congratulate you both most heartily," said the missionary's wife.

"Events have marched, then, while we were stranded on that wretched island?" tittered Isobel. Her voice was rather shrill. She, too, was excited, not quite mistress of herself. She did not know how far Gray's statements might have prejudiced her with the captain; she had already sent de Poincilit a note urging him to deny absolutely all knowledge of the plot to steal the boat, and attribute the American's summary action to his mistaken rendering of the Spanish patois used by the Chilean sailors.

"Yes," laughed Courtenay, ready to put her at ease. "One crowds the events of a month into a day under some conditions. Last night, for instance, I had five minutes' amusement with a steampipe and a double-barrelled gun which will serve all my requirements in the way of physical exercise for a long time to come."

"You feel sure that we shall see no more of the Indians?" asked Isobel, quickly.

"I think so. One never can tell, but if they have the grit to attack us again I shall regard them as first-class fighters."

"Dr. Christobal says they have an astonishing power of bearing pain without flinching," said Elsie, plunging into the talk with a hot eagerness. "The Alaculofs in the fore cabin were afraid of him, thinking he meant to kill them, but, when they found that he wished only to dress their wounds, they followed his actions with a curious interest, as though he were tending some other person's hurts and not their own. And that reminds me. He told me you ought to have that cut on your forehead washed. Let me look at it."

She stood up, and placed the dog on a chair. Lifting Courtenay's cap she brushed back his hair with her fingers, and found that he had covered an ugly scar with a long strip of skin plaster. The tense anxiety in Isobel's face forthwith yielded to sheer bewilderment. These two were behaving with the self-possession of young people who regard the "engagement" stage as a venerable institution.

Of course Courtenay liked to be fondled in this manner. Elsie was at her best as a ministering angel. But he protested against the need of the doctor's precaution.

"No, no," he cried, "you already have one faithful patient in Joey. I wonder he did not wake me earlier so that he might rush off to you. I never have known him play the old soldier before. To see him curled up there, gazing at you with those pathetic eyes, who would think that his teeth met in Alaculof sinews last night? Twice, to my knowledge, he saved my life. And the way he dodged blows aimed at him was something marvelous. He used all four paws then, I assure you."

"Ah, yes," agreed Elsie, blushing again as she recalled the scene in the saloon. "He could have told me the Indians were aboard long before I knew it myself. Dr. Christobal deceived me so admirably that I am not sure yet if I have forgiven him."

"He is a first-rate chap in an emergency," said Courtenay, "though I have a bone to pick with him, too. He promised to call me at eight o'clock, but I expect he and Boyle, or Tollemache, conspired to let me sleep on. I was astounded when I saw the time. What do you think of a skipper who lies abed all the morning, Miss Baring?"

"Gray has told him nothing," she decided at once. "That is very nice of Gray. I must thank him." But she replied instantly, in her piquant way:

"Elsie certainly kept us in the dark about her *fiancailles*, Captain Courtenay; but has not been silent as to your other achievements. If you were not telling us that you have actually slept, I should have cherished the belief that you had not closed an eyelid since the ship struck."

Isobel meant to be on her best behavior. Her pact with the Frenchman was discreditable but smooth words might restrain tongues from wagging until she could leave the ship. Moreover, the vicissitudes of life in these later days were not without their effect. She had known what it was to suffer. She had seen men dying like cattle in the shambles. The shadow of eternity had fallen so closely that twice during the preceding night she was rudely awaked by the shrieking fear of a too vivid dream. These things were not the butterfly flutterings of sunlit Valparaiso. They were of a more ardent order, and her wings had not yet recovered from the singeing.

Courtenay, willing to maintain a fiction which evidently gave her relief, answered lightly that he yet had to earn these compliments, but he hoped to be able soon to fix a date when everybody might bombard him with the nicest phrases they could think of, and end the embarrassing ordeal once for all.

"I went through something of the sort last year on board the *Florida*," he added. "People insist on regarding it as marvelous that a man should strive to do his simple duty."

Suddenly it occurred to him that the topic was unpleasantly analogous to the little French count's cowardly escapades. If one talks of duty, and recognizes its prior claim, what of the man who, in his selfish frenzy, is prepared to leave others to their fate, whether on a wrecked ship or a barren island? So he turned to Elsie again.

"By the way, you have never seen those letters," he said. "I was hunting for them when the alarm was raised last night. Shall I bring them now?"

Elsie gave him a glance of subtle meaning. Her eyes telegraphed "What matters it whether I see them to-day or in half a century? Do I not trust you?" But she only murmured:

"Not now, I am telling Mrs. Somerville and Isobel all the news."

He squeezed her shoulder. Any excuse would serve for those slight pettings which mean so much during early days in wonderland.

"Then I shall resume my rounds. I expect to be received reproachfully by Walker. He made great progress yesterday. Let me whisper a secret. Then you may pass it on, in strictest confidence."

He placed his lips close to her ear.

"I am dreadfully in love with you this morning," he breathed.

"That is no secret," she retorted.

"It is. You and I together must daily find new paths in Eden. But my less poetic tidings should be welcome, also. Walker says he hopes to get steam up to-morrow."

"Well, tell us quickly," cried Isobel, with a show of intense interest, when Courtenay had gone. She had decided on a line of conduct, and meant to follow it carefully. The more sympathy she extended towards her friend's love idyll, the less likelihood was there of disagreeable developments in other respects. That trick of calculating gush was Isobel's chief failing. She was so wrapped up in self that her own interests governed every thought. Courtenay's reference to letters sent a wave of alarm pulsing through each nerve. Though his manner betokened that the affair was something which concerned Elsie alone, she was on fire until she learnt that his "secret" alluded to the restored vitality of the ship.

For once, her expressions of gratitude were heartfelt. Mrs. Somerville even wept for joy. This poor woman after living twenty-five years in the oasis of a mission-house, was a strange subject for storm-tossed wandering and fights with cannibals. Seldom has fate conspired with the fickle sea to sport with such helpless human flotsam, save, perhaps, in that crowning caprice of the waves which once cast ashore a live baby in a cradle.

But the baby's emotions were crude, and probably in no wise connected with the tremors of ship-wreck, whereas Mrs. Somerville, during these full days, was constantly asking herself how it could be possible that she was living at all.

"It will be a real manifestation of Providence if we ever reach England again," she cried, dabbing her eyes with a handkerchief. "I'm sure John and I have said so many a time during the past week. To think of the ship's blowing up in the way she did, it makes me all of a tremble, it does."

"Oh," broke in Elsie, thinking that the information she possessed would help to calm the older woman, "we have made a good many discoveries since--since the boat went away without me, I mean. But do tell me, how did those horrid Chileans manage to cast off the tackle before Mr. Gray or some of the other men were able to stop them? Of course, it is matterless now, in a sense, but at that moment it looked like leaving those on the ship to certain death."

Mrs. Somerville was stricken dumb. The American's shooting of two men on White Horse Island had naturally called for a complete explanation on his part, and she did not know how to answer Elsie's question. Before she could gather her wits, Isobel intervened.

"If you had been in that boat, dear," she said sweetly, "you would realize the topsy-turvy condition of our brains. Even Mr. Gray himself, the coolest man on board, imagined we might sink any moment. So what can you expect of those excitable Chileans? Besides, the thing was done so quickly that we were swept away by the tide before any one fully understood what was happening. Anyhow, you had the best of it, as events transpired. What are the discoveries you spoke of?"

"Well, some one placed dynamite among the coal."

"But who would do such a thing?"

"That is hard to say. The captain believes that the culprit will be found out through the insurance policies. He and the others were discussing the affair one day in the chart-house--soon after the dynamite cartridges were discovered--and you cannot tell how surprised I was to hear him mention Ventana's name in connection with it."

"Ventana's name!"

The blood ebbed away from Isobel's cheeks, leaving her pallid as a statue. There was a gasp in her voice which startled her own ears. Lest her agitation should be noted too keenly, she bent forward and propped her face on her clenched hands, staring fixedly at the distant cliffs in a supreme effort to appear apathetic. Elsie heard that dry sob, but her friend's seeming indifference misled her.

"Yes," she said, wondering a little whether or not Christobal's veiled hint regarding a by-gone tenderness between the two might account for Isobel's hysterical outburst on the night of the ship's break-down. Indeed, so warm-hearted was she that she hesitated a moment before continuing; but she felt that it would be altogether better for Isobel to be prepared for the revelations which the successful end of the ship's voyage would assuredly bring forth. So, pondering unspoken thoughts the while, she told the others exactly what Tollemache, Christobal and Courtenay had said, and even revealed to them that which Courtenay himself did not yet know.

"You remember the poor fellow who got into trouble soon after we sailed from Valparaiso?" she said. "His name is Frascuelo. He was wounded again in last night's fight, but not seriously, and he and I are quite chums. He assures me that he was drugged by a man named Jose Anacleto, who took his place among the coal-trimmers--"

"Oh, Miss Maxwell, come quick!" screamed Mrs. Somerville, for Isobel had lurched sideways out of her chair in a fainting fit, and the missionary's wife was barely able to save her head from striking the ship's rails.

Joey was shot out of Elsie's lap with such surprising speed that he trotted away without any exhibition of lameness. He was quite disgusted, for at least five minutes, but it is reasonable to suppose that a dog of his intelligence would brighten up when he heard the wholly unlooked-for story which Christobal was translating to Courtenay, word for word, as it was dragged hesitatingly out of Suarez.

The Argentine miner had been badly injured during the struggle for possession of the promenade deck. Owing to loss of consciousness, supplemented by an awkward fall, he might have choked to death had he not been rescued within a few minutes. He was very ill all night, and it was not until midday that he recovered sufficient strength to enable him to question the Indians on board.

Courtenay wished specially to find out what chance, if any, there was of the Alaculof attack being renewed. When Christobal assured him that Suarez might safely leave his bunk, he asked the doctor to bring the Spaniard to the fore-cabin, in which the wounded savages lay under an armed guard.

It was obvious that some of the maimed wretches recognized Suarez, notwithstanding his changed appearance, the instant he spoke to them. At once they broke out into an excited chattering, and Suarez was so disconcerted by the tidings they conveyed that he stammered a good deal, and seemed to flounder in giving the Spanish rendering.

"This fellow is telling us just as much as he thinks it is good for us to know," said Courtenay, sternly, when the interpreter avoided his accusing gaze. "Bid him out with the whole truth, Christobal, or it shall be his pleasing task to escort his dear friends back to their family circles."

Being detected, Suarez faltered no longer. A ship's life-boat had been driven ashore lower down the coast. Fourteen men had landed; they were captured by the Indians, after a useless resistance, in which three were killed. The dead men supplied a ghoulish feast next day, and the others were bound securely, and placed in a cave, in order to be killed at intervals, an exact parallel to the fate of Suarez's own companions five years earlier.

But, on this occasion, a woman intervened. Suarez confessed, very reluctantly, that there was a girl in the tribe to whom he had taught some words of his own language. He said that she cooked for him, and caught fish or gathered shell-fish for their joint needs when the larder was otherwise empty. He declared that the relations between them were those of master and servant, but the poor creature had fallen in love with him, and had become nearly frantic with grief when he disappeared. It was difficult to analyze her motives, but she had undoubtedly freed the eleven sailors, and led them over the rocks at low water to the haunted cave on Guanaco Hill. The Indians dared not follow; but they took good care that no canoes were obtainable in which the unhappy fugitives could reach the ship, and they were confident that hunger would soon drive them forth.

Courtenay's brow became black with anger when he understood the significance of this staggering story.

"It comes to this," he said to Christobal. "The men who got away from the *Kansas* in No. 3 life-boat fell into the hands of the savages early on the day of the ship's arrival here. Suarez slipped his cable that night, being aware at the time that eleven white captives were still alive. Yet he said no word, not even when he heard that we had seen one of the boat's water-casks in a canoe. He, a Christian, bolted and remained silent, while some poor creature of a woman risked her life, and ran counter to all her natural instincts, in the endeavor to save the men of his own race. What sort of mean hound can he be?"

Suarez needed no translation to grasp the purport of Courtenay's words. He besought the senor captain to have patience with him. He had escaped from a living tomb, and felt that he would yield up his life rather than return. Therefore, when he saw how few in number and badly armed were they on board the ship, he thought it best to remain silent as to the fate of the boat's crew. In the first place, he fully expected that they had been killed by the Indians, who would be enraged by his own disappearance. Secondly, he alone knew how hopeless any attempt at a rescue must prove. Finally, he wished to spare the feelings of those who had befriended him; of what avail were useless mind-torturings regarding the hapless beings in the hands of the savages?

There was a certain plausibleness in this reasoning which curbed Courtenay's wrath, though it in no way diminished the disgust which filled his soul. What quality was there lacking in the Latin races which rendered them so untrustworthy? His crew had mutinied, de Poincilit was ready to consign his companions in misfortune to a most frightful death on the barren island, and here was Suarez hugging to his breast a ghastly secret which chance alone had brought to light. He strove hard to repress the contempt which rose in his gorge, as it was essential that the broken-spirited miner should not be frightened out of his new-born candor.

"Ask him to ascertain if the Indians believe the white men are still living?" he said. A fresh series of grunts and clicks elicited the fact that the smoke-column seen the previous day on Guanaco Hill had not been created by the tribe. Suarez begged the senor captain to remember that he had spoken truly when he declared that its meaning was unknown to him. Probably, from what he now learnt, the girl who threw in her lot with the sailors had built a fire there.

Courtenay turned on his heel and quitted the cabin. The smell of the Indians was loathsome, the mere sight of Suarez offensive. For this discovery had overcast the happiness of his wooing as a thunder-cloud darkens and blots the smiling life out of a fair valley. There rushed in on him a hundred chilling thoughts, each gloomier than its forerunner. Ravens croaked within him; misshapen imps whispered evil omens; his spirit sat in gloom.

Christobal, well knowing how the demons of doubt and despair were afflicting Courtenay, followed him to the upper deck. Boyle was in the chart-house and

Tollemache. Each man noted the captain's troubled face; from him they glanced towards the doctor; but the Spaniard had undergone his purgatory some hours earlier; his thin features were now quite expressionless.

Courtenay obtained a telescope. With the tact which never failed him, even in such a desperate crisis as this, he handed the doctor his binoculars. Then, both men looked at the summit of Guanaco Hill. Though it was high noon, and the landscape was shimmering in the heat-mist created by the unusual power and brilliance of the sun, they distinctly saw a thin pillar of smoke rising above the trees. Courtenay closed his telescope. He made to approach Boyle, evidently for the purpose of giving some order, when Christobal said quietly:

"Wait! I have something to say to you. You ought to remain on the ship. Let *me* go!"

"You?"

"Yes, I. After all, it is only a matter of taking command. One man cannot go alone. He could not even pull the life-boat so far. Hence, what you can do I can do, and I have no objection to dying in that way."

"Why should either of us die?"

"You know better than I how little chance there is of saving those men. You may deem me callous if I suggest that the reasonable thing would be to forget the miserable statement you have just heard. Oh, please hear me to the end. I am not talking for your sole benefit, believe me. Greatly as I and all on board are beholden to you, I do not propose giving my life in your stead because of my abounding admiration for your many virtues. Well, then since you are so impatient as to be almost rude, I come straight to the point. If you take command of a boat's crew and endeavor to save the men imprisoned over there, you will almost certainly throw away your life and the lives of those who help you. In that event, a lady in whom we are both interested will suffer grievously. On the other hand, if I were killed, she would weep a little, because she has a large heart, but you would console her. And the odd thing is that you and I are fully aware that either you or I must go off on this fool's errand. There is none other to take the vacant place. Now, have I made myself clear?"

"You are a good fellow, Christobal. You revive my faith in human nature, and that is my best apology if I irritated you just now by my attitude. But don't you see that I can neither accept your generous offer nor sail away from our harbor of refuge without making an attempt to save my men?"

"They are not your men. They forfeited your captaincy by their own action. In the effort to succor them you will lose at least one life which is precious to all on board this ship. I am twice your age, Courtenay, and I affirm unhesitatingly that you are wrong."

"Yet you are ready to take my place?"

"I have given you my reasons."

"They do you honor; but you would fail where I might succeed. You are not a sailor. Brave as I know you to be, you are not physically fitted for the rough work which may be needed. I think, too, you exaggerate the risk. The Alaculofs are broken by last night's failure. They will not dare to face us."

"At least spare me an argument which does not convince yourself; otherwise you would depute me instantly for the service."

"Well, you force plain speaking. While I command the *Kansas* I am responsible for the well-being of the ship, her crew, and her passengers. I could never forgive myself if I left those men to the mercy of the Indians. I cannot permit either you or Tollemache to take a risk which I shirk. Boyle and Walker must remain on board--lest I fail. Now, Christobal, don't make my duty harder. Shake hands! I am proud to claim you as a friend."

"Huh!" said Boyle, strolling towards them. "What is it? A bet?"

"Yes," laughed Courtenay, from whose face all doubt had vanished; "a bet, indeed, and you hold the stakes. Have you seen the smoke signal yonder?" and he pointed across the bay.

"Yes. Tollemache found it again, twenty minutes since."

"It means that eleven of our men are there, expecting us to save them. Hoist the ship's answering pennant from the main yard swung out to starboard. Build a small fire on the poop and throw some oil and lampblack on it. If they don't recognize the pennant they will understand the smoke. Get some food and water stowed in the life-boat, and offer five pounds a head to six men who will volunteer for a trip ashore."

"I go in charge, of course, sir?" said Boyle.

"You remain here, and take command during my absence. I want two revolvers for a couple of the crew, and I shall take my own gun. Please make all arrangements promptly. I am going to my cabin for five minutes, and shall start immediately afterwards."

This was the captain speaking. His tone admitted of no contention. Boyle hurried off, and Courtenay went into his quarters.

"What do you think of it?" Christobal asked Tollemache, as the latter appeared to be sauntering after the chief officer.

"Rot!" said Tollemache.

"But what can we do? He is committing suicide."

"One must do that occasionally. It's rotten, but it can't be helped."

Christobal threw out his hands in a despairing gesture. "I tried to stop him, but I failed," he cried.

"Courtenay is a hard man to stop," said Tollemache, vanishing down the companion. The Spaniard was left alone on the bridge. He paced to and fro, deep in thought. He scarce dared probe his own communings. So complex were they, such a queer amalgam of noble fear and base expectation, that he could have cried aloud in his anguish. Big drops of perspiration stood on his forehead when Courtenay came to him.

"For God's sake, don't go," said he hoarsely. "Do you know you are placing me on the rack?"

"Your sufferings are of your own contriving, then. Why, man, there is no reason for all this agony. I have written to Elsie, briefly explaining matters. Here is the letter. Give it to her, if I don't return. And now, pull yourself together. I want you to cheer her. Above all things, don't let her know I am leaving the ship. I'll just swing myself overboard at the last moment. I can't say good-by. I don't think I could stand that."

CHAPTER XVII
A MAN'S METHOD--AND A WOMAN'S

Isobel's drooping was of brief endurance. Elsie and Mrs. Somerville supported her to the stateroom, and there Elsie sat with her a little while, soothing her as one might comfort a child in pain. Once it seemed that the stricken girl was on the point of confiding in her friend, but the imminent words died away in a passion of tears. Elsie besought her to rest, and strove to calm her with predictions of the joyous days they would pass together when the stress and terror of their present life should be a tale that is told.

Isobel, stupefied by some haunting knowledge which appeared to have a vague connection with the misfortunes of the *Kansas*, yielded to Elsie's gentle compulsion, and endeavored to close her eyes. All was quiet in the cabin, save for the sufferer's labored breathing, and an occasional sob, while her wondering nurse smoothed her luxuriant hair, and whispered those meaningless little phrases which have such magic influence on the distracted nerves of woman-kind. There was hardly a sound on the ship, beyond an unexplained creaking of pulleys, which soon ceased.

Mrs. Somerville had gone, in response to Elsie's mute appeal. Somehow, from a piecing together of hints and half phrases, the girl feared a painful disclosure as the outcome of Isobel's hysteria. She was glad it had been averted. If there were hidden scandals in her friend's life in Chile, she prayed they might remain at rest. She had not forgotten Christobal's guarded words. He probably knew far more than he chose to tell of the "summer hotel attachment" between Isobel and Ventana at which he had hinted. But, even crediting that passing folly with a serious aspect, why should the daughter of the richest merchant in Valparaiso fall prostrate at the mere mention of the name of a disreputable loafer like Jose the Winebag? To state the fact was to refute it. Elsie dismissed the idea as preposterous. It was clear enough that Isobel's break-down arose from some other cause; perhaps the relaxed tension of existence on board the *Kansas*, after the hardships borne on the island, supplied a simple explanation.

Through the open port she heard a man walk rapidly along the deck, and halt outside the door. She half rose from her knees to answer the expected knock, thinking that Mrs. Somerville had sent a steward to ascertain if Miss Baring needed anything. But the newcomer evidently changed his mind, and turned back. Then came Courtenay's voice, low but compelling:

"One moment, M'sieu' de Poincilit. A word with you."

The French Count! During the whirl of the previous night, and by reason of the abiding joy of her morning's reverie, she had failed to miss the dapper Frenchman. Once, indeed, she had mentioned him to Isobel, who offered a brief surmise that he might be ill, and keeping to his cabin. Yet, here he was on deck, and possibly on the point of seeking an interview with the lady to whom he had paid such close attention during the early days of the voyage. Perhaps Mrs. Somerville had told him of the fainting fit, and he was about to make a friendly inquiry when the captain accosted him. But Elsie's ears, tuned to fine precision where her lover's utterances were concerned, had caught the note of contemptuous command, and she was even more surprised by the Count's flurried answer in French:

"Another time, M'sieu'. I pray you pardon me now. I find I am not strong enough yet to venture on deck."

"Oh yes, you are, M'sieu'. I want to give you the chance of your life. Mr. Gray has told me of your behavior, and he charitably added that your cowardice and treachery might have arisen from ungovernable fear. Now, if you wish to atone for your conduct, here is an opportunity. I am taking a boat ashore to try to save some of my men who are imprisoned there. There is a fair risk in the venture. The outcome may be death. Will you volunteer to take an oar? That would whitewash your weather-marks."

"It is impossible. I am too feeble. I cannot row."

"Ah, you swine! Can it be possible that you are a Frenchman? What sort of countship is it you boast of?"

"Sir, I am a passenger on this ship--"

Courtenay's voice was raised a little.

"Mr. Boyle," he said, "give orders that if this skunk shows his nose inside the saloon again he is to be kicked out. He can eat his meals in his stateroom, or in the forecabin with the other savages."

Elsie heard every word. She fancied, too, that Isobel was listening, though she gave no sign. But the unknown cause of the captain's anger was as naught compared with the statement that he was about to leave the ship. That stabbed her with a nameless fear. "Love looks not with the eyes, but with the mind;" she saw her idyl destroyed, her sweet dreaming roused into cruel reality. Her understanding heart told her that Courtenay meant to go without bidding her farewell. She had heard the lowering of the boat without heeding; he was already climbing down the ship's side. Soon he would be far from her, perhaps never to return. For he was not one to paint imaginary ills, and had he not told de Poincilit what the outcome of the undertaking might be? Was it his wish that she should remain in seeming ignorance of his mission until it was too late for a parting word? Did he dread the ordeal of telling her his errand? Even he, so strong and resolute, who had so often smiled grim death out of countenance, feared the kiss which might wean him from the narrow way. And she must prove herself worthy of him. She must suffer in silence, trusting the All-powerful to bring him back to her arms.

And then she found Isobel looking at her with frightened eyes.

"Did you hear?" came the tense whisper.

"Yes."

"And you are content to let him go?"

"Ah, God! Yes, content."

"But it is folly. He is the captain. He should not go. We have risked enough already. Who are these men for whose sake he leaves you, and all of us?"

"I know not, nor do I greatly care, may Heaven help me and them."

"Then you should appeal to him to abandon this mad undertaking. It is not fair to you. It is more than unfair to those who have entrusted their lives to his keeping."

Isobel would have risen in her excitement, had not Elsie leaped to her feet.

"Oh, Isobel," she cried, all a-quiver with disdain, "can you not for once conquer the self that is destroying your very soul? Neither by word nor act shall you interfere between Arthur Courtenay and his duty. Would you have him cling ignobly to life like that poor dandy whom he has sent to herd with savages? Be sure he has not forgotten those who are beholden to him. We are his first care. Let it be mine to leave him unhindered in the task he has undertaken!"

Isobel was cowed into silence. Elsie's hero-worship had reached a height beyond her comprehension. She would never understand how a woman who loved a man could send him voluntarily to his death, and her shallow mind did not contemplate the possibility of Courtenay's refusing to be swayed by any other consideration than that which his conscience told him was right.

Thus, at arm's length as it were, they waited until they caught the sharp command "Give way there!" and the plash of oars told them that the boat had really started on its journey shorewards. Then Isobel, glancing furtively at her companion, saw the tears stealing down her cheeks, and the situation came back from the transcendental to that which was intelligible to her lower ideals.

"I am sorry," she whispered, catching Elsie's hand timidly. "I said what I thought was for the best. At any rate, it is too late now."

Too late! The other girl groped blindly for the door. She felt that she would yield to the strain if she did not go on deck and catch a parting glimpse of the man who had become dearer to her than life itself. As she made her way forward, Joey ran to meet her. He was whining anxiously. He seemed to be demanding that sympathy which she alone could give him. In his half-human way, he was asking:

"Why has my master gone away in that boat? And why did he not take me with him? When my master goes ashore he never leaves me on board; what is the reason of to-day's exception?"

On the poop she found Boyle, Christobal, Gray and Walker. A number of Chileans were leaning over the rails of the main deck. All the men were talking earnestly. It was ominous that they should cease their conversation the instant she appeared. One man may conceal his fears, but twenty cannot. Their studied unconcern, their covert glances under lowered eye-lids, told her that they believed the occupants of the life-boat were in gravest peril.

She brushed away the tears determinedly, and looked at the boat, already a white speck on the green carpet of the bay. She could see Courtenay distinctly; some magnetic impulse must have gone out from her, because she had not been watching him longer than a couple of seconds when he turned and waved his hand. She replied instantly, fluttering a handkerchief, poor girl, long after it became impossible for her to distinguish whether or not he returned her signals. In the calm glory of the sunlit estuary, he might have been bent on a pleasant picnic. It was outrageous to think of Good Hope Inlet as a place of skulls; yet she knew that the sea floor beneath the ship was already littered with bodies of the dead. Women would wait in vain for their men to return; why should she be spared?

At last she appealed to Mr. Boyle, who was nearest to her.

"Who is sitting next to Captain Courtenay?" she asked, and she had a fleeting impression that he was anxious for her to speak, so quickly did he answer.

"Tollemache. He shinned down the ladder as the first volunteer; the skipper ordered him to get out, but he said he was deaf. Anyhow, I'm glad he is there. Courtenay ought to have one sure enough white man by his side."

"And what are they attempting?"

"Huh, it's a bold plan, an' I'm not goin' to condemn it on that account. Have you heard this morning's news--how Suarez found out from the Indians that eleven of our crew are hiding in a cave on Guanaco Hill?"

"Something of it, not all. But why--why has Captain Courtenay gone off in such a hurry?"

"Well, Miss Elsie, he figures that an open effort by daylight is the only way to rescue them. They will have seen our signals, and they can hardly fail to sight the boat. When he is close inshore they are sure to make a dash for it, and he hopes to get them off before the Indians wake up to the game he is playing. There are eight men in the boat, and, with eleven others to help, there shouldn't be much difficulty in keepin' the savages at a proper distance."

"How soon--will he--reach the landing-place?"

"Huh, mebbe an hour; an' another hour for the home trip. He'll be aboard for tea."

Boyle uttered that concluding statement a trifle too airily. Elsie, for the first time in her life, knew what it meant to want to scream aloud.

The dog was dancing about excitedly, and whining without cease. She stooped and took him up in her arms.

"Please, Joey, be quiet," she murmured, her voice breaking with a stifled sob.

She turned again to Mr. Boyle, who sedulously avoided her eyes.

"Did Captain Courtenay leave any message for me?" she demanded.

"Huh! Message! Why, he will be away only a couple of hours."

The chief officer's tone was gruff, conveying the idea that women asked silly questions, but his gruffness did not hoodwink Elsie. He had prepared his replies beforehand.

"Surely you will tell me, Mr. Boyle?" she pleaded wistfully.

"Well, I happen to know there's a letter in the doctor's hands. But that is to be given to you in case of accident alone. Isn't that so, doctor? And there's no sign of any accident yet, thank goodness!"

Boyle sighed, like a man who lays down a heavy load. He had successfully engineered Christobal into the conversation.

The Spaniard drew near. He had heard all that had passed, and tried a new line.

"I was rather hoping that you would not put that awkward query," he said, more alive than the sailor to the wisdom of discussing the very topic which offered so many thorns. "Of course, none of us, least of all Courtenay himself, disguises the difficulties which confront him. We have not fought the Alaculofs in two serious battles without learning their tenacity of purpose, and the mere fact that the men hidden in that cleft are compelled to remain invisible shows that they are beleaguered. But the last thing the Indians will expect is the appearance of a boat-load of armed men at this hour, and to take the enemy unawares is the essence of good generalship."

"When am I to have my letter?" she persisted, clinging tenaciously to one clear thought amid the phantasms which thronged her dazed mind.

"Oh, come, now! That is not the hopeless view I want you to take. In writing to you, Courtenay was only providing against a mishap. He would not go to certain death. He has too high a sense of what is due to his position as captain of a ship like the **Kansas**, loaded with a valuable cargo and carrying so many lives. Nor does Tollemache impress me as a would-be suicide. Both men think they will succeed, and they had not any trouble in obtaining a boat's crew of Chileans. So you see, there is a general belief in success, not failure."

She felt that the doctor was talking against time. He had instructions not to give her that letter until there could be no doubt of the fate which had befallen the rescuers. A mist came over her eyes, but she bit her lower lip fiercely, and the white teeth left their deep impress. The dog squirmed uneasily in her arms, and endeavored to lick her face. Joey's anxiety rivaled her own; had he, too, a premonition of evil?

Christobal was watching her intently. It was evident he feared the outcome of any sudden overthrow of her self-control.

"I think," he suggested, with a real sympathy in his voice, "that it would be better if you went to the saloon, or your cabin. Believe me, I shall come to you with every scrap of news. Boyle will see all that happens and we shall know the best, or the worst, within an hour."

"If you would help me," she answered dully, "please take the dog away. He is tearing my heart-strings. Poor little fellow, he makes no pretence."

So Joey was fastened up, much against his will, and his piteous protests no longer added to the girl's agony. She clung to the after rail, and watched the boat, now a tiny dot hard to discern amidst the ripples caused by the inflowing tide. Her intimate acquaintance with the daily happenings of life aboard told her that Courtenay had chosen the last hour of flood for his effort, thus gaining the advantage of the ebb in the event of the life-boat's being pursued by canoes on the return journey. By degrees, a tender little sprig of hope peeped up in her dulled consciousness. The boat was very near the distant rocks, and there was neither sight nor sound of the Indians. Could it be that they were afraid--altogether broken and demoralized by the slaughter of the preceding night? How quickly the acts of this drama shifted their scenes! Sixteen hours ago, she and Christobal were actually participating in the defense of the ship's last stronghold; now, the broad decks resembled the inner spaces of some impregnable fort, while the war was being carried into the enemy's territory. Yet the mortal peril which overshadowed them was threatening as ever. Life seemed to be doled out grudgingly, by minutes.

Suddenly she had a breathless desire to know why Courtenay was so sure that the men to whose help he had gone were really members of the crew. Christobal, dreading her despairing questions, was standing in the position he had occupied before Boyle dragged him into prominence. The chief officer was bracing a telescope against the ensign staff, and keeping the lifeboat in a full field. Gray, she noticed, was not looking towards Guanaco Hill, but swept all parts of the coastline constantly with his binoculars. The Spaniard's field-glasses were slung around his neck. He was not using them. He appeared to be deep in thought. More often than not, his glance rested on the eddy created by the swirl of the current past the ship's quarter. With a species of divination, she guessed somewhat the nature of his reverie. The notion stung her into a sort of fury. To quell it, she must speak again.

"Will you tell me now what it was that Suarez found out?" she murmured.

The doctor quickly appreciated her need of material for further thought. She wanted to appraise at their true value all things affecting that daring enterprise, bringing the evidence to the bar of her hopes, and nerving herself to hear the crudest testimony as to its dangers. He was glad to be able to beguile the next half hour with his recital. He suppressed no detail except his own willingness to take Courtenay's place in the boat. Notwithstanding his slight affectations, he was a man of finely-tempered judgment. He saw now that Courtenay could not have accepted his offer, nor was it likely that the men in the boat would follow any other leader than the captain. He even smarted a little at the knowledge. A super-sensitive honor led him to fear that his successful rival might suspect him of vaingloriousness. Herein Christobal did himself an injustice, and Courtenay a greater one, as he was fated soon to learn.

When Elsie heard of the duplicity practised by Suarez it was good to see the hot indignation which reddened her brow. She realized that the man was unscrupulous enough to remain silent concerning the captured sailors, whose unhappy fate had contributed, in no small degree, to the chance which brought him to safety. She instantly fastened on to the theory that the Indians paid their first nocturnal visit to the ship in the belief that the vessel would prove as easy a prey as the castaways, whereas Suarez must have fallen beneath their stones and rude hatchets if he had attempted to board the **Kansas** in broad daylight. With all a woman's single-mindedness, she regarded the Argentine miner as being directly responsible for Courtenay's hazard, nor would she listen to Christobal's mild protest that nothing could have been done earlier, no matter how outspoken Suarez chose to be.

The Spaniard encouraged her to debate this point--anything was better than the dumb pain of thought--but their talk ceased abruptly when a muttered exclamation from Gray sent Walker flying to the charthouse. Forthwith the trumpet shriek of the siren sent its wild boom across the silent waters. Elsie needed no ex-

planation of this tumult. Otter Creek was not so far distant that canoes quitting its
shelter could not be seen with the naked eye. She counted sixteen putting forth in
a cluster, and they all made for the adventurous life-boat.

"That is exactly what our captain expected," Christobal was ready to assure her.
"He was certain he would reach the head of the bay before the Indians awoke to the
meaning of his scheme. By this time, unless his plan fails, the men on shore should
have joined him, no matter what number of savages may seek to oppose their passage to the boat. The only doubtful question is-- Will he be able to beat off the
rascals who are now cutting his line of retreat?"

"Huh!" growled Boyle, "the skipper's out of sight now. Gone into a small creek
or something of the sort. Hope he heard the horn. Let her rip!" he added in a
loud shout over his shoulder, and again the siren flung a warning to the foot of the
mountain range.

It was evident that the wonderful eyesight of the Indians practically equalled
the range of the telescope. The men in the canoes were aware of the lifeboat's disappearance, and their wet paddles flashed in the sun as they tore across the three
miles of open water which separated the southern promontory from the inner shore
of the island. After a phenomenal spell of fine weather in that storm-swept latitude,
the atmosphere was transparent and bright as that of Stornoway on a clear day in
December. The rays of the sun were reflected from many a blue glacier and ice-
covered slope. Even the green of the higher belt of firs was dazzling in its emerald
luster, and the copper-hued beeches beneath shone in patches of burnished gold.
Elsie was sick at heart with the knowledge that red-eyed murder was stalking its
prey under the resplendent mantle spread by nature over a scene of rare beauty. In
an agony of apprehension she followed the progress of the canoes. Creeping nearer
Boyle, she whispered:

"For Heaven's sake, say the life-boat is visible again!"

He held up a hand to enforce silence. A deep hush fell on the ship.

"Listen!" he muttered, so low that Elsie alone caught the words. "Can you hear
firing?"

She thought she could distinguish an irregular patter of dull reports, and the
behavior of the Indians showed that additional excitement was toward. Many of
them stood up and waved their arms, possibly as a signal to their allies on shore.

The canoes raced madly. Where speed was vital the rough-hewn native craft were far swifter than the solidly-built lifeboat, with its broad beam and deep draft.

And that was all. Though they strained their eyes and spoke with bated breath, never a sight of boat or canoes was obtainable for hours after the latter were swallowed up by the trees which shrouded the creek at the foot of Guanaco Hill.

Isobel Baring, moved by genuine pity for her distraught friend, tried to induce her to leave the deck. But she shrank away, terrified by the fire which blazed from the blue eyes resting on her for an instant. Mrs. Somerville came, but she, too, was repulsed. Elsie spoke no word. She hardly moved. She clung to the rail, and gazed at the deepening shadows with the frozen stare of abiding horror. All things around her were unreal, fantastic; she dwelt in a world peopled by her own terrible imaginings. The smiling landscape was alive with writhing shapes. She fancied it a monstrous jungle full of serpents and grotesquely human beasts. The inert mass of the *Kansas*, so modern, so perfectly appointed in its contours and appurtenances, crushed her by its immense helplessness. The dominant idea in her mind was one of voiceless rage against the ship and its occupants. Why should her lover, who had saved their lives--who had plucked the eight thousand tons of steel fabric from the sharp-toothed rocks time and again--why should he be lying dead, disfigured by savage spite, while those to whom he had rendered such devoted service were coolly discussing his fate and speculating on their own good fortune? That thought maddened her. Her very brain seemed to burn with the unfairness of it all. When Christobal made a serious effort to lead her away, she threatened him with the fierceness of a mother defending her child from evil.

But relief was vouchsafed in the worst throes of her agony. It was some poor consolation to let her sorrow-laden eyes rest on the far-off trees which enshrouded him. What would befall her when night came, and the ship drew back out of the living world into the narrow gloom of deck and gangway, she could not know. She felt that her labored heart would refuse to bear its pangs any longer. If death came, that would be sweet. Her only hope lay in the life beyond the grave. . . . And what a grave! For her, the restless tides. For him! Surely her mind would yield to this increasing madness.

Boyle or Gray had never relaxed their vigil by her side. It was Gray who made the thrilling discovery that the canoes were returning. As the fleet crossed the bay it could be seen that they were towing the life-boat. But never a sign of any prisoners could the most careful scrutiny detect. The boat was empty; it was easy to count every man in the canoes as they passed into Otter Creek. And there were wounded Indians on board many of them. That was a significant, a tremendous, fact. There had been hard fighting, and the boat was captured, but some, if not all, of the crew must have joined their comrades in the sanctuary of the haunted cave. The accuracy of this deduction was proved by the presence of the smoke column on the hill. Indeed, the opinion was generally held that its spiral clouds were denser than at any previous hour, thus showing that the defenders were endeavoring to make known their continued existence.

Elsie awoke from her trance, but, in returning to life, she was transformed into a stern, resourceful, commanding woman. Her face had lost its gentleness; the pleasant curves and dimples of mouth and chin had hardened into a sort of determination; even her slight, graceful figure seemed to assume a certain squareness which betokened her resolve to act as her lover would have acted were he the watcher from the ship and she the prisoner pent behind that screen of rock and wild forest.

None suspected the mighty force which worked this resolution in her nature. She conducted herself with a cunning that was wholly foreign to her character. Her first care was to hoodwink her companions into the belief that the strain of the day had passed. She accepted a cup of tea brought by Isobel, expressed her sorrow that if by word or look she had given cause for offence, and entered eagerly into the pros and cons of the debate which sprang up as to the best course to pursue on the following day.

Everyone agreed that nothing could be done that night. If the pillar of smoke were visible at sunrise, and Walker could possibly manage to fire the boilers, Boyle suggested that some sailors in the jolly-boat should sound a channel along which the vessel itself might steam slowly towards Guanaco Hill. That, in itself, would be a move of considerable value. If they could lessen the distance between the shore and the ship, each yard thus gained would help the prisoners and impose a stronger barrier against the Alaculofs, who would probably be daunted when they found that the vessel's mobility was restored.

This proposal was deemed so excellent that they all dined in vastly better spirits than any of them anticipated. Christobal, puzzled out of his scientific senses by

Elsie's change of manner, kept a close eye on her. He was amazed to see her eat a better meal than she had eaten for days, and she was normally a quite healthy young person, with a reasonably good appetite.

Boyle and Gray took the first watch, from eight o'clock to midnight. Christobal and Walker shared the next one; by four o'clock it would be daylight, so the doctor was retiring early to his cabin when he met Elsie, by chance as it seemed. She was self-possessed, even smiling, with a certain dour serenity.

"The day's doings have tired me," she said. "I am off to bed. Will you rap on my door soon after dawn?"

"Yes," he replied, secretly marveling at her air.

"I plead guilty to a slight feeling of nervousness," she went on. "Is your revolver loaded? Would you mind lending it to me? I think I could sleep more soundly if I had a reliable weapon tucked under my pillow."

A whiff of suspicion crossed Christobal's mind, but he brushed it aside as unworthy. At five o'clock that day he certainly would not have granted her request. But now, since the new hope had sprung up that Courtenay was alive, it was absurd to doubt her motives.

So it came to pass that Diego Suarez, lying asleep in his bunk, awoke with a start to find a shrouded figure bending over him.

"Is that you, Senor Suarez?" asked a voice, which he recognized instantly as belonging to the Senorita Maxwell.

"Yes," said he, drowsily.

"Have you the witch-doctor's clothes you wore when you came on board the ship?"

"But yes, senorita."

A hand, slight but strong, grasped him by the shoulder. He felt the rim of a revolver barrel pressed against his forehead.

"Get up, then! Dress quickly in those clothes, and come out on deck. By the side of your bunk you will find tins of black and white paint to smear your face and hands. At the slightest refusal on your part to do as I bid you--if you utter a cry or make any noise to attract attention--I shall kill you without another word."

The soft voice had a steely ring in it which persuaded the man from Argentina that he had better obey. In less than five minutes he emerged from the doorway.

The corridor in which his cabin was situated led into the saloon. Elsie awaited him. A lamp, dimly lighting the gangway, revealed her face. Suarez thought he had to deal with a mad-woman. The dog, standing by her side, sniffed at him gingerly, but a muttered "Be quiet, Joey!" prevented any outburst, every fox-terrier being a born conspirator.

"What do you wish me to do, senorita?" began Suarez, thinking to placate her until he could obtain assistance.

"You must obey me in silence," she whispered tensely. "You must not even speak. One syllable aloud on deck will mean your death. Walk in front of me, up the main companion, and go straight to the ship's side."

"But, senorita!--"

The hammer of the revolver began to rise under the pressure of Elsie's finger on the trigger. The man's hair rose even more rapidly. His nerve was broken. He turned along the corridor in front of her, not knowing the instant a bullet might crash into his head. The girl followed so closely that she almost touched his heels. The dog would have trotted in front, but she recalled him.

When Suarez reached the port rail of the promenade deck, Elsie breathed:

"Climb, quickly, and go down into the canoe by the rope ladder you will find there."

"The canoe!" gasped he.

"Quick! One, two,--"

Up went Suarez over the rail. He found the top-most rungs of the ladder. As he descended, the revolver followed his eyes. When his head was level with the deck the order came:

"Take the dog and go down."

"I cannot, senorita."

"You must try. You are going down, dead or alive."

He did try. Joey scuffled a little, but Suarez caught him by the neck, and made shift to descend. Elsie was already on the swaying ladder when Boyle's voice rang out sharply from the spar-deck:

"Below there! Who is there?"

"I, Mr. Boyle," she answered.

"You, Miss Elsie? Where are you?"

"Here; not so far away."

She was descending all the time. She had cast loose the rope which fastened the canoe alongside, and her difficulty was to hold the ladder and at the same time, by clinging to the mast, to prevent the canoe from slipping away with the tide. The revolver she gripped between her teeth by the butt.

Boyle, puzzled by the sound of her voice, ran from the side of the bridge down the stairs and across the deck. He was a second too late to grasp the top of the mast as it drifted out of reach. He heard Elsie utter a low-voiced command in Spanish, and the dip of a paddle told him that the canoe was in motion.

"For the Lord's sake, what are you doing?" he roared.

"I am going to save Captain Courtenay," was the answer. "You cannot stop me now. Please hoist plenty of lights. If I succeed, look out for me before daybreak. If I fail, good-by!"

CHAPTER XVIII
A FULL NIGHT

Boyle was very angry. It was a situation which demanded earnest words, and they were forthcoming. Elsie understood them to mean that she need not be in such a purple hurry to disappear into the darkness without the least explanation; thereupon she bade Suarez back the canoe a little.

"I am sorry it is necessary to steal away in this fashion," she said, and the coolness of her tone was highly exasperating to a man who could no more detain her than he could move the *Kansas* unaided. "I have a plan which requires only a bit of good fortune to render it practicable. I have two assistants--Suarez, whose aid I am compelling, and Joey, who is quite eager. There is no use in risking any more lives. If I do not return you may be sure the worst has happened."

"But what is your plan?" roared Boyle. "It may be just sheer nonsense. Tell me what it is, and I swear by the Nautical Almanac I shall not prevent you from carrying it out if it has any reason behind it."

"I am going to collect all the Indian canoes," was the amazing answer. "I know it can be done, from what Suarez has said. Once we have the canoes in mid channel, we can set most of them adrift, and bring Captain Courtenay and the others back to the ship in four or five which we will tow to Guanaco Hill. And now, good-by again!"

"One moment, Miss Maxwell," broke in Gray's quiet voice from the upper deck. "You can't engineer that scheme with a one-man crew, and he sick and unwilling. I am going with you. You must take me aboard, wet or dry."

"I am well armed, and shall admit of no interference," she cried.

"I promise to obey orders."

"If I wanted you, Mr. Gray, I should have sought your help."

"It is one thing or the other--a wriggle down a rope or a high diving act."

"You have no right to impose such an alternative on me."

"I hate it myself, and I can't dive worth a cent. You will hear a beastly flop when I strike the damp."

"Mr. Boyle--I call on you to hold him."

Boyle explained luridly that the American was doing a balancing act on the rail eight feet above his head. Elsie, taking her eyes off Suarez for an instant, discerned Gray's figure silhouetted against the sky. She yielded.

"There is a rope ladder fastened to the lowest rail, near where the canoe was moored," she said.

"Is there to be any catch-as-catch-can business, Boyle?" demanded Gray.

"No. All this is d--d unfair to me."

"You have my sympathy, friend, but you can't leave the ship. Now, Miss Maxwell, come alongside. Boyle is going to be good. He doesn't mean half he says, anyhow."

As the canoe slipped out of the dense gloom of the ship's shadow, Elsie heard the wrathful chief officer interviewing the Chilean sailors on watch on the main deck fore and aft. That is to say, he stirred them up from the bridge with a ritual laid down for such extreme cases. Not yet had he realized the exceeding artifice which the girl displayed in throwing him and all the others off their guard. She had maneuvered Suarez into the canoe with the fierce and silent strategy of a Red Indian.

The Argentine squatted on his knees in the bows, Gray placed himself amidships, and Elsie sat aft, holding the revolver in her right hand and the dog's collar in her left. The American groped for and found a paddle, which he plied vigorously.

"Guess you'd better discourse," said he over his shoulder, when the light craft was well clear of the ship.

"You understand Spanish, I think?"

"Yes."

"Please tell Suarez to cease paddling and listen. Don't move. I can trust you, but I may have to shoot him."

"Best hand me that pop-gun, Miss Maxwell. The gentleman in front seems to have a wholesome respect for you already; anything you say goes, where he is concerned. I am taking your word for it his name is Suarez, but he looks, and smells, more like an Indian."

"I forced him to dress in his discarded clothes. He may be able now to scare any of the savages we come across. But why should I give you my weapon, Mr. Gray?"

"Because I can hit most things I aim at, whereas you are more likely to bore a hole through me as a preliminary. Moreover, you have the dog with you, and even the wisest dog may bark at the wrong moment. You must have both hands at liberty to choke his enthusiasm."

"Do you pledge your word to go on with my scheme?"

"That is what I am here for."

"Take the revolver, then."

"Sure it's loaded?"

"Quite sure. I have fifteen extra cartridges, but, as I have practised refilling it in the dark, give it to me if you have occasion to empty it."

"You seem to have thought this thing out pretty fully?"

"I intend to succeed. Now, please, I must explain what I want Suarez to do."

Speaking in Spanish, slow and clear, while the canoe drifted steadily up the bay with the rising tide, Elsie unfolded her project. Behind the guardian cliff of Otter Creek a ridge of rocks created a small natural harbor. It was the custom of the Alaculofs, when the weather was calm, and they meant to use their craft at daybreak, to anchor most of their vessels in this sheltered break-water. At other times the canoes were drawn ashore, but she reasoned that such a precaution would not be taken during the present excitement. That was the first part of her program--to capture the entire fleet, including the life-boat. In any event, she intended to go next to the hidden cleft at the foot of Guanaco Hill, trusting to the dog's sagacity to reveal the retreat where she believed that her lover and many of his men were hidden. If a squad of Indians mounted guard there, the reappearance of Suarez in his war paint, backed by the alarm of a night attack from the sea, might mystify the enemy sufficiently to permit of a landing, while the frequent reports of the revolver would certainly lead to a counter demonstration by Courtenay. Suarez was the only man on the *Kansas* who could act as guide, and the penalty of his refusal would be instant death. She had provided a strong, sharp knife to cut the thongs which fastened the canoes to their anchor-stones. For the rest, she trusted to the darkness. It was her fixed resolve to succeed or die.

Gray listened to the girl's cool statement with growing admiration. The plan began to look feasible. It came within the bounds of reason. The odds were against it, of course, but the law of probability is seldom in favor of a forlorn hope. Suarez, too, making the best of a situation which gave him no option, agreed that they had a fair chance if once they got hold of the canoes. Nevertheless, he warned them that he knew nothing of the surroundings of Guanaco Hill. He believed there were no reefs on that side of the inlet, but he had never visited it. Their greatest peril lay amid the almost impenetrable trees which grew down to the water's edge. On his advice, Gray unshipped the mast and threw it overboard. Then silence became imperative. If aught were said, they must speak in the merest whisper.

The canoe darted forward again with stealthy haste. The night was clear, though dark. The stars helped them to distinguish the outlines of the shore now coming rapidly nearer. As they crept round the southern cheek of Point *Kansas*, the Argentine ceased paddling, and placed a warning hand on Gray's arm. The cliff was so high and steep that its shadow plunged into deepest gloom the water at its base. Suarez, however, had imbibed a good deal of savage lore during his enforced residence on the island. He stretched well forward over the bows, held a paddle as far in front as possible, and thus not only guided the drifting canoe by an occasional dip of the blade, but trusted to it for warning of any unseen rock.

There was a cold breeze on the surface of the bay, but the dog was the only one who shivered, and his tremors arose from excitement. At last they felt a slight bump. The Argentine had found the reef he was searching for; by watching a star it was easy enough to follow the southerly bend taken by the canoe in skirting this barrier, while their ears caught the murmur of the swift current amid the numerous tiny channels of the rocks. Suddenly this swirl and hum of fast-flowing water ceased. Elsie and Gray became aware that Suarez was cautiously drawing himself inboard again. Then his paddle dipped with a noiseless stroke; the canoe was inside the Alaculof harbor.

The midnight blackness was now something that had a sense of actual obstruction in it. It seemed that a hand put forth would encounter a wall. The tide was here, but no perceptible current. For all they could tell to the contrary, they might have been floating in Charon's boat across some Stygian pool.

For a minute or two, Elsie's brave heart failed her. Here was a difficulty which desperate courage could not surmount. There might be dozens of canoes moored on all sides, but to discover them in this pitch darkness was so obviously impossible that she almost made up her mind to abandon this part of her enterprise. Yet the narrow-beamed Fuegian craft she was in would hold only four more occupants, and that with a certain risk and unwieldiness. She was as determined as ever to cross the bay and endeavor to communicate with the imprisoned men. But she recognized the absurdity of the thought that Courtenay and Tollemache would consent to escape in the canoe and leave the others to their fate, even if such a thing were practicable. Oddly enough, the one person whose daring might reasonably be suspected, gave no signs of the pangs of doubt. Suarez pushed forward resolutely. He knew what Elsie had forgotten--that in each canoe used by the Indians there was a carefully preserved fire, whose charcoal embers retained some heat and glow all night. The first intimation of this fact was revealed by the pungent fumes which environed them. Elsie could not help uttering a little gasp of relief. There was a slight movement in front. Gray leaned back and touched her hand.

"Suarez says," he whispered, "that you are to be ready with your tow ropes. As he secures each canoe he will pass it along to me. You will be able to see its outlines by the dim glimmer of the fire. But how will you manage about the dog? He may cause an alarm."

Much to Joey's disgust, he was forthwith muzzled with a piece of rope, not that this device would stop him effectually from barking, but Elsie thought he would so resent the indignity that he might pay less heed to outer circumstances. She needed no warning that Indians were near. The Argentine miner's description of the community which dwelt on Otter Creek made her understand that there were hundreds within hail.

A great joy leaped up in her when the first canoe came under her hand. It was quite easy to manipulate the painter-rope. The stem had a notched knob provided for this very purpose, and there was a stern-post against which a steersman might press a paddle and thus swerve the canoe in any direction. But it was slow work. The craft were moored without any semblance of order, yet Suarez was forced to secure them in a definite sequence, or a string of half-a-dozen would become unmanageable.

When the second canoe was made fast Gray bent towards the girl once more.

"I have been listening to the tick of my watch," he breathed against her ear. "I reckon it has taken ten minutes to collect two dug-outs. Unless we mean to remain all night we must let up on the cutting adrift proposition."

"I agree," she murmured. "But we must have two more."

He told Suarez of the new development, which was essential, though it added to the danger of the enterprise. By sheer good fortune, however, they blundered against the life-boat. A dog barked, and Elsie had a thrilling struggle with Joey, who was furious that this unlooked-for insolence should go unanswered. The sleepless cur who yelped ashore speedily subsided, but it appeared to be an age before Suarez moved again. He knew, better than his companions, how ready the Indians were to note such sentinel challenges. Had the alarm continued, the whole village would have been aroused, and, if the attack on the canoes were suspected, the water would swarm with vengeful savages.

Elsie found the painter of the life-boat coiled in its proper place. Soon she experienced a steady pull on the rope. Her little fleet was in motion. Gray began to help in the paddling. Ere long they came under the influence of the tide, and she heard the ripple of the water against the planks of the boat. Then Suarez called a halt and a parley.

It would be far better, he advised, to use the oars in the heavy boat than attempt to tow it across the strong current from a canoe. They would gain time and be safer. So they climbed into the life-boat, but continued to tow the canoes.

And now they saw the mast-head light of the **Kansas**. Boyle had also caused the side lights to be slung to davits, and the white, red, and green lamps made a triangle in the obscurity, though its base seemed to be strangely near sea level. Even a big vessel like the Kansas shrinks to small proportions when she is a mile or more distant at night. She becomes indivisible, a mere atom in the immensity of the black waters; it demands an effort of the imagination to credit her with wide decks, streets of cabins, and cavernous holds. In one respect the exhibition of the port and starboard lights served them most excellently. Guanaco Hill was directly astern of the ship; they had absolutely no trouble in maintaining a straight line for their destination, all that was necessary being to keep the mast-head light in the exact center of the green and red points.

Suarez, somewhat weak from his knock on the head over night, was not equal to the strain of continued exertion, so Elsie and Gray took two oars each, and allowed their companion to rest. When, judging by the surrounding hills, they were half way across the inlet, Gray stooped low in the boat, struck a match, and looked at his watch. It was long after one o'clock! There could be no doubt whatever that the dawn would find them far from the ship, no matter how fortunate they might be in their further adventures.

It was well for Elsie that she had learnt how to scull when in her teens, and that her muscles were in fair condition owing to her skill at tennis. Even so, she feared that she could never hold out against the sustained stress of that pull across the bay. The heavy boat, intended to be rowed by six men, had the added burthen of four canoes. It was back-breaking work; but she neither faltered nor sighed until Suarez said:

"Let me take your place now, senorita. In ten minutes we shall be at the mouth of the creek, though heaven only knows how we shall find it."

He did not exaggerate in thus expressing his fear. Time and again they neared the shore, only to hear the tidal swell breaking heavily on the rocks. The lights of the *Kansas*, fully three miles away, could only tell them that they were in the neighborhood of the place where Courtenay had last been seen in this identical boat. The least divergence from the line given by the position of the ship meant a difference of hundreds of yards at such a distance, and there was an ominous lightening of the gloom, accompanied by a dimming of the stars, when Gray hit on the idea that the powerful current had probably carried them a good deal southward of the point they were aiming at. He suggested that they should boldly pull a quarter of a mile or so against the tide and then try their luck. Their progress, of course, became slower than ever, and Elsie began to despair that they would ever find the mouth of the stream which ran through the cleft in the hill, when she suddenly saw the luminous crescents which heralded the sunrise over the inner mountain range. They could not be visible unless there was a break in the cliffs in that locality.

"Pull in now," she whispered tensely, and, with a little further effort, they found that the boat was traveling not against but with the tide, which was flooding a small offshoot of the main estuary.

Precaution became not only useless but impossible. They were all worn out.

Nothing but the most inflexible determination on the part of Elsie and Gray, eked out by a certain desponding fear of both of them felt by Suarez, had sustained them thus far. They went on, and on; they swept rapidly into the jaws of a precipitous defile, the lofty crests on either hand coming momentarily nearer against the brightening sky. It did not seem credible that this sheer cut through the heart of a gigantic hill could continue for more than a few yards, nor that anything save a bird could find foothold on its steep sides. Yet the current flowed smoothly onwards, through a wealth of vegetation which clung precariously to every ledge and natural escarpment.

Joey, embarrassed by his gag, nevertheless managed to emit a warning growl. Then the boat crashed into a canoe, and a hoarse yell of alarm came from beneath the lowermost trees, whose dense foliage flung a pall over the water. Gray was seized with an inspiration. He grasped the canoe as it bumped along the gunwale, and held it down on one side until it filled and sank. He sent another, and yet a third, guzzling to the bottom before the outburst of raucous cries from both banks showed there were Indians here in some force.

Stones, too, began to hum around them; some struck the boat, but the greater number whizzed unpleasantly close to the heads of the two men and the girl, proving conclusively that they were visible to the unseen enemy. Gray whipped forth the revolver and fired twice. The second time a shriek of pain told that he had hit one of their assailants. The two reports made a deafening din in that place of echoes. They appeared to stir the Indians into a perfect frenzy, and it was evident, by the sounds, that the islanders had not much liberty of movement on the narrow strips of land they occupied on both sides of the gorge.

Elsie caught some significant splashing behind her.

"They are swimming towards the canoes," she screamed.

Telling Suarez to pull for all he was worth, Gray, clambered to the stern of the boat and emptied the revolver at what he took to be the black heads of the swimmers.

"Quick! Load it again," he said, and Elsie obeyed with a nimbleness and certainty that were amazing.

The American fired three more shots before he was satisfied that the canoes were untenanted and not cut adrift. They were now leaving the pandemonium behind, and Elsie, bethinking herself of the dog, freed him from that most objectionable muzzle. Joey forthwith awoke the welkin with his uproar, but, although the girl strained her ears for some answering hail, she could detect nothing beyond the bawling of Indians at each other across the narrow creek, and the repeated echoes of the dog's barking.

About this time Gray began to suspect that the tide was bearing them onward at a remarkable rate. In the somber depths of the cleft or canon it was difficult to discern stationary objects clearly enough to obtain a means of estimating the pace of the stream. But the rapid dying down of the hubbub among the savages gave him cause to think. He asked Suarez to cease pulling. The canoes behind came crowding in on the more solid boat, and an oar held out until it encountered some invisible branch was rudely swept aside. In a word, they were being impelled towards an unknown destination with the silence and gathering speed of a mill-race.

An expert engineer, though his work may have little to do with sea or river, cannot fail to accumulate a store of theoretical knowledge as to the properties and limitations of water in motion. Gray knew that the quickened impulse of the stream arose from the tidal force exerted in a channel which gradually lessened its width. The boat was traveling at sea level. Therefore, there could be neither rapids nor cataract in front; but the steady rush of the current, now plainly audible, could not be accounted for simply by the effort of the tide to gain a passage through a mere by-way, as the boat was now nearly half a mile from the estuary, and the velocity of the current was increasing each moment.

"We must endeavor to reach the bank and hold on to the branches of a tree," he shouted in Spanish. "Down with your heads until the boat strikes, and then try to lay hold of something."

There was no time for explanation. He seized an oar; a powerful stroke swung the boat's nose round. By chance, he used the starboard oar. All unknowing he spun a coin for life or death, and life won. They crashed through some drooping foliage and ran into a crumbling bank. Gray unshipped the oar and jammed it straight down. It stuck between stones at a depth of three feet, and the life-boat was held fast for the time. The canoes hurtled against each other, but were swept aside instantly. When the noise ceased, they plainly heard the swirl of the water. In their new environment, it had the uncanny and sinister hiss of some monstrous snake.

"Everybody happy?" Gray demanded coolly.

"I am clinging to a tree trunk," answered Elsie.

"Bully for you. Make fast with a piece of rope. But be careful to provide a slip-knot, in case we have to sheer off in a hurry. Can you manage that?"

"Quite well."

Elsie was fully aware that the leadership of the expedition had gone from her. She was not sorry; it was in strong hands. Suarez, too, secured a stout branch, and passed a rope around it.

"Now, silence! and listen!" said Gray.

They soon detected a curiously subdued clamor from the inner recesses of the cleft. At first almost indistinguishable, it gradually assumed the peculiar attribute of immense volumes of distant sound, and filled the ear to the exclusion of all else. It was like nothing any of them had heard before; now it recalled the roar of a mighty waterfall, and again its strange melody brought memories of a river in flood. But the dominant note was the grinding noise of innumerable mill-stones. It cowed them all. Even the dog was afraid.

"Guess we tied up just in time," exclaimed Gray, feeling the need of speech. A little sob answered him. Elsie was beginning to admit the sheer hopelessness of her undertaking.

"Now, cheer up, Miss Maxwell," said he. "All the water that is going in must come out by the same road. At the worst, we can skate back the way we came and take our chance. But it will soon be broad daylight, and I'll answer for it that if Captain Courtenay is yet alive he is not between us and the mouth of the inlet, or he would have contrived some sort of racket to let us know his whereabouts. Now, I propose that our friend in the bows be asked to shin up the cliff and prospect a bit. He ought to know how to crawl through this undergrowth. Fifty feet higher he will be able to see some distance."

Elsie agreed miserably. She was crushed by the immensity of the difficulties confronting them. Expedients which looked simple beforehand were found lamentably deficient to cope with wild nature on the stupendous scale of this gloomy land. Suarez, too, was very reluctant to leave the boat, but the American adopted a short cut in the argument, offering him the alternative of climbing ashore or of being thrown overboard.

So the Argentine adopted the less hazardous method, and climbed to the bank. A splash, and a scramble, and a slight exclamation from Elsie told that the dog had followed. Soon the swish of leaves and the crackling of rotten wood ceased. Suarez might be out of earshot or merely hiding for a time, intending to return with news of an impassable precipice. There was a crumb of comfort in the absence of the terrier. Joey would either go on or come back to them at once.

Gray felt that the girl was too heart-broken to talk. He listened to the rhythmical chorus of that witches' cauldron in the heart of the defile, and watched the gray light slowly etching a path through the trees, until it touched the fast-running water with a shimmer of silver.

Neither of them knew how long they remained there; at last, a straining and creaking of the boat warned them that the water level was rising and the ropes needed readjusting. It was now possible to see that Elsie had made fast to a fallen tree; its branches were locked among the gnarled roots of the lowermost growth above high-water mark. Already there was a distinct lessening in the pace of the current, and Gray fancied that the distant rumble was softer. It would not be many minutes before the neighboring rocks were covered; high tide, he knew, was at 3.15 A.M. He forebore to look at his watch, lest the girl should note his action. That would imply the utter abandonment of hope.

It might be that his mind was too taken up with the weird influences of the hour, or that Elsie's senses were strung to a superhuman pitch. Be that as it may, it was she who sprang to her feet all a-quiver with agitation.

"Do you hear?" she whispered, and her hand clutched Gray's shoulder with an energy which set his heart beating high. He did not answer. He had heard no unusual sound, but he was not without faith in her.

"There!" she panted again. "Some one is hailing. Some one cried 'Elsie.' I am sure of it."

"Guess you'd better toot 'Arthur' on the off chance," said Gray.

Almost the last thing she remembered was the sound of her own wild scream. There came back to her a stronger shout, and the bark of a dog. She had a blurred consciousness of a whole troupe of men scrambling down the choked ravine, of glad questions and joyous answers, of a delirious dog leaping on board and yelping staccato assurances that everything was all right in a most wonderful world. Then she found herself in Courtenay's arms, and heard him say in a rapture of delight:

"I owe my life to you, dear heart. That is the wonder of it. No need to tell me you ran away from the ship. I know. One kiss, Elsie; then full speed ahead for the **Kansas**. By the Lord, to think of it! You here! At the very gate of the Inferno! Well, one more kiss! Yes, it is I, none other, and fit as a fiddle. Never got a scratch. There, now; I really must see to the crew. We must be ready for the turn of the tide."

CHAPTER XIX
WHEREIN THE KANSAS RESUMES HER VOYAGE

The events of the next hour were shadowy as the dawn to Elsie. She knew that her lover placed men in each of the canoes, that the life-boat itself was crowded, and that it began the seaward journey after the others had started. She followed his explanation that if one of the lighter craft got into difficulties at the Indian barrier, the big, heavy boat would be able to extricate it. But she feared neither Indians nor sea. Had Courtenay proposed to sail away into the Pacific she would have listened with placid approval. She was by his side; that sufficed. For the rest, they lived in the midst of adventures. What did it matter if they were called on to run the gauntlet of one more ambuscade--or a dozen, if it came to that?

But they sped out of the twilight into the morning glory of the open bay, and never a savage hoot disturbed the echoes. Some of the Alaculofs had dragged a couple of canoes from beneath the trees and raced off toward the village; others had followed a coast path known only to them, while, if there were watchers by the side of that mysterious river which flowed both ways with the tide, they kept a silent vigil, awed by the force arrayed against them.

As the life-boat emerged into the estuary under the vigorous sweep of six ash blades, Elsie's wondering glance rested on the brown plumpness of a three-quarters naked girl who was gazing at Suarez with wistful, glistening eyes, much as Joey was regarding his master. In the intense, penetrating light of sunrise, the bedaubed and skin-clothed Argentine was the most unlovely object that ever captivated woman. Yet he satisfied the soul of this Fuegian maid, so what more was there to be said?

Courtenay caught the happy little sigh, half laugh, half sob, with which Elsie announced her discovery of the idyl in the canoe.

"We owe a lot to that young person," he said. "None of us could make out a word she uttered when first we saw her. She loses what small amount of Spanish she can speak when she becomes excited, and it was sheer good fortune that some of the crew were with her when she swung herself down the side of the cliff to warn us of our danger; otherwise she might have been shot. I suppose Suarez told you what to expect?"

"You might as well be talking Alaculof yourself for all I can follow what you are saying," murmured Elsie happily.

"Then how did *you* know where to tie up? *We* went too far. We lost the boat that way, and my gun as well. We had to jump for it, and it was only the boat's stout timbers which enabled her to live through that boiling pot in the volcano. The native girl said that no Indian-built craft ever came back."

"Excellent!" said Elsie. "When we reach the ship I shall write down everything you tell me. After a time I shall begin to understand."

Whereupon, Courtenay took thought, and explained that the channel which flowed through that amazing cut in the cliff led to the crater of an extinct volcano, into which the sea poured twenty feet of water each tide. An almost everlasting maelstrom raged within, as the water entered by a side-long channel, and sent a whirlpool spinning with the hands of the clock until the enormous cistern was full, and against them until it was empty. The sailors had taken refuge on a wide, sulphur-coated ledge high above the vortex, and the presence of several skeletons showed that many an unfortunate had sought a last shelter there against pursuit. Every Alaculof knew of this retreat, but few dared approach it, as the roar of the water far below appalled them. There was only one path; when the hunters closed that their prey was safe. The alternative to capture was death by starvation. The Chileans, and he himself during the past fourteen hours, had subsisted on a bag of dried berries stolen by the girl when she first led the sailors thither.

"Didn't you see how eager we all were to search the lockers?" he asked. "But the rascals had cleared every scrap when the boat fell into their hands again with the falling tide."

She nestled close to him.

"I saw nothing," she whispered. "My mind held but one thought--that you were alive, though, indeed, I was mourning you as dead. But now I am restored to my senses. I think I can grasp what happened. Did Joey find you?"

"Yes. You can guess my bewilderment when he sprang on top of me. I was lying down; I heard our sentries shouting, but paid no heed. As a matter of fact, Elsie, I, too, had abandoned hope. I could see no chance of escape. Great Heaven! To think of your coming to my rescue! What made you do it?"

"Please go on. Tell me all. You shall hear my story afterwards."

"Well, I jumped up, and Joey nearly fell into the crater with delight. I was just in time to save Suarez from being shot. Luckily he was a long way behind the dog, and I recognized his make-up. The guard, who belonged to the original lot, naturally thought he was an Indian. And you ought to have seen that blessed girl skipping around when she set eyes on him. We must give her money enough to fix her up as his wife if the *Kansas* gets off."

"If--"

There was a world of belief in that one word. Could any one doubt the ultimate hap of that thrice fortunate ship? Had not Mr. Boyle said her captain was a lucky man? Elsie laughed aloud in her joy, for the queer notion occurred to her that her grumpy friend would surely have some remarkable story of the one-legged skipper of the *Flower of the Ocean* brig, wherewith to point the moral and adorn the tale of the *Kansas* and her commander.

Though Courtenay did not allow ten seconds to pass without a glance at the charming face by his side, he, nevertheless, had a sharp eye for events elsewhere. He saw smoke rising from the funnel of the ship; a line of flags dancing from the foremast told him that Boyle had discovered them as soon as they were clear of the deep shadow of Guanaco Hill. But there were anxious moments yet in store. A fleet of canoes put off from Otter Creek. There was every prospect of a fight before they reached their fortress. They had a long two miles to travel, and the Indians could attack them ere they covered half the distance.

Gray and Tollemache were sitting together in the fore part of the boat. When they had met in the canon they had merely exchanged a hearty grip, and Gray's inquiry if his friend was O.K. had elicited the information that his general state was "Fair." But the sight of the sparkling bay had unlocked even the Englishman's lips, for he was telling his friend some of the adventures of the previous afternoon, when he viewed the black dots darting forth from behind Point *Kansas*.

"Here they come again," he growled. "I never have seen such persistent rotters. And this time we're in a fix."

A long blare from the ship's siren thrilled their hearts, but the excitement became frantic when three short, sharp blasts followed, and every sailor knew that the chief officer had signalled: "My engines are going full speed astern."

That was a pardonable exaggeration, but the *Kansas* was certainly moving. They could see the white foam churned up by her propeller. With one accord they cheered madly, and the oars, double-handed now, tore the life-boat onward at a pace which outstripped even the shallow canoes.

Then the Indians did a wise thing. They spared many of their own lives, and, perchance others of greater value to the world, by ceasing to paddle. The unlooked-for interference of the great vessel was too much for them. They merely stared and cackled in amaze, while the small flotilla dashed towards the towering black hull, and Boyle lowered the gangway in readiness to receive the captain, his bride elect, and a good half of the passengers and crew.

Courtenay lost not an instant of favoring tide and fine weather. When Boyle told him that Walker could work the engines under easy steam, he dashed up to the bridge three steps at a time. With his hand on the telegraph, he superintended the hoisting on board of the life-boat and two of the canoes, which he meant to carry away as trophies--be sure that Elsie's own special craft was one of them. Meanwhile, Boyle saw to the safe stowing in the remaining canoes of the wounded Indians in the fore cabin, and a few furnace bars attached to a rope anchored them in mid channel, whence their friends could bring them to shore later.

At last, the captain of the *Kansas* had the supreme satisfaction of hearing the clang of the electric bell in the engine-room as he put the telegraph lever successively to "Stand By," and "Slow Ahead." Gradually the ship crept north, gaining way as the engines increased their stroke and the full body of the ebb tide made its volume felt. Round swung the *Kansas* to the west, just as the sun cleared the highest peak of the unknown mountains. Courtenay had not forgotten his bearings. Although he had men using the lead constantly, he did not need their help. Once clear of the reefs which he had seen when the vessel first ran into the inlet, he made straight for the pillar rock, and rather raised the hair of the man at the wheel, not to mention most of the people on deck, by the nearness of his approach to that solitary buoy set in the midst of a broken sea. How good it was to feel the steady thrust of the pistons, the long roll of the ship over the swell! And then, when Elsie brought him his breakfast, and stood by his side as he watched the set of the tide with unwavering eyes, what a joy that was, to listen to her story of the night's wanderings, and to know that, with God's help, their Odyssey was nearing its end!

For every sailor is a fatalist, and in the unwritten code of the sea the law runs that once a ship has undergone her supreme trial she has the freedom of the great highway for that voyage, though she girdle the earth ere the dock gates open.

But best of all was it to hear Elsie tell how Dr. Christobal had handed her a bulky packet, in which she found Courtenay's words of farewell, together with those wonderful letters which fate had held back from her twice already. They were only glowing epistles from the hundreds of passengers on the *Florida*, but six of them were proposals from enthusiastic ladies, all well dowered, and eager to give their charms and their cash to the safe keeping of the man who had saved their lives. It was with reference to some joking comment by Courtenay on these missives that his sister wrote to congratulate him on having escaped matrimony under such conditions. Elsie, brimful of high spirits, amused herself by teasing him with nice phrases culled from each of the six.

Long before noon the *Kansas* cleared White Horse Island. There was a ticklish hour while Courtenay and Boyle looked for the shoal. When its long, low sandspit was revealed by the falling tide, the ship took thought of her agony there, and traversed those treacherous waters with due reverence. Thenceforth, the run was due south until eight bells, when, for the second time within a fortnight, the captain set the course "South-40-East."

A stiff breeze blowing from the south-west, and heavy clouds rolling up over the horizon, showed that the land of storms was repenting the phenomenal frivolity which had let it bask in sunshine for an unbroken spell of ten days. But the gale which whistled into Good Hope Inlet that night carried with it no disabled and blood-stained ship. Mr. Malcolm, who got his diminished squad of stewards in hand as though the vessel had quitted port that day, served dinner promptly at two bells in the second dog watch--by which no allusion is intended to an animal already gorged to repletion--and wore a proper professional air of annoyance because everybody was late, owing to the interesting fact that the half-minute fixed dashing light on Evangelistas Island had just been sighted.

Elsie noted that Count Edouard de Poincilit came with the rest, and sat beside Isobel. Courtenay put in an appearance later to partake of a hasty meal. He gave monsieur a black look, but, of course, catching Elsie's eye instantly, he meekly sat down and said nothing--nothing, that is, of an unpleasant nature. All good ladies will recognize such behavior as one of the points of a man likely to become a model husband.

Dr. Christobal and Gray were in great form, while Tollemache actually told a story. When the captain sent Boyle down from the bridge, Elsie made Tollemache repeat it--a simple yarn, detailing an all-night search for a Devonshire village, which he could not find because some rotter had deemed it funny to turn a sign-post the wrong way round.

"Huh, that's odd," said Boyle. "Reminds me of a thing that happened to a friend of mine, skipper of the *Flower of the Ocean* brig. Brown his name was, an' he had a wooden leg. The day his son an' heir was born, he dropped into a gin-mill to celebrate, an' his stump stuck in a rope mat. He swore a bit, but he chanced to see on one of the half doors the name 'Nosmo,' an', on the other, 'King.' 'Dash me,' says he,' them's two fine names for the kid--Nosmo King Brown'--a bit of all right, eh? So he goes home an' tells the missus. After the christenin', he took a pal or two round to the same bar to stand treat. That time the two halves of the door were closed, an' any ass could see that the letters stood for 'No Smoking.' Well, the other fellows told me his language was so sultry that his prop caught fire."

So all was well with the *Kansas*.

*   *   *   *   *   *

Crawling quietly into the Straits of Magellan at daybreak, the ship put forth her best efforts in the run through the narrows. Passing Cape San Isidro, she signalled her name, and it was easy to see the commotion created by her appearance. The real furore began when she approached Sandy Point. A steam launch puffed off hastily from the side of a Chilean warship, and the commander brought the news that he had been sent specially from Coronel to search the western coast line thoroughly for the *Kansas*. He was about to return that day, to report his failure to discover any trace of the missing vessel, and he listened in amaze while Christobal gave him a succinct history of the ship's doings. At the end, Courtenay presented him with a photograph of Elsie's chart, to which many additions had been made by her under her lover's directions. The position of the shoal, and of Pillar Rock, together with the set of the tidal current, were clearly shown, and it is probable that Good Hope Inlet, notwithstanding its dangerous approach, will be thoroughly surveyed one of these days. Then, perhaps, more may be heard of those lumps of silver and copper ore which the savages hurled at the *Kansas*.

The cruiser hurried away, under forced draft, to report from Coronel, the nearest cable-station. Thence she would go to Valparaiso, so she carried a sheaf of letters, and one passenger, Frascuelo. Finding that he could not execute the needed repairs at Sandy Point, Courtenay decided to make for Montevideo, where he would be in telegraphic communication with Mr. Baring. He was fortunate in finding a shipwrecked crew on shore, awaiting transport to England. He secured a full complement of officers and engineers, and the *Kansas* reached the chief port of Uruguay without any difficulty.

A sack-load of telegrams awaited the ship. The Chilean man-of-war put into Valparaiso, after calling at Coronel, nearly three days before the *Kansas* dropped anchor on the east coast. Hence, there was time for things to happen, and they seized the opportunity. The copper market had turned itself inside out; the firm of Baring, Thompson, Miguel & Co. had rebounded from comparative ruin to a stronger financial state than ever, and Senor Pedro Ventana, after shooting a man named Jose Anacleto, had considerately shot himself. Evidently, Frascuelo lost no time when he went ashore; Mr. Baring, too, reported that the dynamite wrapper had been traced to Ventana's possession.

When Isobel Baring heard this final item she fainted so badly that Dr. Christobal thought it advisable she should be taken to a hotel while the ship remained in port. But she vetoed this proposal determinedly when she recovered her senses, and straightway confessed to Elsie that Ventana was her husband. She had foolishly agreed to marry him privately, and Anacleto had witnessed the ceremony. Within a month, she regretted her choice; there were quarrels, and threats; ultimately, an agreement was made that they should separate. Her father knew and approved of the arrangement. He could not afford to break openly with Ventana, and it must have been a dreadful shock to him when he learned that the scoundrel had plotted not only to destroy the ship but to murder his wife at the same time.

"So you see," she added with a wan smile, "I did not give serious thought to your troubles, Elsie. Ventana could never have married you while I was alive."

Elsie's cheeks reddened.

"I never told you he asked me to marry him," she said. "It would have been just the same had he done so. As it was, I feared the man. Now you know why I ran away from Chile. If I permitted another impression to prevail, I acted for the best. But the unhappy man is dead; let us endeavor to forget him."

"His memory haunts me with an enduring curse," cried Isobel, bitterly. "Among my papers I had some letters of his, the marriage certificate, and his written promise not to molest me. On that awful night when the ship was disabled, I went to my cabin and secured them, or thought I did. At any rate, I could not find them when we landed on White Horse Island, and, from hints dropped by that wretched little adventurer, de Poincilit, I feel sure they have fallen into his hands. Believe me, Elsie, I was half mad when I helped him to steal the boat."

"Steal the boat! What boat?"

"Has not Captain Courtenay told you?"

"Not a word."

"Ah, he is a true gentleman. But you forget. You heard what he said to de Poincilit before he went to the Guanaco canon?"

"Yes; I did not understand. Oh, my poor Isobel, how you must have suffered, while I have been so happy."

"If only I could recover my papers--"

"May I ask Arthur to help?"

"He knows the worst of me already. One more shameful disclosure cannot add to my degradation."

"Isobel, how little you know him!" Thus spoke Elsie, after fourteen days. Truly there is much enlightenment in a hug!

Monsieur le Comte Edouard de Poincilit, to his intense chagrin, found that a ship's captain has far-reaching powers when he chooses to exert them. Rather than enter a Montevidean jail, where people have died suddenly of nasty fevers, he not only restored the missing documents but submitted to a close scrutiny of his own belongings, which resulted in the pleasing discovery that he was not a French count, but a denizen of Martinique--most probably a defaulting valet or clerk. No one troubled to inquire further about him. His passage money was refunded and he was bundled ashore. Courtenay's view was that he had heard, by some means, of Isobel's intended departure from Valparaiso, and deemed it a good chance of winning her approval of his countship, seeing that such titles are not subjected to serious investigation in South America. Suarez took his Fuegian bride up country, where Mr. Baring and Dr. Christobal established them on a small ranch.

Isobel renewed her voyage somewhat chastened in spirit. But her volatile nature soon survived the shocks it had received. By the time the *Kansas* put her ashore at Tilbury, to be clasped in the arms of a timid and tearful aunt, she was ready as ever for the campaign of glory she had mapped out in London and Paris.

And she was a success, too. Her father's victory over the copper ring, her own adventures, which lost nothing in the telling, and her vivacious self-confidence, carried her into society with a whirl. Recently, her engagement to an impecunious peer was announced.

*　　*　　*　　*　　*　　*

Captain Courtenay, R.N., and his wife are not such distinguished personages, but their romance had a sequel worthy of its unusual beginning. They were married quietly a week after the *Kansas* reached London. There was some war scare in full blast at the moment, and a Lord of the Admiralty who deigned to read the newspapers thought it was a pity that a smart sailor should not risk his life for his country rather than in behalf of base commerce. So he looked up Courtenay's record, and found that it was excellent, the young lieutenant's reason for resigning his commission being the necessity of supporting his mother when her estate was swept away by a bank failure. The Sea Lords made him a first-rate offer of reinstatement in the service, at a higher rank, without any loss of seniority, and they went about the business with such dignified leisure that Dr. Christobal had time to find out, through men whom he could trust, that Elsie's small estate in Chile contained one of the richest mines in the country. He secured a bid of many thousands of pounds for it, and advised Mrs. Courtenay to accept half in cash and half in shares of the exploiting company.

Hence, there was no need for Courtenay to decline a new career in the magnificent service which Mr. Boyle once sniffed at, and Elsie became a prominent figure in that very select circle which clusters around the ports mostly favored by his Majesty's ships.

It was not unreasonable that Gray should go back to Chile to take charge of Elsie's mine, nor that Mr. Boyle should become captain and Walker chief engineer, of the **Kansas**, but there was one wholly unexpected development which fairly took Elsie's breath away when she heard of it.

She was with her husband in London. While passing the National Gallery one day, she remembered the picture by Claude which deals with the embarkation of Saint Ursula and her Eleven Thousand Virgins. A painter herself, Elsie had an artist's appreciation of the vanity which led Turner to bequeath his finest canvasses to the nation with the proviso that they should be placed cheek by jowl with those of his great rival, the Lorrainer. So a fat fox-terrier was given in charge of a catalogue seller, and they passed up the steps.

It was a students' day, and the galleries were crowded with embryonic geniuses. Courtenay waxed sarcastic anent the rig of Claude's ships; he was laughing at the careless grace with which several of the Baozan maidens were standing in a boat just putting off from a wharf, when a lady cried sharply:

"George, how careless of you! You are sitting on my mahl-stick."

"Sorry, my dear," said a tall thin man, rising from a camp-stool.

"Good gracious, it's Mr. Tollemache," whispered Elsie.

"Gad, so it is. Let's hail him."

Tollemache's solemn face brightened when he heard the hail. He introduced his wife, an eminently artistic being who answered to the name of Jennie. She at once enlisted Elsie in an argument as to atmospheres, but Tollemache drew Courtenay aside.

"Got married when I reached home that trip," he explained. "The wife comes here every Thursday, an' I have to carry the kit. Rather rot, isn't it?"

"It is certainly a change from stoking the donkey-boiler, and bowling over Alaculofs like nine-pius."

"That's what I tell her, but she says the Indians were Boeotian, and the landscape, as I describe it, had the crude coloring of the Newlyn school, which she abominates. She thinks Turner might approve of Suarez in his black and white stripes, but the Guanaco crater reminds her of Gustave Dore, who always exaggerated his tone values. I learn that sort of gabble by heart. Jennie's a good sort, yet sometimes she talks rot--"

"George," said Mrs. Tollemache, "pack up my portfolio. We are going to lunch with your friends. Mrs. Courtenay and I have so much to talk about. We find we think alike on many points. I am delighted to have met your wife, Captain Courtenay. My husband raves about her."

"So do I, ma'am," cried Courtenay, gallantly, yet with a subtle glance at Elsie which told her he meant what he said.

The Codes Of Hammurabi And Moses
W. W. Davies

QTY

The discovery of the Hammurabi Code is one of the greatest achievements of archaeology, and is of paramount interest, not only to the student of the Bible, but also to all those interested in ancient history...

Religion   **ISBN: *1-59462-338-4***   **Pages:132**

MSRP $12.95

The Theory of Moral Sentiments
Adam Smith

QTY

This work from 1749. contains original theories of conscience amd moral judgment and it is the foundation for systemof morals.

Philosophy   ISBN: *1-59462-777-0*   **Pages:536**

MSRP $19.95

Jessica's First Prayer
Hesba Stretton

QTY

In a screened and secluded corner of one of the many railway-bridges which span the streets of London there could be seen a few years ago, from five o'clock every morning until half past eight, a tidily set-out coffee-stall, consisting of a trestle and board, upon which stood two large tin cans, with a small fire of charcoal burning under each so as to keep the coffee boiling during the early hours of the morning when the work-people were thronging into the city on their way to their daily toil...

Pages:84

Childrens   ISBN: *1-59462-373-2*   *MSRP $9.95*

My Life and Work
Henry Ford

QTY

Henry Ford revolutionized the world with his implementation of mass production for the Model T automobile. Gain valuable business insight into his life and work with his own auto-biography... "We have only started on our development of our country we have not as yet, with all our talk of wonderful progress, done more than scratch the surface. The progress has been wonderful enough but..."

Pages:300

Biographies/   **ISBN: *1-59462-198-5***   *MSRP $21.95*

The Art of Cross-Examination
Francis Wellman

QTY

I presume it is the experience of every author, after his first book is published upon an important subject, to be almost overwhelmed with a wealth of ideas and illustrations which could readily have been included in his book, and which to his own mind, at least, seem to make a second edition inevitable. Such certainly was the case with me; and when the first edition had reached its sixth impression in five months, I rejoiced to learn that it seemed to my publishers that the book had met with a sufficiently favorable reception to justify a second and considerably enlarged edition. ..

Pages:412

Reference   ISBN: *1-59462-647-2*   *MSRP $19.95*

On the Duty of Civil Disobedience
Henry David Thoreau

QTY

Thoreau wrote his famous essay, On the Duty of Civil Disobedience, as a protest against an unjust but popular war and the immoral but popular institution of slave-owning. He did more than write—he declined to pay his taxes, and was hauled off to gaol in consequence. Who can say how much this refusal of his hastened the end of the war and of slavery ?

Law   ISBN: *1-59462-747-9*

Pages:48

MSRP $7.45

Dream Psychology Psychoanalysis for Beginners
Sigmund Freud

QTY

Sigmund Freud, born Sigismund Schlomo Freud (May 6, 1856 - September 23, 1939), was a Jewish-Austrian neurologist and psychiatrist who co-founded the psychoanalytic school of psychology. Freud is best known for his theories of the unconscious mind, especially involving the mechanism of repression; his redefinition of sexual desire as mobile and directed towards a wide variety of objects; and his therapeutic techniques, especially his understanding of transference in the therapeutic relationship and the presumed value of dreams as sources of insight into unconscious desires.

Pages:196

Psychology   ISBN: *1-59462-905-6*   *MSRP $15.45*

The Miracle of Right Thought
Orison Swett Marden

QTY

Believe with all of your heart that you will do what you were made to do. When the mind has once formed the habit of holding cheerful, happy, prosperous pictures, it will not be easy to form the opposite habit. It does not matter how improbable or how far away this realization may see, or how dark the prospects may be, if we visualize them as best we can, as vividly as possible, hold tenaciously to them and vigorously struggle to attain them, they will gradually become actualized, realized in the life. But a desire, a longing without endeavor, a yearning abandoned or held indifferently will vanish without realization.

Pages:360

Self Help   ISBN: *1-59462-644-8*   *MSRP $25.45*

QTY

The Rosicrucian Cosmo-Conception Mystic Christianity *by Max Heindel*   ISBN: *1-59462-188-8*   **$38.95**
The Rosicrucian Cosmo-conception is not dogmatic, neither does it appeal to any other authority than the reason of the student. It is: not controversial, but is: sent forth in the, hope that it may help to clear...   New Age/Religion Pages 646

Abandonment To Divine Providence *by Jean-Pierre de Caussade*   ISBN: *1-59462-228-0*   **$25.95**
"The Rev. Jean Pierre de Caussade was one of the most remarkable spiritual writers of the Society of Jesus in France in the 18th Century. His death took place at Toulouse in 1751. His works have gone through many editions and have been republished...   Inspirational/Religion Pages 400

Mental Chemistry *by Charles Haanel*   ISBN: *1-59462-192-6*   **$23.95**
Mental Chemistry allows the change of material conditions by combining and appropriately utilizing the power of the mind. Much like applied chemistry creates something new and unique out of careful combinations of chemicals the mastery of mental chemistry...   New Age Pages 354

The Letters of Robert Browning and Elizabeth Barret Barrett 1845-1846 vol II   ISBN: *1-59462-193-4*   **$35.95**
by Robert Browning and Elizabeth Barrett   Biographies Pages 596

Gleanings In Genesis (volume I) *by Arthur W. Pink*   ISBN: *1-59462-130-6*   **$27.45**
Appropriately has Genesis been termed "the seed plot of the Bible" for in it we have, in germ form, almost all of the great doctrines which are afterwards fully developed in the books of Scripture which follow...   Religion/Inspirational Pages 420

The Master Key *by L. W. de Laurence*   ISBN: *1-59462-001-6*   **$30.95**
In no branch of human knowledge has there been a more lively increase of the spirit of research during the past few years than in the study of Psychology, Concentration and Mental Discipline. The requests for authentic lessons in Thought Control, Mental Discipline and...   New Age/Business Pages 422

The Lesser Key Of Solomon Goetia *by L. W. de Laurence*   ISBN: *1-59462-092-X*   **$9.95**
This translation of the first book of the "Lemegton" which is now for the first time made accessible to students of Talismanic Magic was done, after careful collation and edition, from numerous Ancient Manuscripts in Hebrew, Latin, and French...   New Age/Occult Pages 92

Rubaiyat Of Omar Khayyam *by Edward Fitzgerald*   ISBN: *1-59462-332-5*   **$13.95**
Edward Fitzgerald, whom the world has already learned, in spite of his own efforts to remain within the shadow of anonymity, to look upon as one of the rarest poets of the century, was born at Bredfield, in Suffolk, on the 31st of March, 1809. He was the third son of John Purcell...   Music Pages 172

Ancient Law *by Henry Maine*   ISBN: *1-59462-128-4*   **$29.95**
The chief object of the following pages is to indicate some of the earliest ideas of mankind, as they are reflected in Ancient Law, and to point out the relation of those ideas to modern thought.   Religion/History Pages 452

Far-Away Stories *by William J. Locke*   ISBN: *1-59462-129-2*   **$19.45**
"Good wine needs no bush, but a collection of mixed vintages does. And this book is just such a collection. Some of the stories I do not want to remain buried for ever in the museum files of dead magazine-numbers an author's not unpardonable vanity..."   Fiction Pages 272

Life of David Crockett *by David Crockett*   ISBN: *1-59462-250-7*   **$27.45**
"Colonel David Crockett was one of the most remarkable men of the times in which he lived. Born in humble life, but gifted with a strong will, an indomitable courage, and unremitting perseverance...   Biographies/New Age Pages 424

Lip-Reading *by Edward Nitchie*   ISBN: *1-59462-206-X*   **$25.95**
Edward B. Nitchie, founder of the New York School for the Hard of Hearing, now the Nitchie School of Lip-Reading, Inc, wrote "LIP-READING Principles and Practice". The development and perfecting of this meritorious work on lip-reading was an undertaking...   How-to Pages 400

A Handbook of Suggestive Therapeutics, Applied Hypnotism, Psychic Science   ISBN: *1-59462-214-0*   **$24.95**
by Henry Munro   Health/New Age/Health/Self-help Pages 376

A Doll's House: and Two Other Plays *by Henrik Ibsen*   ISBN: *1-59462-112-8*   **$19.95**
Henrik Ibsen created this classic when in revolutionary 1848 Rome. Introducing some striking concepts in playwriting for the realist genre, this play has been studied the world over.   Fiction/Classics/Plays 308

The Light of Asia *by sir Edwin Arnold*   ISBN: *1-59462-204-3*   **$13.95**
In this poetic masterpiece, Edwin Arnold describes the life and teachings of Buddha. The man who was to become known as Buddha to the world was born as Prince Gautama of India but he rejected the worldly riches and abandoned the reigns of power when...   Religion/History/Biographies Pages 170

The Complete Works of Guy de Maupassant *by Guy de Maupassant*   ISBN: *1-59462-157-8*   **$16.95**
"For days and days, nights and nights, I had dreamed of that first kiss which was to consecrate our engagement, and I knew not on what spot I should put my lips..."   Fiction/Classics Pages 240

The Art of Cross-Examination *by Francis L. Wellman*   ISBN: *1-59462-309-0*   **$26.95**
Written by a renowned trial lawyer, Wellman imparts his experience and uses case studies to explain how to use psychology to extract desired information through questioning.   How-to/Science/Reference Pages 408

Answered or Unanswered? *by Louisa Vaughan*   ISBN: *1-59462-248-5*   **$10.95**
Miracles of Faith in China   Religion Pages 112

The Edinburgh Lectures on Mental Science (1909) *by Thomas*   ISBN: *1-59462-008-3*   **$11.95**
This book contains the substance of a course of lectures recently given by the writer in the Queen Street Hail, Edinburgh. Its purpose is to indicate the Natural Principles governing the relation between Mental Action and Material Conditions...   New Age/Psychology Pages 148

Ayesha *by H. Rider Haggard*   ISBN: *1-59462-301-5*   **$24.95**
Verily and indeed it is the unexpected that happens! Probably if there was one person upon the earth from whom the Editor of this, and of a certain previous history, did not expect to hear again...   Classics Pages 380

Ayala's Angel *by Anthony Trollope*   ISBN: *1-59462-352-X*   **$29.95**
The two girls were both pretty, but Lucy who was twenty-one who supposed to be simple and comparatively unattractive, whereas Ayala was credited, as her Bombwhat romantic name might show, with poetic charm and a taste for romance. Ayala when her father died was nineteen...   Fiction Pages 484

The American Commonwealth *by James Bryce*   ISBN: *1-59462-286-8*   **$34.45**
An interpretation of American democratic political theory. It examines political mechanics and society from the perspective of Scotsman James Bryce   Politics Pages 572

Stories of the Pilgrims *by Margaret P. Pumphrey*   ISBN: *1-59462-116-0*   **$17.95**
This book explores pilgrims religious oppression in England as well as their escape to Holland and eventual crossing to America on the Mayflower, and their early days in New England...   History Pages 268

www.bookjungle.com *email: sales@bookjungle.com fax: 630-214-0564 mail: Book Jungle PO Box 2226 Champaign, IL 61825*

QTY

The Fasting Cure by **Sinclair Upton**   ISBN: *1-59462-222-1* **$13.95**
In the Cosmopolitan Magazine for May, 1910, and in the Contemporary Review (London) for April, 1910, I published an article dealing with my experiences in fasting. I have written a great many magazine articles, but never one which attracted so much attention... New Age/Self Help/Health Pages 164

Hebrew Astrology by **Sepharial**   ISBN: *1-59462-308-2* **$13.45**
In these days of advanced thinking it is a matter of common observation that we have left many of the old landmarks behind and that we are now pressing forward to greater heights and to a wider horizon than that which represented the mind-content of our progenitors... Astrology Pages 144

Thought Vibration or The Law of Attraction in the Thought World   ISBN: *1-59462-127-6* **$12.95**
by **William Walker Atkinson**   Psychology/Religion Pages 144

Optimism by **Helen Keller**   ISBN: *1-59462-108-X* **$15.95**
Helen Keller was blind, deaf, and mute since 19 months old, yet famously learned how to overcome these handicaps, communicate with the world, and spread her lectures promoting optimism. An inspiring read for everyone... Biographies/Inspirational Pages 84

Sara Crewe by **Frances Burnett**   ISBN: *1-59462-360-0* **$9.45**
In the first place, Miss Minchin lived in London. Her home was a large, dull, tall one, in a large, dull square, where all the houses were alike, and all the sparrows were alike, and where all the door-knockers made the same heavy sound... Childrens/Classic Pages 88

The Autobiography of Benjamin Franklin by **Benjamin Franklin**   ISBN: *1-59462-135-7* **$24.95**
The Autobiography of Benjamin Franklin has probably been more extensively read than any other American historical work, and no other book of its kind has had such ups and downs of fortune. Franklin lived for many years in England, where he was agent... Biographies/History Pages 332

Name	
Email	
Telephone	
Address	
City, State ZIP	

☐ **Credit Card**   ☐ **Check / Money Order**

Credit Card Number	
Expiration Date	
Signature	

Please Mail to: Book Jungle
PO Box 2226
Champaign, IL 61825
or Fax to: 630-214-0564

ORDERING INFORMATION

web*: www.bookjungle.com*
email*: sales@bookjungle.com*
fax*: 630-214-0564*
mail*: Book Jungle PO Box 2226 Champaign, IL 61825*
or PayPal *to sales@bookjungle.com*

Please contact us for bulk discounts

DIRECT-ORDER TERMS

20% Discount if You Order
Two or More Books
Free Domestic Shipping!
Accepted: Master Card, Visa,
Discover, American Express